T0245785

Skyscraper

TAHSİN YÜCEL

SKYSCRAPER

translated by Ender Gürol

Talisman House, Publishers
2013 · Greenfield · Massachusetts

Copyright © 2013 Tahsin Yücel, Ender Gürol, and the Kalem Literary Agency. Originally published in 2006 in Turkish by Can Yayınları as *Gökdelen* by Tahsin Yücel © Tahsin Yücel © Kalem Literary Agency

Manufactured in the United States of America

13 14 15 7 6 5 4 3 2 1 FIRST EDITION

Book designed by Samuel Retsov

Published in the United States of America by
Talisman House, Publishers
P.O. Box 896
Greenfield, Massachusetts 01302

Grateful acknowledgment is made for the generous support given to the publication of this book by the Turkish Ministry of Culture.

ISBN: 978-1-58498-200-5

Skyscraper

I.

HE HAD NOT BEEN TIED DOWN.

He sat bolt upright on the straight wooden chair, the only one in the room. No one had prevented him from sitting on the chairs to his left and to his right.

He was apprehensive and perplexed, petrified, looking blankly across the room. They were all broad-shouldered with black hair, narrow foreheads, thick eyebrows, beady eyes, aquiline noses, drooping moustaches, and pointed chins. Each wore a dark suit, a white shirt, and boots as pointed as their chins. They stood around a long rectangular table, speaking singly or simultaneously, sometimes in muffled voices, sometimes harshly. What was remarkable was that what they said could not be understood, no matter how loudly they spoke. It was difficult to know how many of them there were since they continually shifted position so quickly and so often that it was all but impossible to keep track of what they were doing. One in the front row moved to the row behind, and one who was in the second row moved to the front while a new one appeared among them or disappeared — one could not be sure.

Seated in his wooden chair, he tried to count them and figured there were eight, then ten, or nine, and sometimes just seven.

It took quite a while for them to line up in a single row behind the long table, their faces toward him. The man in the middle lost no time in stepping forward. "Look, Can," he said. "Tell me exactly. What is today's date? The day, the month, and the year."

He did not have a powerful voice, nor was it loud, yet it echoed interminably in Can's ear.

Can recoiled with a shudder but was not discouraged. He did not stir but waited for the echoes ringing in his ears to die away before he answered. Only then did he notice that he was wearing a pair of old, tightly fitting pyjamas and that the man with the black moustache standing before him clasped a holster with a gun on his belt. Can had not to slightest idea how to answer the question. His head bent like that of a penitent boy as he waited for the man's next move.

The man also waited, then raised his voice, repeating his question. "I'm waiting, Can! The day, the month, and the year?"

Can felt his heart suddenly begin to pound wildly. Frightened, he glanced here and there around the room. There was neither a door nor a window. As for the number of the men, he could not tell exactly whether there were eight, nine, or ten standing there, each with his right hand on his gun. They leaned forward to hear him speak, their looks slowly growing harsh and disparaging. As if this were not enough, their number suddenly increased. Dozens of frowning men with drooping moustaches in similar uniforms stared at him, their hands on their guns. He felt he was about to lose consciousness.

The same voice boomed out, "Come on, my learned friend. Tell us the day, the month and the year! The sooner you do, the better!"

With great effort, Can tried to pull himself together. "I don't know, sir," he muttered. "I'm very sorry, but I don't know."

With a roar of laughter, the man who was cross-examining him caught him by the neck and threw him toward his colleagues. "Just look at this man! He is said to be one of the cleverest lawyers in Istanbul, yet he is unable to tell the day, the month and the year!"

As if they had received a message that Can himself did not hear, the ring of men closed in and began to talk in low voices. Can tried to listen and held his breath, but his pounding heart prevented him from hearing what they said. After a few minutes, however, he heard one of them say in a loud and squeaky voice, "Are we to question this man who does not ever know the day, the month and the year! As if we had nothing better to do! Let's drop it and send him back to prison to rot."

Can saw them scowl disdainfully before they dissolved in hysterical laughter reminiscent of the cries of animals. It curdled his blood. Just then one of the men with drooping moustaches whose stealthy approach he had failed to notice punched him in the chest. He rocked back and forth, tried to find something to grasp but, failing, fell backward onto the ground. He saw one of his slippers dangling from a foot while the other skittered ahead a few yards. He tried to reach it, but either the man who had punched him or one of the others had placed his foot on his chest. "Stay where you are, you bastard. Either you answer our question, or forget about ever seeing your wife again."

With difficulty, Can sat up. The floor was wet and stone-cold. His head between his hands, he tried to think. Nothing like this had ever happened to him before; he could remember neither the day, nor the month, nor the year. Instead, his mind wandered to dates like July 14th, 1789, the French revolution, or May 29th, 1453, the conquest of Constantinople, or October 20th, 1448, the decisive battle of Kosova, or January 28th, 1881, the day Dostoyevsky died. That was not all. Dates, some of which he had learned in his history class at school, some he happened to have memorized, flocked into his mind, each of them giving him momentary relief. Sitting on the wet, cold floor, wearing pyjamas, feet naked, he found that this exercise of his memory helped him to draw his mind away from the men with dark hair and black moustaches in black suits. Just as he was about to recall Kafka's birth date, the man who had been interrogating him pressed the pointed heel of a boot onto the toes of Can's right foot and said, "Yes, my learned friend, I'm ready to hear you speak the date in question." Whereupon, without a moment's hesitation, Can uttered, "July 3rd, 1883, Prague!" No sooner had he said this than all the men in dark suits began indiscriminately kicking him in his head, chest, back, stomach, arms, legs, testicles.

Suddenly a miracle occurred: a kick in the stomach threw him high into the air, which made him close his eyes, and he fell back with a deafening and blood-curdling roar onto a soft surface, where he remained motionless, not daring to open his eyes.

When he finally looked, he found himself stretched on his bed beside his wife Gül, who, calm and composed, was reading a newspaper.

Instead of saying "Good morning" or "Any interesting news?" or even "I've had a horrible dream!" he anxiously glanced at his wife and asked, "Will you tell me, dear, what day is today, the month, and the year?"

His wife put aside the paper and sat up. She stared at him for a moment before asking, "What's the matter, dear? Is it one of those nightmares again?" She put her hand on his forehead. "Is it Smerdyakov again?"

Can pulled a long face. "Pooh!" he said simply.

Years ago, after he had finally given up his revolutionary activities, he was haunted by Smerdyakov in his dreams and imagination whether in his sleep or in broad daylight, whether at home, in the street, or at the office. After a series of pointless acts, Smerdyakov would take him by the arm and lead him by force into the room of Fyodor Pavlovitch Karamazov where he was compelled to watch Smerdyakov murder the old man. When the man was eventually overcome by an epileptic seizure and fell on the ground, Can, highly agitated with fear and disgust, would open his eyes, breathing rapidly in short gasps while sweating profusely as if he had run all the way from Russia and cry, "That's enough! Enough! I say!" His wife would turn on the light quickly and ask, "Smerdyakov, again?" To which he would reply, "Yes, him! This has gone on long enough! He'll end up killing me. I can't stand him any longer."

Can took the glass of water his wife had brought him and drank it down. "But," he went on, "they were grotesque people, much worse than he. You worry helplessly about the date without being able to remember the day, the month, and the year. They may well have been Smerdyakov's offspring."

"Come, dear; don't be stupid. For one thing, Smerdyakov had no children. How can you, as an admirer of Dostoyevsky's, someone who read The Brothers Karamazov at least twenty times, say this?"

"Well! Maybe he was married later, why not, and had children. A host of children and an endless number of children's children. And ..."

"Are you serious? Are you still dreaming?"

"No," he said, "I am perfectly awake. Look, I'm touching you now, see? And I am aware of the fact that I'm touching you. Yet... as if…"

He suddenly realized that he was still at a loss for the answer to the question put to him by the men in his dream, which made him shudder as if a bolt of electricity had passed through his body. He looked into his wife's eyes. "You haven't answered my question," he said.

Gül, bewildered, stared at his face. He smiled strangely.

"O, yes, that question," she replied. "This is the 17th of the month of February in the year 2073." And then she added, "The date of the umpteenth session of the Varol case. It must have gotten on your nerves."

As soon as he heard her say February 17th, 2073, he smiled pleasantly and took a deep breath as if he had recovered something valuable.

"Indeed! February 17th, 2073! How the devil could I forget? Yes, dear, it is. Thanks a lot; splendid! February 17th, 2073, yes, splendid! February 17th, 2073. Capital! Capital, indeed!"

His sense of exaltation astonished him. He could not account for it, since February 17th had no associations for him. February 17th, 2073, was an ordinary day of the year, a dreary day like any other day of the year, and realizing this, he felt his exaltation disappear. It was true that he had had a bad dream. A dream could be colorful, disturbing, or even funny. At times, in a dream one might not be able to remember one's name, job, wife or the day, the month, and the year, but not being able to recall the day, the month, and the year when one was wide awake called for an explanation. Could it be that he had continued to dream while fully awake? Was he suffering from a loss of memory, a transient amnesia perhaps? Or one that was ongoing? Fearful of the second possibility, he fixed his eyes on his wife's and repeated his question.

"I've told you, haven't I? February, 2073, twenty to eight," she said. "Are you trying to be funny? Trying to pull my leg?" She folded the paper and laid it on her lap, her finger pointing to the date. "See? There it is!" she said and laughed.

Can smiled faintly. "A fleeting darkening of mind," he murmured. "It was an awful dream. Smerdyakov proliferated. Multiple replicas of him. They were even more aggressive than he. You know, dreams leave a lasting influence on me. Thank God, it's over now."

"Sure. Come, let's have our breakfast," she said. "I hope you haven't forgotten what you have on your agenda today?"

Can seemed to collect his thoughts, his eyes wandering over the headlines as if the answer to her question were there, and then smiled broadly. "In the morning at a quarter to eleven, I'll appear in court to defend Varol. The case file is ready. And in the afternoon I have a discussion with Temel from New York." So saying, he straightened up, took his watch from the night table, and glanced at it. It was five past eight. He looked surprised and, after hesitating a moment, turned to his wife. "Strange!" he said. "It's been such along time since Varol was detained, but only today, February 17th, 2073, did I remember it." He wondered whether this long and unwarranted detention lay behind his dream.

He shaved quickly and dressed. Crossing the drawing room, he took his seat at the breakfast table. "Isn't it funny? Up until now, the first thing that came into my mind every morning when I woke was Varol in detention, but today it's taken me at least half an hour before I could remember it and only after you hinted at it."

A forced smile appeared on his wife's face but quickly vanished. "Don't worry; you'll conjure him up ten, twenty, perhaps fifty times during the day. You'll be seeing him in person as well. It seems that this case has thrown you into total confusion. You'd better pull yourself together."

"But, we're such close friends," he said with a sigh, spreading his bread with yellow stuff and then something purple. He sipped his tea. "Just think. Isn't it unfair? During the entire time — six years — when we sat on the same bench in class, never did I see him lie or cheat. You and I, we took part in student demonstrations at the university, threw stones at the police, broke windows, set cars on fire, while not once did he commit any such offence and remained the epitome of honesty, impartiality, and conscientiousness both at home and in public, everywhere. Yet he has been in the jail a couple of years while we are as free as birds. So are criminals, thieves and anarchists. They happen to be the freest citizens in the country..."

Can had stopped eating, just as he was about to start ranting. The tingling sound of the tea cup and teaspoon stopped him.

"Oh, come on! You know very well there's nothing new in what you're saying. You're saying it to me, remember! The people who threw him into jail are well aware that Varol Korkmaz is not guilty of anything!"

"So?"

"You yourself told me yesterday that his guilt is the fact that he is innocent!"

Can sighed. "Yes, that has to be the most likely explanation. He's guiltless," Can said and added, "yet, there seems to be injustice in this. Varol Korkmaz is not the only guilty person in this country. While a host of them are roaming around, *he* is left to waste away at the Tuzla penitentiary. It has been two years now since he was arrested." She broke into a laugh. "You don't expect them to coop up all of the common people at the same time, do you?"

She grew silent, staring at her husband, waiting for a reaction, and then, frowning, said, "Finish your breakfast first. Remember we are among the lucky few who can eat real bread."

"I know. Wheat is grown in greenhouses, and greenhouses are owned by foreigners. But I'm not obliged to eat it. I've got no appetite."

"As you like. But try to forget your Smerdyakov dream and defend your case successfully. If some airhead allows you to take up his cause, do what you can," she said glancing at the clock on the wall. "But, hurry up. It's past nine already. Are you taking the spaceshuttle or would you rather drive?"

Can collected his thoughts: "I'd better drive," he said. "I don't know why, but the spaceshuttle has begun to bother me recently. To board such a small aircraft upsets me. It wobbles, and when it opens its wings after it's launched, it gets on my nerves somehow. Suppose it failed to open those wings. Just the thought makes me shudder. There's always the chance that might happen, isn't there?"

"Are you going to drive yourself?"

7

"My mind is confused today. Please call Mustafa and ask him to get the car from the garage and wait for me in front of the building. I'll be there shortly."

A few minutes later, he stood at the door to the apartment with his portfolio.

He was about to leave when his wife said, "Make sure not to get tangled up in your dreams during the trial." He was about to say, "You always make a mountain out of a molehill," but he stopped himself and, although he usually said goodbye with a kiss, satisfied himself by simply blowing one in her direction and headed for the elevator.

Can and his wife lived three floors from the top of the tallest skyscraper in Istanbul, and from where Gül looked down, he seemed like a miniature toy figure about to open the door of a miniscule black car almost as small as he while another tiny figure rushed to open the door for him. Having made sure that Can was comfortable settled in the back, he passed around the car to the driver's seat and set off at great speed. The car grew more and more distant and disappeared.

Gül took a deep breath. "This case has thrown him off balance," she murmured. "I hope he'll reap the benefits even though it's been so long."

Much the same thought crossed Can's mind as he reviewed the file for his friend Varol's case on his laptop one final time, but he had a feeling in his bones that the situation was not going to change. At times it was difficult to keep his temper in check and smother a cry of protest as he addressed an imaginary person beside him — someone who would be qualified to judge the case. "No! Oh, no! This is too much!" he said. "We have seen enough of tribunals, of judges and prosecutors who have been bought with promises of preferment or a limousine. He stopped suddenly, his eyes riveted on a particular document on the laptop.

They had reached the courts of justice and, as the driver opened the car door, saying, after a brief pause, "We've arrived, sir!" he got up, his eyes still fixed on the maddening document, and started up the stairs to the building.

Five lawyers in their robes waited for him at the door to the court-room. A clerk came running to help him with his robe, but he hardly noticed this, nor did he see that people were staring at him curiously. He drew his assistant, Sabri, aside, a man in whom he had full confidence, and showed him the document. "Have you seen this?"

Sabri smiled. "I have, sir," he said. "The old girlfriends of the suspects, their school diplomas, the awards and orders received from their respective organizations: it looks as if these are to be used as collateral evidence. It looks as if innocence has become a dream."

"Indeed!" Can snorted. "This case will drive me mad!" he added. "Never have I heard or experienced such a thing. They have confiscated all his possessions on a pretext that cannot be proved. They've taken all his possessions, the bank, the factory, the house, the farm, the car, whatever he had. Now they ride in his car, occupy his house, consume his wines, and extend generous credit to their associates in his former bank. What they want is to pass a law declaring that his assets shall be considered forfeited, effective as of a particular date, and then release Varol, who has no fault other than having acted as their adviser."

Sabri looked about, smiling. "Please, sir, lower your voice, or they might pass another law against us." He held his employer by the arm, leading him towards the stairs. "However," he continued, "such an action would be worthless, since, as you know, they have already sucked dry all his assets."

One could not be sure if Can were listening or not. He rushed head-long, quickening his pace.

Sabri held him back. "You're going in the wrong direction, sir. Our trial is in the second courtroom to the left, and I'm afraid we're a bit late."

They entered the courtroom where the trial was to be held. Three judges, the prosecutor, the accused without his handcuffs, counsels for the plaintiff and for the defense, the newspaper reporters, and the audience had already taken their places. Can and Sabri squeezed in among the lawyers for the defence on the left side of the room. The presiding judge declared the session open and gave the floor to lawyers to express their opinions on the fourth expert's report regarding the latest state of affairs related to the seizure of the bank and its branch offices. The lawyers, without going into detail, merely stated that the situation was clear to everyone and that the report was a merely a duplicate of earlier ones, while stressing that the statement of accounts presented by the bank and its branch offices was most probably far from reflecting the true state of affairs, and that the operational deficit had caused the treasury to sustain considerable loss. They added that such reports delayed the case. They gave their opinion regarding the need to release the accused and not to afflict them further.

Can expressed the same opinion but with more emphasis, using well chosen, assertive language. As he expanded on his arguments, he grew nervous, and his indignation made him more aggressive. "Since capital punishment has been abolished, you can't hang these men, and having held so long already, why not sentence them in some fashion or other so this case can finally be closed?"

To this, the chief justice, Cahit Güven, who was nationally famous for his role in this particular case, suddenly flew into a rage. "Am I to understand that you claim these sixteen individuals in the dock have been pointlessly detained?"

Can seemed not to have been affected by Güven's words.

No, your honor, I said nothing of the sort. As a matter of fact, in the course of the past two years, we have learned by rote that guiltlessness is actually guilt. I am perfectly in agreement with you in this respect," he answered.

This infuriated the chief justice still more and led him to raise his voice. "What does my learned friend mean exactly?"

Can managed a weak smile. "I said nothing wrong, sir. I dare to hope you have not forgotten that you mentioned in the previous session that it looks suspicious that such a vast conglomerate in 2073 should have not a single foreign partner. This was their fault! A miracle not to feel the need for foreign partners! Your very words, sir."

"True, so I said, and in all seriousness, I say it once again before my nation and my God. These men whom you are defending have adopted a course of action contrary to expected procedures. They must have wicked intentions they are trying to conceal from us."

"Intentions — that you have been doing your best these past two years to unearth and judge."

"Exactly!"

"In other words, you are looking for some vague offence. To corroborate your arguments, your experts, working on the same premises, try similar semantically unsound arguments concluding with the formula 'in all probability' so that these men are kept at the Tuzla prison — and all because of a strong personal conviction that they are guilty 'in all probability.'"

The chief justice banged his fist on the desk. "You are overstepping yourself, sir! Do you realize what you're saying?"

Can was not the same man as one whose eyelids had barely been able to open this morning. He was now where he felt perfectly at home and where his mind worked extremely well.

"I apologize if I have unintentionally committed an impropriety, sir. I'm not going to take much of your valuable time, but there is a question that keeps puzzling me and that I would like to bring to your attention and discuss."

"Out with it then! Make it brief!"

With a faint smile, Can argued that the case involved sixteen people who were accused of having caused extensive damage to the state and the nation and that this entailed the seizure of a bank and its fourteen branches and that given the fact that the only way to recover the damages in question would be to sell the said bank with its branches, the best thing would be to sell those assets as soon as possible and release the accused, thus allowing them to return to their respective jobs.

Responding to the chief justice's quizzical expression, Can proceeded, "To take an obvious example, the salary of the person at the head of the organization in question is six times that of his counterpart now being detained. The salaries of the new officers in lesser positions are at least three times those of their predecessors, not to mention the new cars they have been granted. The new administrators have added five soccer players to the teams of two sport clubs, and scholarships have been awarded to the children of persons connected to cabinet ministers — and don't forget the circumcision feasts held twice a year — which all together have led the organization to the brink of insolvency."

Can spoke so moderately and convincingly that the judges and the prosecutor listened intently, so much so that one of the judges seemed to smile approvingly and even nodded once.

"Here is our compelling evidence, your honor," Can said, taking a file from his briefcase and handing it to the chief justice. He drew a deep breath and went on talking with a winning smile. "Under the circumstances, we seem to be facing a difficult case, the nature of which would be difficult to underestimate. For if it is needlessly protracted, both the bank and its branches will be bankrupt. Therefore, would it not be appropriate to close the said institutions right away, release these men, and replace them in the dock with their replacements? Can it be that the offence committed by the defendants is their reluctance to be profligate?"

Güven sat motionless for a minute or two, staring at Can, and after deliberating with the other judges, turned back to him and said, "You are wasting our time. What you have been saying is beside the point and has no relevance to the case." Before anyone could contradict him, he called out, "Varol Korkmaz!" as if reprimanding him. Korkmaz stood up, and the judge pointed with his chin to the spot where he was supposed to stand.

Korkmaz threw back his head and marched boldly to the spot indicated. He looked thin and shrunken. Frowning, the chief justice gazed at him for a while before speaking, and just when it seemed he would be content merely to stare at him, he made him swear that what he would be saying would be the truth and nothing but the truth. Then he asked whether he knew a woman named Aynur Alpay.

Korkmaz staggered as if he had been hit by an invisible fist. He made no answer but fixed his eyes on those of the chief justice — eyes in which no one dared to look deeply. The chief justice turned to look at another of the accused, the general manager Ahmet Alpay.

"Why did you blush, Alpay? I wasn't addressing you," Güven said and turned to Korkmaz, repeating his question. "I asked whether you knew Aynur Alpay."

"I did, sir." Korkmaz replied, lowering his eye.

"How long have you known her?"

"Twenty-five years, sir."

"Are you certain?"

"Sir, I am positive."

"How come you're so sure? Do you mean that you remember everything that happens?"

"I think so, Sir."

"Wouldn't you think rather that this might be due to the importance you attribute to the acquaintance rather than to your memory?"

"That can't be disputed, Sir."

"If I understand correctly, you were deeply in love with her?"

"I was."

"Have you slept with her?"

"I don't think this is the place to discuss that, Sir."

"I see. Well then, why did you not marry her? Why did you abandon her?

"I was not the one who did, Sir."

Can tried in vain to interfere, but his assistants held him back whenever he tried. The judge saw this and could not help smiling. He turned to the accused again. "Why then?" he inquired. "Why did she marry him after all your efforts? Was it because she tried to fix a lucrative business for you while carrying with you? Was this the way things were arranged in your organization?""When we parted, Ahmet Bey had not yet even started working in our bank, we did not know him," rejoined Vural Korkmaz. "Such incriminations hardly become your honor."

The judge banged on his desk again. "Don't forget you are being tried here, not I."

Can dashed forward, and his assistants made no attempt to hold him back. "Your honor, I don't see the relevance of your questions to the case!" he shouted. "Only five minutes ago you said that stealing by persons appointed by the administration were beside the point, and yet you are trying now to involve the relationship of two young people twenty-five years ago. Is this relevant to the matter in hand?"

"Calm down. You don't have the floor."

"I haven't asked for it, your honor! But I don't think you should be doing this."

His fists clenched, the judge shouted defiantly and banged on his desk. "One more word, and I'll throw you out! Or in!"

Can heard the first sentence but the rest was buried in sounds from noises from the hallway as he rushed from the courtroom."

Even the lawyers on the right disapproved of the way one of the most renowned defence lawyers in the country was being treated. The audience by the door reported that the celebrated lawyer said as he left, "This cannot go on. A cross-examination like this is inadmissible." As he walked briskly to his car, he said, "In my student years, those who committed crimes against young people with witnesses could never be found. Tufan, my close friend, was one of the victims. The newspapers printed over and over the photograph showing the man in the act of shooting Tufan two yards away, but the photograph was not corroborated by other evidences and so was considered inadmissible in court. But things had changed now; anyone at odds with the government has his property seized and is detained."

Just before getting into his car, Can turned to his assistant Sabri and asked, "Why not privatize justice as they privatize everything? I'm sure things would run more smoothly then."

Sabri smiled gently. "Just imagine, " he said to himself, "these words are uttered by our last Marxist!" but before he found an opportunity to express his view of the matter, he saw his boss rush up to a shabby looking, stout man with greenish eyes and a snub nose and fervently embrace him. "Well! Weren't you inside?" Sabri was surprised to hear him display such close intimacy. He bid his chauffeur leave and got in Can's car and watched him from a distance.

Can held the man in a tight embrace before stepping back to have a look at him. "You know what, Rıza, the cell seems to have done you good, and you look fine! When were you released?"

"Nine days ago. Can you imagine, I have been free nine days."

"You can be free for nine years if you remain a good boy," Can said. "But your hanging around the court doesn't look good. What are you looking for?"

"The parking lot attendant is a good friend of mine from prison, and I was looking for you."

"You could contact me elsewhere. This place is not healthy for folks like you."

"I don't care. You know nothing scares me. I like to pick up the gauntlet. It's left for me to prove the communists haven't died out in Turkey, even in the 2070s."

"Every new pamphlet, as soon as it's printed, gets you arrested and imprisoned. It doesn't serve its purpose."

"To my mind, it does In this way I prove that Marxists aren't extinct, even not in the 2070s. The only problem is having the face of a boxer. Puny cops take special delight in beating me up."

Can laughed. "Isn't it rather Quixotic? I mean the way you play the game?" he asked. "How many persons do you expect have the slightest idea that an important figure named Marx once existed?"

Rıza made a wry face. "I don't care! I am dedicated to the cause, I don't care whether there is anyone left in the country who knows him or not. I don't know about you, but I am determined to stick to my beliefs. Moreover," he went on, "your Don Quixote owed his fame to Cervantes's language. My Don Quixote is my own creation! He owes his existence to my own words and conduct."

Can's indignation had subsided; he seemed to be in good spirits now.

"Well, I must congratulate you on that, comrade," he said, adding, "but I have other fish to fry now. I hope we'll see each other again. Stop by any time you want to talk."

Rıza Koç clasped his arm. "Just a moment! I've been waiting here for quite some time, looking forward to seeing you. I've risked being seen here for your sake. I need money."

"Any forthcoming publication?"

"Yes, an ambitious project!"

"For the sake of good old days, I thought perhaps you..."

"I understand," he said, cutting him short. He got into his car, took out his check book, scribbled something on one of the checks before tearing it out. Having alighted from his car, he walked towards his friend and handed it to him. "I think that'll do."

Rıza Koç glanced at the figure: "Enough and to spare!" he commented and added, "One can never tell, I may well come back to knock on your door once more."

"You're welcome. But try not to get arrested. We're getting on in years," Can said as he got into his car. As the car emerged from the garage into day light, he felt somewhat relieved. "Strange," he said to himself, "my resentment a while ago seems to have disappeared. Probably due to Rıza, who's made me conscious of the fact there still is a Marxist in this country." He brooded over it for some time. No, this was not a conference with a terrific effect. To make sure that he was all right, he slid aside the bullet-proof window pane separating the chauffeur and asked Mustafa how he and his family were.

"Thank you, Sir; we are all fine, thank God!"

However, Can hardly heard Mustafa's answer. He put his hand on Sabri's and, resuming his line of thought before Rıza had interrupted him, said, "Yes, my dear Sabri, I'm sure, privatized justice would apply the law better than Doğan. It would supplement and modify the rigor of common law. And their dispensation will gain a legitimacy." And he added, "Why not, after all?"

Sabri made no answer. Can had called Rıza the "last Marxist," exactly the word Sabri would have applied to Can.

II.

TO HAVE WORKED OUT A PLAN, even though it was hypothetical, brought Can some peace. As he entered the Tezcan Law Office on the 98th floor of the pink skyscraper 25-C, some 300 or so feet higher than the Manhattan Building, he felt relieved. In front of the entrance, it occurred to him that his blue-eyed, attractive private secretary İnci, who was well-informed and even tempered and whose sphere of knowledge included even his recent encounter with Rıza, might share his sense of relief. Smiling, he approached her, put his right hand on her shoulder, and stood there for some time before suddenly asking, "İnci dear, what date is it today; could you please tell me the day, the month, and the year?"

Hesitating briefly, İnci, who always had her wits about her, answered, "February 17th, 2073, and a beautiful day it is!" She let her eyes rest on her smiling boss for a moment. "Anyway, it's a day like any other," she added.

Can suddenly felt a wave of anxiety wash over him and momentarily blacked out. For years, he had dreamt of having a daughter. Gül's answer to that had been, "I don't want to bring a child into a world in which butterflies face extinction." He had to acquiesce. Yet the dream lingered. Years later, when he saw İnci for the first time, he imagined her to be the daughter he had wanted. He moved nearer to her. "Not exactly, İnci," he said. "An hour ago, a celebrated judge accused Varol Korkmaz of having had a love affair twenty-five years ago, when you were born."

İnci, trying to lighten the situation with a broad smile asked, "Did I understand you? Are you saying that Korkmaz slept with this woman twenty-five years after he was drawn to her?"

"Not exactly, he had fallen in love with her twenty-five years ago and slept with her. But the woman married somebody else," Can explained.

Having made sense of the situation, İnci replied, "As you always say, Sir, this is Turkey." "It seems clear that that the chief justice doesn't know about statutes of limitations. Twenty-five years is a long time."

"Indeed!" he confirmed, his hand resting on her shoulder. "Twenty-five years is a long time. As a matter of fact, it is also twenty-fine years since Tufan was killed. Despite the fact that the photograph that appeared in nearly all the newspapers clearly shows the man shooting at him from a few feet away, the culprit was never caught. On the other hand, the fact that Varol Korkmaz made love to this girl twenty-five years ago has been brought up in court, although somewhat late."

"As you always say, Sir, this is Turkey."

Can felt prostrate. He doubted whether he had enough energy to reach his office, yet, having held himself straight for a couple of minutes, he pulled İnci to him and kissed her. "You know," he said, I've always wanted to have a daughter like you." Taking a deep breath, he headed to his office.

İnci followed. "Sir, Temel asked me this morning to let him know as soon as you arrived, and he's asked about you three times since."

Can pulled a long face. "I haven't arrived yet, dear. I'll let you know as soon as I do."

"What am I supposed to say, if he calls me again?"

"You can tell him that you'll let him I've arrived as soon as I have! The same holds true for the other staff."

"Just as you say," she said, making for the door.

Before she reached it, Can cleared his throat and inquired whether there was anybody missing among the staff. Instead giving a direct answer, she went out, only to come back with a tiny gadget in her hand. "Except for nine of our lawyers at trial, including Sabri, thirty-eight lawyers, four reporters, twenty-nine clerks, and five attendants have reported for duty," she rejoined.

Can slumped down into one of the armchairs beside his desk, and leaned back, his eyes closed. "Something about me feels strange today," he reflected. "My thoughts are all muddled. First, I forget what day it is and have to ask Gül for it. Then I lack the reserve the court requires. And now I've asked İnci to tell one of our important customers a lie. And why? For God's sake, why? Am I still somehow under the influence of that dream? Is it owing to some pathological change in my brain?" For ten minutes or so, he tried to remember what his father and uncle had said and done before they died. Occasionally he would smile only to frown again. Finally he straightened himself. "Nonsense!" he shouted. "I am not their age yet!"

He laughed at his own words, thinking it would make his friends laugh at him. From his early years at primary school until February 17th, 2073, everybody judged him to be a successful, honest, and creative person. His postgraduate years at the Faculty of Law in Istanbul, crowned with a degree from Sorbonne, were memorable. His academic records were exemplary despite his involvement in demonstrations against conservative and capitalistic regimes and the bourgeois order of things. He spearheaded "reformist students' organization" and was keenly interest in Dostoyevsky and Marx to whose works he had with relish devoted much time. He smiled as if he were telling a story about the past rather than remembering it. "Oh those days! The idealized past when the notion of fear was alien to us!" he murmured. He remembered vividly for the umpteenth time Tufan snatching the pistol from the belt of that colossal cop who tried to take him away, and directed it at him; he thought that the best and the most significant days of his life was back then. However, the period that followed was not less stimulating; for instance, in 2050 when he began his career, he mainly defended the leftist children from wealthy middle class families who had been arrested and imprisoned on charges of violence against property. This had earned him his reputation. Interviews with him became headline news. His picture appeared on the front pages and every other day on television screens. When he took the floor in a trial, he argued his case eloquently, referring to the number and contents of particular provisions of the applicable law and to the venue and the date of the incident concerned without having to consult the file before him, while the audience lapsed into silence and everybody, including the judge himself, listened with great interest. Judges, prosecutors, lawyers, plaintiffs, and defendants would marvel at the way he took up a case, laying due emphasis where required and constructing flawless sentences that shed light on the dark corners of the background to the action. The aforementioned gentlemen, spellbound by the impassioned plea he put forward, blamed themselves for having failed to reach that conclusion themselves. Without prevaricating or begging judges for mercy claiming that the accused had just acted like youths breaking shop-windows, setting fire to expensive cars, retaliating against tear gas with gases even more noxious. These things should be seen as intimations of the great revolution, the source for which was concealed not in the proletariat (of whose very existence had become doubtful) but in capitalism itself, the source of all evil. He knew that that young people of both sexes, the children of middle class families, would soon be set free when the trial was over and would return to their homes not as pioneers and heroes but knowing that they were the products of capitalistic system. In three years, he was instrumental in affecting the release of so many middle class children, having convinced the judges that their militant activities were just natural and ordinary events. Eventually these activities had stopped and the young people themselves had resumed their middle class lives, engaged in the businesses run by their parents, leaving him, so to say, the only faithful leftist around — with the exception of Rıza the fool. A few years back, at a dinner given in his honor at a restaurant at Bebek by his senior classmates, a friend he had not seen for many years had, by way of joke, said, "Bravo, my friend, how clever of you to express the ideas of your youth as if you were talking about a close friend of yours, somewhat foolhardy, and making money from it!" "Nonsense!" he had replied, "I've never changed. I've always been faithful to 'the ideas of my youth' as you say." To this, his friend responded sardonically that he was fully conscious of this, but he was serious about his friend's abiding leftist sympathies even as late as 2073.

The fact that he had made a fortune thanks to captains of industry like Temel and had become the most renowned lawyer in the country was not a result of his political convictions but hard work. He often reminded Gül of the wide chasm separating his past from the present. He drew a deep breath. Even if one were the last lawyer upon the earth, one would still be at a loss to transmit one's thoughts, especially to Gül ... even after so many years of a shared life. He recollected their long discussions, talk about Dimitri, Ivan, Alyosha, Shatov, Raskolnikov, Nastasia, Netochka, prince Myshkin, Iefimov and Golyadkin. "Beautiful days they were, all the same!" he thought. "Private courts had not yet been formed by special decrees."

He stood up and went to the window: the sky was crowded with tiny spaceshuttles whose droning went on, a contrast to the automobiles, somewhat like household flies, among which one could see, quite by chance, a couple of human figures even tinier than flies. He had the fleeting impression that what he saw was the actual state of things, which, having lingered briefly, suddenly vanished. "How absurd and senseless!" he observed. "In order to conceive of the importance of one's existential moment, it seems one should be able to say, at the beginning of the day, what the date is. He went back to his desk and, having pressed one of the dozens of the blue buttons before him, asked İnci to tell Temel that he had 'just stepped in' and was at his disposal.

Within five minutes Temel entered briskly without knocking and sank into the club chair that Can had been occupying. Having dispensed with such courtesies as 'Good morning' or 'How are you?' he tackled the problem that had lately become an obsession with him.

"Your colleagues told me that the man had our case deferred again, and the next hearing is in two months," he said. "It's evident that he's against us."

Can smiled. "I believe you're exaggerating. You said you wanted to be present at the hearing but that you were leaving a week from Tuesday for America and would be away for six weeks. Under the circumstances what else could poor Tansu do? He insisted that the hearing take place on Monday, but his lordship was reluctant to hear cases then, as he reserved Saturday, Sunday, and Monday for rest, since the work came in bursts, he claimed, all week"

"Has he the right?"

"It's not a question of right. By virtue of his authority, he is entitled to decide which days he will hold a hearing; thus, Monday is an off-day. Who would object to his passing the time studying the files or sitting idle, if he preferred that?"

Temel snorted like a horse. "Suppose he decides against me, there's no way to oppose him, is there?" Without waiting for an answer, he went on, "My affairs are in limbo since the beginning the foundations for the sixteen skyscrapers depends on His Lordship's decision. I have other reasons for concern as well."

Can loved a witty exchange. "Come on, Temel dear, what's sixteen skyscrapers compared to 150 you've already built or are building right now!"

This changed in no way Temel's countenance or demeanor.

"You know perfectly well that I am trying to convert Istanbul into another New York. The site of that house has special importance in my overall scheme. A judge takes it into his head to sit back on Monday in the city where I am working to build it anew from the ground up. And apparently nobody can have a say in this."

"Nobody, I'm afraid," Can replied. He noticed his guest's lips tremble, an sign of his anxiety; he got up and approached him, putting a hand on his shoulder. "Did it ever occur to you," he said, "that the man's strategy might simply be to defer the case indefinitely for your own good, that is, until the other party is fed up and admits defeat?"

Temel shrugged his shoulders.

"Even so, what's that to me? That lot with the house and garden is preventing me from erecting neat rows of sixteen skyscrapers just like those in Manhattan. You know, it's been two years that I've been waiting for a decision. This year I got permission to pull down at least six buildings that had been declared parts of an historic district. Yet, that old pig-headed man is intractable. The funny thing is that the house itself has nothing historical about it. It's not fair. Not sportsmanlike!"

Can flashed a smile. He was no longer the man an hour ago who was fiercely indignant. He patted his client on his bald head. "Don't take it to heart! I know that your plan involves lofty ideals: you want to make a new New York out of old Istanbul. But you know damn well that the erection of these sixteen skyscrapers is not critical to the overall plan. In the meantime, why not go ahead with the other buildings?"

"Have I not been telling you that this is my favorite spot, the most beautiful site of Istanbul, the choice of the people. Once my skyscrapers soar, we will have perfection."

"Symmetry and uniformity!"

"However, I've another compelling reason: the idea of a Statue of Liberty erected at Seraglio point flashed into my mind right there. As I've repeatedly said, it's the ideal place to have a spectacular view of it. It would be like a lookout tower on a summit, affording a panoramic view of the entire city."

Can burst out laughing. "How do you know?" he said. "You've never been there. Or did your spaceshuttle hover sixty or seventy feet above, giving you an aerial view?"

Temel sighed. "I've been in and out of it so many times in my dreams. Moreover, don't forget, I'm an architect. I've got the power of imagination."

Can seemed to wink as if he saw someone else in the room. "Anything more?"

"No. I'd like to occupy one of the apartments in the skyscraper to be built there with a view, close-up, of the greatest Statue of Liberty in the world. The fact that I, Temel Diker, can't do this drives me mad. I suffer from a lack of sleep."

Can wanted to point out that the location in question was the site of a home, not just a plot of land, but he gave up the idea. He went back to sit at his desk. Propping his chin on his hand, he fixed his eyes on his visitor. The man in front of him had always been an object of derision to him. His achievements, wealth, and respectability as a businessman had seemed not the result of some intelligent and clever hotshot. His sole merit was his determination, firmness, and persistence. At least as far as skyscrapers were concerned. On his way to the airport returning home after two weeks in New York back in the 2060s, he had spoken with a young compatriot from the Black Sea who had shown him around New York "By God! They've done a good job, these infidels!" he said. "They've turned their building sites to good account. Trust me, I'll do the same for Istanbul. As soon as I'm back I'll set to work!" Those very words were repeated to another friend who met him at the airport. Within a week of his return to Istanbul, he gave orders to pull down twenty or so luxurious apartment houses, some finished and some half-finished, while designing a prototype for the skyscrapers he had in his mind. The fact that he announced his ambitions to everybody that came his way earned him the nickname "New Yorker." No matter what might arise, he made a point of spending each April 22nd to May 8th in New York, but New York had become a mere frame of reference, emptied of content. Having built a several skyscrapers on the model of those in New York, he decided at the beginning of 2068 to be more systematic and, assisted by his specialists' unremitting efforts, created a new prototype not to be compared to those in New York in terms of size, height, and speed of construction. He was determined to convert Istanbul into an inimitable city of skyscrapers. He moved along with the development of his ideas without making any concession, loathing a middle course. With the support of some influential people dedicated to the cause, he had already created ten or eleven per cent of his El Dorado. Can, who couldn't help laughing at such ambition, stood in awe of Temel's achievements. Some writers had claimed that Istanbul had already changed, but this was long before Temel had entered the scene. He felt that the city in question, thanks to his determined efforts, would assume an identity even more unique than before. In fact a comparison would be irrelevant.

"Let's go ahead with the other buildings," he said, with a wan smile.

Can was well aware that Temel had a special attraction for this small plot of land, a sentimental attachment even greater than the desire to convert Istanbul into a second New York. He interpreted the present roadblock as a wicked impediment to his private venture and to free enterprise, and he was profoundly upset over this thoughtless act. The resident of the property was an ordinary, 70-year-old, man, who strongly wanted to continue living on his plot of land containing a ramshackle house, three pine trees, a mulberry tree, a pomegranate tree, and a stunted hazelnut tree, and would not hear of tempting offers, no matter how substantial. "I have inherited this house from my brother. My two sons were born here, my wedding was celebrated here, and my wife died here. I won't sell it for the world!" he insisted. Can had told him repeatedly that the property was rightfully Temel's, that he had bought it, and that there was no legal recourse. Temel, furthermore, was a big client. He couldn't be disregarded. Although Sabri had argued that acting on Temel's behalf would "undermine their reputation and make them an object of ridicule," he had set the law in motion, challenging arguments preferred in the name of "public interest." Perhaps because the judge was well acquainted with both Temel and Can, he had not dismissed the plaintiff's claim on the grounds that his argument was "untenable." On the other hand, all the lawyers in Can's office agreed that seizing the teacher's property, even at a fair price, was not acceptable. The law had been tweaked, or violated, already. "No, it flies in the face of reason!" they said. And when Can cited the Varol Korkmaz case, reminding them of the latter's imprisonment for the last two years, they retorted, "That's quite a different matter altogether. *Amicus curiae*; the litigant is the Prime Minister!" The only solution seemed to be the teacher's death.

"If you ask my opinion, we are working in vain," Can said, "We can never win our case. The chief-justice is the type who is kindly disposed, but he procrastinates pronouncing judgment so not to give the impression that Temel has lost his case against an aging teacher, living on borrowed time."

Hearing this, Temel straightened up. "You don't say!"

"The situation speaks for itself. We would do better to forget the whole thing. It's become the talk of the town. The whole situation appeals to the public's sense of the ridiculous, as you can see by looking at the tabloids. We must be carefully not to undermine our reputation."

"You think so?"

"That has to be the inescapable conclusion!"

"Yet I could have the house and the garden and the pompous old man living there laid flat, level to the ground, and, believe me, I've got the means to do it. I can also see to it that the property is expropriated, if I have to."

Can stood up, approached him, and, placing a hand on one of Temel's shoulders, said:

"Come, come, Temel, founder of a big city! You can't possibly veer off in a new direction, straying from the path that's earned you a venerable name. You'd discredit yourself."

"You think so?"

"I think so. You know well enough that this is the way I look on life."

They were silent for a moment. Can, a smile lurking in the corner of his lips, gazed at Temel, whose eyes were fixed on a spot on the opposite wall and looked blank. Suddenly he turned toward his lawyer. "Why not start an action against the government?"

"On what grounds?" Can asked, laughing.

"O, I don't know. Grounds are never lacking in Turkey. You can had the justice impeached for failing to expropriate the land on which that ramshackled shack stands."

Can shook his head despondently. "This is quite unrealistic."

"He's proud of the way his place infects the beautiful atmosphere of that area while I sacrifice my whole life to build a city that would make New York envious."

Can again shook his head despondently. "Your plea is personal; in other words, it's contingent. A contingent justification would leave you nowhere. What you'd need is a communal justification."

27

"What's that?"

"The right of the individual to live."

"The right of the individual to live?"

"Exactly. I've told you repeatedly that pollution in the environment has long since reached a peak. We are besieged by microbes and viruses. Unless a solution is found we shall soon be witnessing the extinction of everything, including the human species. It follows that the solution would be to soar as high as possible in the air and breathe what's up there. The only thing that remains is to instil this into the brains of the authorities," said Can with a smile.

"I don't see why this should be so difficult," Temel retorted. "It's plain as plain can be." Then he added, "Have you lately seen a pigeon, a sparrow, or a swallow in the sky?"

Can curled his lips. "No, I haven't. They've vanished from the face of the earth, and so have the butterflies. Of all the many insect species that once adorned the earth, there remains only the housefly. Nevertheless, convincing others of the reality is the most difficult thing in the world."

Temel frowned. "I don't see why it should be difficult," he rejoined. "The solution is easy. Let them appropriate the old man's house in return for an attractive price and sell it to me at an exorbitant price. There have been precedents for things like that."

Can laid his hand on his friend's shoulder once again.

"Don't think that this idea has not occurred to me before; as a matter of fact, I've had recourse to a good many lawyers. The house is very small and the teacher is obstinate. It looks as if there are people behind him that help to strengthen his convictions. Media people, probably. If we get actively involved in this business, I'm afraid we can't avoid being exposed to their criticisms, and we'd risk facing their censure in other matters. Moreover, as you may well know, they have privatized all of the country's assets. Our mineralogical resources, thickly wooded areas, rivers, ports, factories, hospitals, universities, primary schools, and so forth have been put up for public auction. If they were now to appropriate this property, it could lead to vicious rumors."

"You were the one who used to say that the press, blindfolded, supported these big shots, weren't you?"

"I was, in fact. But they did so for their privatization schemes, not appropriating someone else's property. You can't deny the that you yourself are favorably disposed towards such things since it is to your own advantage."

"Just imagine! I have the courage to pull down monuments, yet I am defeated in the presence of a shanty!"

Can picked up a blond hair from his lapel and threw it away. "My friend, we are governed by a democracy in which the feasibility of anything and everything can be evaluated. However, our needs, even if endorsed, would cost us a couple of skyscrapers. Better wait some time more." He suddenly grew thoughtful as he remembered something that he had told to Sabri as they left the courthouse after the trial. He fixed his eyes on the ceiling and remained silent for a few minutes. Then he smiled and took Temel's right hand and held it tight. "I think that there should be a way out after all," he whispered, as if he was disclosing a secret, "although I have my doubts."

"A way out?"

Can remembered Varol Korkmaz in the prisoner's dock, his answers under interrogation related to his love affair and his comment to Sabri that "private opinion couldn't be worse than under the Doğan regime." He moved closer to Temel and spoke softly. "The privatization of judgment, that is of the administration and procedural law, like everything else. In the strictest sense of the word, selling totally an activity controlled by the government to private investors, to some big shot like you."

Wherever the present inspiration came from — the amusing article he had read in the *Illustrated Agenda* a few days ago, Temel's observations, the angry words whispered to Sabri, or more likely the way Korkmaz sat in the prisoner's dock while being interrogated — the idea had been lingering at the back of his mind since he was a young practicing lawyer imbued with leftist ideals: confronted by the fact that the country's every imaginable asset had been put up for sale by administrative authorities, especially when they sold his alma mater, Istanbul University, to a well established smuggler, he had concluded that "the time will come when these brutes will privatize even the dispensation of justice." Without the least compunction, he had said that in a period when even mountains and rocks were being privatized, the administration should, in order to be consistent, privatize justice. To those who opposed his suggestion, he replied, "In a country where everything has been privatized, why should justice alone should be an exception? Why not privatize the entire judiciary, the police, even the cabinet? When they were distributing the country's riches, they either forgot justice or considered it irrelevant. However, before long you'll see it on the agenda." He had his listeners in stitches and was himself euphoric. Whenever someone strongly opposed him, he argued further with increased humor, saying that since the country is run by bigwigs with discretionary authority, this kind of privatization would settle their affairs more effectively. At such moments, arguing as he had when he was young, he grew sentimental, believing that his reasoning was sounder and arguments more ingenious than ever.

This time, speaking with Temel, he felt, if somewhat ironically, that the privatization of justice was an effective means to a desired end, but hearing Temel seriously ask whether such an ingenious design was feasible, he realized he had gone too far. "Well!" he declared, staring at the ceiling. After brooding over the situation, he said, "For God's sake! Is there anything left that has not been privatized? Nowadays even the police and the army are educated and trained in educational establishments run by the powers that be. Under the circumstances, justice also should be entrusted to the care of our administrators." A good ten minutes elapsed between Temel's question until Can answered. Although Temel seemed to endorse it first, he could not help asking, "That may well be, but how am I to draw any benefit of it? Will this enable me to get that piece of land from that man?"

Can's replied immediately, "Just imagine that you have purchased the institution of justice and appointed me at its head! Who would challenge us anymore?"

The mere thought held Temel spellbound. He straightened up as if all the fat in his body had been converted into muscle. But then he began to doubt. "It's all very well," he said, "but will the whole thing be within our power?"

Can was quick to answer. "Why not? The power will be concentrated in our hands. In the meantime, we can release Varol from prison." So saying, lost in thought, he gave rein to his imagination until Temel asked who Varol was. "One of my oldest and closest friends," he replied with a frown. "For the last nineteen and a half years he has been in jail without knowing what his offence was."

"I see, I remember him now," said Temel. "All right, why not? The man shall be released. Men of sense should approve such a design, but will *they* do so?" Temel's qualifying Can's friend as a "man," an object, offended him as if considering him as a petty detail.

"It's been nineteen years and six months, and I've done everything in my power. All my attempts have been in vain. The presiding judge sits on his throne of rock, impassive. There is not the slightest chance that he will change."

"Will they do so?" Temel asked again, paying no attention to Can's comments.

Can resumed his line of thought. "Why, just think of the power we've been selling at rock bottom prices, including our mineralogical riches, without discriminating between natives and foreigners. What's more, the people who do this praise themselves for what they've done. Do you think they'll be stingy when they sell the broken seats, bad benches, and outdated computers in the court?"

"Do you mean to say that we'll be able to buy at a bargain price?"

"Don't worry. It might be no more than the price of one or two sky-scrapers."

"It's settled then," said Temel and began to expand upon his plans, as if the plot had already been realized. Considering that there would be no further impediment, no historical, geographical, æsthetic, or environmental concern or restriction, it would be easy to turn Istanbul into a second New York. "Ten years will do it," he said.

Can listened to Temel without really believing him. "What about your Statue of Liberty?" he asked. "What are you going to do about it?"

"A child's toy, once we have what we want," Temel replied. "You may remember that the Statue of Liberty in New York Bay, dedicated in 1886, took ten years to see the light of day. But this was in the distant past. In the meantime, science and technology have advanced at a tremendous pace, so much so that in fact in no time I'll be erecting another three or four *Statues of Liberty*. The architect that made...."

"The sculptor," Can corrected.

"Well, yes, a sculptor... That sculptor Bartholdi who began his work in 1875 would certainly be astounded were he to see where we are today in terms of technology." He continued smiling broadly. "A shrewd fellow he was! He modelled the face of the lady after his mother. Mine will be a replica of Madam Nokta."

"And who is she?"

"My mother."

"Bartholdi was a sculptor, you know. Your involvement with the new Statue of Liberty will be limited to paying for it."

"So much the better! As a matter of fact, my mother is far more beautiful than Bartholodi's mother was." So saying, he took from his briefcase a photograph, and, before handing it to Can, gazed at it with admiration, as if he was seeing it for the first time.

"My mother," he said. "The only picture I have of her."

The photograph shook in Can's hand.

"But...but..." he muttered, "she truly is beautiful...breathtaking indeed! So beautiful in fact that one is inclined to ..."

"She is, or was, to be exact," Temel confirmed with a strange smile that made him look at least ten years younger. "I did not know her. She died when I was six months old," he added with a sigh. "One thing is certain though. She was apparently the beauty queen of the village. They said they had never seen anyone like her."

"Absolutely! This forehead, this nose, these eyebrows, and these eyes..." Can's voice shook like his hands. "So unassertive and unassuming that one is inclined to qualify it as a real person, and yet one might take her for an idol..." Suppress his feelings, he asked Temel, "Can I keep this until tomorrow? I'd like to show it to Gül."

"Of course, you can. You can keep it if you want to," Temel said. "Our boys have made photocopies of it, magnifying, enlarging, blowing it up, and they even made color copies."

"Thank you," said Can. He wanted to change the subject but continued to gaze at the picture and asked, "Are you positively determined to erect your statue at Seraglio Point?"

"It is an excellent site to vie with the New York harbor. Moreover, given the fact that I don't wish to demolish Topkapı Palace, I'll build a wall to hide it."

Can had difficulty keeping from laughing. "That idea crossed your mind then?"

"It did."

Can burst into laughter. "I see that you have considered everything. By God, no one can match your cunning. But why Topkapı Palace? One of our historical monuments of vital importance. It's a beautiful edifice as well."

"Maybe. But it threatens the integrity of Istanbul."

"Don't you think that in fact you're the one who violates that integrity?"

"Not exactly. It had changed for the worse long before I got here. My concern now is to redeem its wholeness. A wholeness in line with modern trends, a homogenous unity. Once my scheme is implemented it will give people the impression that the city has had this aspect from eternity, a sense of totality that will not allow their memories to travel back in history or to venture towards a distant future, a sense of totality that will enable them to live in a continuous present."

Can smiled. "You've let yourself go again, my dear Temel. Your desire to make something extreme possible has been awakened." After a moment's consideration, he said, "I think you have an obsession. You are haunted by the idea to build towers like the one in Babel and fill the world with them. "Maybe because ..."

He did not finish his sentence.

"Yes, because?" replied Temel.

Can wanted to say that Temel's passion for tall elongated skyscrapers was an overcompensation for his bulk and protruding belly but gave up the idea. "Because you are a rare example."

"Maybe so," Temel said as an image of the teacher's house surged up again in his imagination. Then he continued, "But let's get back to the subject. How are we going to go about this?"

"About what?" asked Can.

"About appropriating the teacher's property."

It had occurred to Can to think seriously about it. Not only was he still undecided about whether such an undertaking was advisable, the very thought had been off the cuff like asking İnci about the day, the month and the year and then kissing her. Although he did not yet take the idea seriously, he said. "Just think on the number of things we have achieved. There is no reason why we should miss our mark this time, provided, of course, that we work out our plans properly."

"There is no denying that what we have done already was what looked right," Temel confirmed, as he gave rein to his imagination, but they had missed the target and failed to convince the teacher. On the other hand, no one could deny that their relations with the state bureaucracy had always been harmonious. Can had enthusiastically endorsed Temel's plan to make Istanbul a second New York, even more monolithic than the prototype. Although people had humorously nicknamed him "New Yorker" out of pure jealousy, he had considered the idea of erecting a Statue of Liberty at Seraglio Point good and needed and had already set to work.

"There's money galore, thank God! Don't worry about that! I'm confident that the rich would be willing and eager to pay any price in order to own of an apartment in a skyscraper. Those who have purchased one will be eager to buy another. At the moment there are already fourteen high-rise apartment buildings almost ready for people to move in."

"If everything runs according to plan, we won't require staggering sums for the project."

Temel moved his chair closer to the lawyer and asked, "Well, tell me what your plans are?"

Can smiled mysteriously. He remembered a humorous article he had read a few days ago. "Easy!" he said, "Wait! Not even an hour has passed since we conjured up this vision. I have only a rough idea about to go about it. Here's a thought that just occurred to me, but it's better than nothing."

"Where do we start?"

"The illogicality of the fact that justice is still in the hands of the State while everything else has been privatized."

"What do you mean by 'illogical'?" asked Temel, who appeared to be confused. He could not bring himself to believe in the feasibility of a privatized system of justice as he could not conceive of the lawyer's idea to be anything but an extended metaphor involving in all probability certain amendments.

But Can was serious, explaining, "Illogical, indeed! As you may well know, ever since the close of the last century, everything has been privatized and sold, preferably to foreign nationals or, failing that, to local heavyweights — in other words, to the subcontractors of the former. We've sold mountains, rocks, rivers, seas, harbors, airports, ships, airplanes, trains, railroads, bridges, plants, an infinite variety of industrial waste, and all sorts of rejected material, educational establishments, stadiums, and so forth. The Prime Minister pays an annuity to an Israeli tycoon to help him continue to occupy his position. Considering that everything is owned and run by individuals, why on earth shouldn't justice follow suit? What is there to prevent justice from being privatized as well? And my chief justification to make it so will be cohesiveness!" His voice was shaking, and he was short of breath. "Yes," he reiterated, "the cohesiveness of the established order!"

There was a smile on Temel's face "You speak like a confirmed leftist, but you speak the truth. Indeed, there should be no impediment whatsoever to privatization under the circumstances." However, even though he did not deny the likelihood that Temel's plan would succeed, he still as at a loss how this scheme could be brought to fruition.

"What you say will come true in the end. But what exactly shall will our interest be in this venture? Do you mean to say that we'll be in a position to appropriate the old man's property?"

Can felt almost certain that if justice were privatized — in other words, if it were entrusted to them — the problems Temel raised would easily be settled. For instance, no one could protest against erecting the Statue of Liberty at Seraglio Point, and even if there were opposition, they could turn a deaf ear to it. Yet there was another risk, for another employer might mess things up; in a situation where regulations are subject to modifications, even New York could be razed to the ground within a couple of weeks, but in a situation where demolition is interpreted as revolution, and revolution as demolition, to be a leader seemed a brilliant idea.

"In all probability our plans will work out," Can said.

"How?"

"I don't know exactly now. Time will tell."

Temel said nothing for a while. Then he did what was usual in situations when others were to make decisions that would involve him: he tapped three times on the breast pocket in his jacket where he kept his checkbook, repeating the words he used whenever the situation presented itself. This might be an act of encouragement that might also be a challenge. "I'll be your accomplice," he said.

A thought suddenly flashed in Can's mind. Asking his wife about the date, the month and the year could be the beginning of the scheme he was planning. In short "this very moment" could be the beginning of a new era, and his countenance beamed with delight. "Temel, mark this date, February 17th, 2073."

"What's so special about it?"

"Special? I'm told that the seventeenth skyscraper at Maçka is nearing completion. Is that true?"

Temel seemed puzzled. "Indeed! But what has this to do with these plans today?"

"I just wanted to be sure, that's all," he answered. No sooner he had uttered these words than a host of bright ideas began to race across his mind at incredible speed. He was no longer a thinker now, nor was he developing a scheme in his mind; his thoughts mixed with memories, designs, and visions, all mixed together, descended on him. In his mind, Cüneyt, an old friend, was telling him, "You need money to buy a nice flat on the umpteenth floor of that blue skyscraper; where do you find it?" Can repeated the same words softly at least twenty-five times before pressing the tiny intercom button on his desk.

"İnci dear, be kind enough to call Cüneyt from *The Globe*?"

III.

CROSSING THE THRESHOLD OF *THE GLOBE*, Can felt sure that his friend, whom he had not seen for the last four or five months, would be glad to see him. In fact, people rose from their seats and greeted him with the utmost deference. It was evident that his visit was expected not simply by Cüneyt and the office boys but by the whole staff, including the reporters and the accountant, and, last but not least, the owner of the paper. "What's the reason for this reception?" he asked himself. "Could it be because I'm Temel's lawyer? Or is it because I censured the judge this morning? Or simply because I'm Can Tezcan?" He did not answer his questions but continued, "Whatever the reason, this welcome is a good sign." If he could persuade his friend that his scheme had potential, the matter could be settled easily. *The Globe* was both a tabloid press, like *The Liberty*, with pictures and pin-ups, but thanks to the owner's connections plus his land, goods, money, and investments, coupled with the paper's many columnists, *The Globe* was able to make the public believe the most improbable things, too good to be true. There were times when the owner strayed from the party line, while at other times siding with the powers that be, yet it was undeniable that he also played a significant role in concluding things by never taking "no" for an answer. The paper echoed Cüneyt Ender, an exemplary newspaperman, dexterous in honestly adopting new courses when circumstances dictated and masterful in arguments. There was no reason why he should make a mistake this time.

Can and Cüneyt briefly reviewed what had happened that morning in court and reminisced about their long-standing friendship. Actually their idiosyncrasies and their views of life had differed considerably when they were young and still did. Back then Can was a militant university student while Cüneyt was a young correspondent who preferred to look at facts from a distance, but his job had led him, more often than not, to be involved with leftist students who were long-standing friends and whose thoughts and acts made their way, at least in part, into his articles. After social unrest declined, he wrote books about the missions and the psychological make-up of his friends, much as if he were one of them. Now that their politics had been reduced to mere bluster and swagger, they considered him to be one of them. Moreover, they preferred to listen to their political actions as he recorded them, perhaps because of the way he stretched the truth. Can concealed his feelings, giving free rein to reminiscences, sometimes qualifying them as mere pranks. They talked about how they shot their guns into the air amid a cheering crowd and how they chanted slogans against the government: "To the bitter end!" and "Revolution, the only solution!" They recalled how Can snatched the pistol from the belt of a police officer and, directing it to him, fearlessly in spite of his puny stature. They remembered how the American consul, who had been kidnapped and, despite circulars posted everywhere, wasn't seen for three weeks, made a dash for the police force, with her reddish false hair falling in waves over her shoulders, in a sleeveless pink blouse, a pink miniskirt, and high heeled pointy shoes. They retold this three times over, adding more details each time. They burst into laughter, declaring with some nostalgia, "Oh those days!"

Glancing at his friend, Cüneyt sighed, "Of all things consigned to oblivion, you snatching the gun from the belt of the superintendent of police and getting Tufan Şirin away from him will be remembered best." After a moment's pause, he added "Poor thing! Shot before the end of the year. And only because you were not with him."

Can's eyes filled with tears. "Tufan wrote a poem about the struggle. He himself did not know how to fight. His main mission in life was to write poetry," he said regretfully. "My warning to him had always been to stay in the rear guard, but it was all in vain."

Cüneyt smiled wryly. "I used to poke fun at his name, Şirin, meaning 'comely.' I told him that he bore a name that meant the opposite of his real nature. He proved to be neither a poet nor a hero."

After another moment's silence, Cüneyt spoke, "Apparently, Varol Korkmaz was never involved. He preferred to remain aloof. Furthermore, he harangued people about loyalty to the state and obedience to law. Now he happens to be on the inside, and we're not. Since you made so much noise this morning, it looks as if no progress has been made. True?"

"Apparently," was the answer. "As matter of fact, I want to get your opinion about it."

"You are his lawyer. You are acquainted with the niceties of the case."

Can sighed again. "In order that a lawyer be acquainted with all the details of a case, there must be more than there is so far. There is neither documentary evidence nor statements that would incriminate him, only groundless accusations leading nowhere. Such 'news' reaches you, the media, first — before it reaches judges and lawyers. And then you publish it without looking into whether it's true."

"Correct!" said Cüneyt. "We can't take pride on that account. But the men were very repulsive, and Mevlut Aga was very insistent."

Can suddenly leaned towards his friend and said softly, "I'm up to something that may put an end to such problems once and for all. As a matter of fact, the reason for my visit was to speak about it."

Cüneyt started and leaned back in his the chair. "I don't suppose you'll set me against these men," he said. "As you know well, they are not people to be trifled with. A single telephone call from Mevlut Aga would be enough to fire me."

Can smiled. "I don't think that my program will have such nasty consequences, my friend!"

"Well, then tell me about it!"

His eyes fixed on the ceiling, Can was lost in thought for a moment. Then, looking towards his friend, he acted as if he were going to make a joke. "My dear Cüneyt, in order that real democracy may take root in this country, justice must be privatized as soon as possible."

Cüneyt found himself stammering, something he had not done since his student days. "Is this the wild product of your imagination?" But he stopped and caught himself. "You've stunned me, I must say! Is this a new kind of reform or revolution?"

Can stood up. "Indeed! It's a reform, a drastic reform. Or rather it will be a radical and wide ranging reform, if it succeeds."

"How in the world did this occur to you?"

"Well, it is simply based on the *laissez faire laissez passer* principle. If everything is privatized, if all the lawyers and the entire police force are trained in private academies, it would be out of place if justice remained a state institution, wouldn't it? Don't you see this, given the present state of affairs?"

"What's wrong with the way things are now?"

"Today justice is sometimes off-the-record and sometimes it's constitutional. To be precise, at times it looks as if it's run privately, and at times it has a public flavor, but more often than not, it looks like a private enterprise. Everything depends on the administration, not even on the administration as such, but on the man who rules the country. In other words, it is private under the guise of public authority. No, even more than private, it is an individual's will. In other words, it is the worst of all possible systems, the most corrupt. Didn't we see that this morning? Don't you think so?"

Cüneyt did not answer immediately and stared at the ground. He doubted whether his newspaper, which strongly supported the ruling party, would acquiesce to this proposal. Further, he took his optimistic view of the future with a grain of salt. All the same, he tried to smile. "How did you arrive at this conclusion?"

Can did not expect the question. He looked for a reasonable answer, a concrete illustration. The figures of the Prime Minister and some cabinet ministers rose before him followed by voting taking place in the Grand National Assembly as well as in certain trials.

"If particular laws are passed every now and then in a country, it follows that justice and public administration have already been privatized," he said. "That's how things stand in our case. It often happens that people in power wish they had thought about alternative courses of action. They insist that their point of view is accepted at all events, usurping all the rights of the judiciary and its administrators. Only a blind man could fail to see what goes on. If you ask my opinion ..."

"Easy now!" said Cüneyt, "You are going too far! All those laws you mention were passed not behind closed doors, but in the open in the National Assembly! Which means they are legislated by the state, by representatives of this community."

Can restrained his anger with great difficulty. He was about to get up and leave. "If these laws had been passed behind closed doors, we would still believe that they at least followed the rules. It would not have compromised their dignity," he said.

"Do you mean to say that our administrators lack a sense of propriety?"

"Please, Cüneyt, let's leave aside such sentiments and try to see the facts," said Can, "In this country laws are passed every minute to be substituted before half a year has passed for new ones that contradict them. In this, new levels of justice are established and new private judges are appointed with a view to bringing judgments in line with the expectations of the powers that be. It follows that nothing is on sure ground, let alone justice. Even legislators themselves are not protected from it. Is this so difficult to understand?"

Can ranted and raved and spoke with conviction. The things he said might have crossed his mind at some point, but they were not his considered judgments, and he felt as if he were giving someone else's views. That in turn gave him the satisfaction of being able to determine the causes and effects while not feeling personally responsible for them. Meanwhile, Cüneyt began to feel that Can spoke the truth. He was no longer listening to the arguments of the renowned lawyer but to the passionate militant of the 2050s he had known in his youth. Nevertheless, he could not bring himself to see any connection between, on the one hand, establishing new courts of justice and passing new laws, and, on the other, privatizing justice.

"My dear Can," he said, "it seems to me that the enactment of a legislator and the privatization of justice are two very different things. Do you think that laws enacted by the legislature would be executed better by private institutions?"

"Most likely," said Can. "Most likely."

"Why?"

"Because all sorts of contradictory elements will be eliminated in the system. Like everything else, justice will also pass into the hands of private individuals. Even though the wheels of progress may not run as smoothly as one would wish, statements that contradict themselves will vanish."

"Is this all?"

"Sooner or later justice will take a turn for the better, for the judges will be well paid. They will get money both from the plaintiff and from the defendant and will be meticulous about their job so that they do not discourage people."

"How can you be so sure? You know better than I the state of affairs between the state and private institutions. We are witnessing every day the fact that they work together robbing the public, especially when these private institutions are entrusted to people outside the country. Don't you think that the same thing would happen to justice?"

"No, Sir!"

"So be it! But under the circumstances, don't you think that justice will be a commodity, be converted into a commodity?"

"Is this not the usual way? In a place where everything of value is converted into a commodity? In our twenty-first century, everything has been absorbed by commerce."

Cüneyt continued to listen to his friend as if the militant of twenty-five years ago were speaking. Whether or not he endorsed his views and ideas did not matter, since his arguments, observations, excitement, and so forth commanded admiration. Cüneyt did not quite know what to think or what to say. "Tell me where the person who would purchase justice is," he said.

Can smiled. "Me, for instance."

Cüneyt was confused. "You! Are you kidding? The whole institution together with its army of judges and prosecutors?"

Can continued to smile. "What a question!" he said. "Just like the multitude of plants, mines, woods, universities, hospitals, airlines, roads, and railroads. Justice will be no different; in other words, cheap. Further, for those already, there's no extra cost. It's up to you to hire them or ignore them. What's more, the government will get rid of having to pay salaries to thousands of men. I don't understand why a journalist like you cannot understand this."

Cüneyt ignored that last remark. "Justice is a different matter," he said. "You'd still need an enormous cash flow."

"I gave myself as an example. I didn't say I would be the buyer. As a matter of fact, I couldn't," said Can. "Were I to undertake such a venture, the number of people who would be willing to back me up would be considerable or at least those who would put up the money and appoint me the head."

"Who, for instance?"

"For instance, Temel, a wealthy client of mine ..."

"The skyscraper tycoon?"

"You said it. Any objection?"

"Why, no. He is reputed to be extremely rich. The skyscrapers he has erected are indeed beautiful. But is he not something of a wheeler-dealer?"

"He has the fantastic ambition to convert Istanbul into a completely modern city, a city even more homogenous, more orderly and functional than New York."

"How?"

Can thought for some time. "I don't know how to put it," he said finally. "All I can suggest for the moment is something similar to Thomas More's *Nusquama*. Or a counterpart of it, tuned to our century. According to his plans, all the skyscrapers will be uniform, having the same design and height. The only thing that will differ will be their colors and numbers. There will be no trees or gardens between them. Each will be almost 2,000 feet high."

"What about the old structures? Especially the old skyscrapers?"

"They will all be pulled down."

"When?

"At the first opportunity."

Cüneyt had difficulty containing himself. "No! No! No! This is presumptuous!" he said straining his voice. "And you think you'll be able to live in such a city?"

After some thought, Can observed, "Temel's Istanbul is not my ideal, but there is no doubt that it will be far better and more attractive than the present unpleasant scene. In a sense it will be the utopian capital dreamed by Thomas More."

Cüneyt stood up, exasperated. "No! It has no chance whatsoever!" he said. "What does it have to do with More's utopia?"

Can was going to say, "One can see that you haven't read More," but he kept his peace. "For heaven's sake, Cüneyt! Temel's vision is more easily realized and in keeping with our age than More's utopia. As you may remember, the houses in More's capital were a long line of uniform tenements. His utopia also heralded the middle class and advised men and women to wear the same uniform, so that men and women and the unmarried and the married could be told apart. Today we see that house and roads tend too look alike, clothes have become unisex, and people dress in uniforms: the married and the unmarried, male and female are no longer easily told apart. Even if they were, nobody would care."

"You're grossly exaggerating!" Cüneyt said, frowning. "By the way, is Temel also an utopian and a philosopher?"

"Neither the one nor the other," replied Can. "But he's got creative instinct and genius."

"And a lot of money?"

"Right, but he made his fortune himself. His grandfather was a tailor. They were the best tailors making hunting clothes in Trabzon. Temel changed professions. He became a building contractor and has so far erected the best and the most solid high-rise buildings."

"How did that happen?"

"Wise entrepreneurs, wealthy investors gave him the lion's share of the businesses from the beginning, and then he changed course and established lucrative relations with public organizations and hired a leading lawyer like me."

"So he's all money?"

"Far from it," said Can, bursting into laughter. "You are wrong if you think that Temel sets too high a value on money. He is simply devoted to Istanbul, the Istanbul of his imagination. He'd sacrifice huge sums if he believed that he would be nearing his objectives. He might sacrifice five skyscrapers for a small piece of land."

"His ruling passion?"

"It is. A fascinating passion that inspires fear and respect at the same time."

"Looks like it," said Cüneyt with a smile. "On the other hand, one cannot deny that he has a flair for business. His indifference to money hasn't kept him from making lots of it."

After a moment's consideration, "Maybe you're right," said Can. Then he added, "It has been a century now that in this country every party that came to power created its own wealthy class. As for our ..."

Cüneyt cut him short. "Thank God! The Turkish public, endowed with common sense, sees to it that each party falls from power before the new elections."

"Indeed! The fact that the public has always brought to power parties who have successfully generating their own money class proves what I say. But wait, you've interrupted me. The interesting thing about Temel is his talent in increasing his wealth in every successive election. Who knows, he may make huge sums of money. And he has another good point: he has taken up my cause. He is a true patriot. He reads your articles and often says that a thinker like you ought to view the world from the window of one of his skyscrapers. You are mentioned often in our conversations."

Cüneyt smiled. "Frankly, I wouldn't say "no" to a large and comfortable apartment in one of his skycrapers," he said sighing and added, "And I would like to travel between my home and my office in a spaceshuttle."

"These are things altogether possible nowadays, especially for a reputable columnist for *The Globe*," said Can. "You name it, and it's yours."

"You think so?"

"I think so!"

Cüneyt's interest had been aroused. "These are the words of revolutionaries. Had they had the opportunity to hear what you're saying, even Danton and Saint-Just would have endorsed this fantasy," he said. Looking at his former militant comrade, he said, "Do you sincerely believe that this privatization idea is relevant. In other words, are you serious about your dreams? Do you have reliable partners?"

Can nodded. "Yes. But I can't do it all by myself. I, or to be precise we, wish you'd help us."

Cüneyt's interest increased. "How am I supposed to contribute?"

"One of your articles, a single one of those seminal and provocative articles of yours would set off a chain reaction."

"You think so?"

"I am serious! My dear Cüneyt, Temel shares with me this opinion. Both your identity and the reputation of your paper are of paramount importance."

"Then all right! Why not, after all? I could even get it ready in time for tomorrow's issue," replied Cüneyt.

He took out some whiskey, ice cubes, glasses, and hors d'oeuvres. The two men toasted their success and began discussing the details of their plan. After nearly three-quarters of an hour, believing everything to have been finalized, they resumed their memories of their schooldays.

By the time Can left, he had finished three drinks of whiskey. Standing before the door of the elevator, they embraced each other warmly.

"It's good to get together even though we don't do it often. One's horizon expands," Cüneyt said.

"We must do this more often," said Can.

"You know what, when you first mentioned the privatization of justice, I thought you were kidding. I said it was too much. Now it seems that what we've spoken about dates back years."

"I know. I understand you perfectly well. I often experience such things. Quite unconsciously, I go back to my adolescence and find myself viewing the world in the light of the logic of that era. As a matter fact, I think that revolution is innate in us. It is part of our nature, of our primitive self, of Freud's *Id*. At such moments, it emerges from God knows where only to shrink back again. We are veterans of war. We should be ready to come together to give our society cohesiveness through the privatization of justice."

"Indeed, veterans of war! And we are committed to our cause," confirmed Cüneyt. "I do believe in your ideology, in the privatization of justice." Three drinks of whiskey did not prevent him from thinking that the human skill in bringing together the most irreconcilable things was a miracle.

"You may remember Montesquieu's famous definition of law: 'Laws are the necessary connections arising from the nature of things,'" said Can.

"In other words?"

"In other words, you're right; the privatization of justice is a reform. You couldn't possibly apply laws formulated at the beginning of the nineteenth century to mid-twentieth century."

"Certainly. The world is becoming global."

"Is the process continuing?"

Cüneyt laughed." Our pundits say so. Not for nothing did we adopt you as our leader when we were young. Do you remember Rıza Koç? Your disciple? A sharp-witted fellow."

"You mean the last Marxist? I met him a few hours ago," said Can.

"Oh no!' said Cüneyt. "Wasn't he in jail?"

"No longer! He has served his term apparently."

"Where did you see him?"

"In the parking lot at the law courts."

"What was he doing there? Summoned?"

"He never responds to summons. He is usually arrested."

"Well then, what was he doing there?"

"Waiting for me. To borrow money."

"God knows for what purpose! And you gave it to him?"

"I did."

"I wish you hadn't. He must be in pursuit of some strange business again. He'll get caught."

"I believe he takes delight in such exploits. Sometimes I also have such a funny feeling. Rıza is perpetuating an old revolutionary tradition. He writes political pamphlets and distributes them clandestinely, just think, in 2073! The last revolutionary in Turkey! He is determined to carry the flag to the bitter end."

"And you support him in his cause? These days when you would like to see justice privatized and pass into the hands of the powerful."

Can smiled. "Man is a paradoxical animal," he said. "You yourself said this in one of your articles, if I remember correctly."

"Correct! Infallible memory," said Cüneyt.

The elevator was already there, and soon Can was leaving the building. He saw his chauffeur waiting for him, his hand ready to open the rear door. He headed for the car. No sooner had he taken his seat than he remembered Tufan Şirin again. Cüneyt's behavior had endeared him to Can still more. Back in the troubled years, Cüneyt had written at least five articles for his paper demanding that those who had been responsible for Tufan's death be found. His last article, Can remembered, bore the title of "The Poet's Blood." "It received no response at the time, but after all it had appeared in a leftist paper," Can said to himself. Tufan surged up once again in his imagination. Can had not been as intimate

49

with him as he had been with Varol Korkmaz and Rıza Koç. Yet they had both been aggressively active in the same cause on many occasions, had taken part in celebrations, had sang marches together, had banded together, and had pursued the enemy and taken flight when the necessary. He wrote beautiful poems.

Can happened to be in Paris when he heard of the shooting. Tufan's death had grieved him to the heart, his image lingering in his imagination for days on end and made him cry. Yet now with the exception of a few elderly men, nobody remembered him. Can tried to revive his appearance in his imagination. The face was there all right, but there was something missing. "Life is ignoble!" he said before realizing that the image Tufan Şirin had already vanished into thin air.

Can returned to the subject at hand. He believed that somehow his ambitious plan had already begun to take shape thanks to his knowledge, creativity, and persuasiveness. As he recalled the inspiration that had come to him, he felt proud. Even half of the justifications he had given would be sufficient with enough to spare, he told himself.

Back in his office, he broke into a smile and dialed Temel's direct line. As soon as he heard Temel's voice saying "Hello," he merely said, "Can speaking, everything is all right!" and hung up. And as if there were someone who had asked why he had hung up, he said, "Let him think about it!" and dissolved into laughter.

As he stepped in the elevator at home, he found another justification for his scheme. "It takes me less than a minute to go up 130 floors. To free the city from all those bumpy and twisty roads and quaint buildings, each uglier than the other, building skyscrapers was the solution, liberating both the city and its inhabitants. Just like the privatization of justice. Temel's beatific smile flashed in his imagination. He smiled in return.

When he stepped out of the elevator on the 128th floor and entered his apartment, the same happy and beatific smile lingered on this face. A glass of raki in hand, he sat in his armchair facing the panorama of the city and the vast sea. Gül thought that her husband was about to make a joke. Seeing that he didn't, she sensed that he had something enigmatic on his mind that he preferred to keep to himself. Given the fact that he had not been able to have Varol Korkmaz released, she found it difficult to account for his smile.

"Can, dear, there's something strange about you. Your behavior this morning seems to continue. You look as if you did not know your own mind," she remarked.

Can laughed. "I don't know my own mind, eh? Quite the opposite, darling. Were I to tell you what it's all about, you'd go mad!" And before she could react, he began telling her about Varol Korkmaz's trial, followed by an account of his meetings with Temel and Cüneyt. Having told her everything, which took a full hour, he asked her to get him a glass of raki and a big glass of water.

As if there were nothing to wonder about in all this, Gül, without saying a word, went to the kitchen, and, having duly done as her husband asked, she resumed her seat.

"A new craze! You're a fool! Or a mere child! To engage in great utopian dreams has become a habit with you."

Her comment was received with derisive laughter. "This may explain my wise choice in entering the legal profession and the success I have achieved!"

Gül did not change her position or the tone of her voice. "So far everything has met your expectations. Facts have met your fancies. But everything might suddenly alter course. Don't you think this time you are weakening the foundations of the law? You are planning to take property from the hands of its lawful owner in order to give it to speculators. In other words, and you chop off the limb you're sitting on. Nowhere else has such a thing ever been dreamt of!"

"Wait a moment, Gül!" he interrupted. "Hold on!" He had always attached great importance to his wife's views. He held her in high esteem as a jurist, and yet he did not allow her to finish her sentence. "Just wait!" he repeated. "Please consider every one of my arguments on its own merits and see if there are any flaws in them."

"None, as a matter of fact. All your premises are valid enough in their own contexts, yet they contradict everything else, all social values and in particular law as such. You want, on the one hand, that everybody be like you, while, on the other, you make up wild dreams."

Can was grieved to hear this. "Please, don't say so. Tell me what you always say when you are in the mood. Tell me that I'm always right and endowed with creative genius."

Gül thought that she had overstepped her bounds but stuck to her arguments.

"You *are* always right. You *are* a creative genius, but this is something different!" she said, affectionately. "What you've been telling me is wrong and fallacious. A destructive scheme. You can induce no one to embrace such a proposition. You'll be the laughing stock of the public."

"You are wrong," said Can. He seemed quite serious and sincere in his excitement. "You get me wrong. It's been ages since I have recaptured my youth. I can now place in their proper contexts all the capitalists and their theories, consistent in their inconsistencies, and living amid their fallacies, by showing them their inconsistencies, thus endowing them with their true identities. Who knows, perhaps my venture may lead them to their inescapable end."

"Espousing their ideology and supporting them in their inexorable logic."

"Not exactly! By consciously remaining distant and aloof."

"In your capacity as Temel's lawyer, living in one of the largest apartments in the highest skyscraper in Istanbul and wallowing in riches?"

Can looked as if a sharp pain had shot up his leg. However, Gül was accustomed to such behavior in him, which surfaced whenever he was opposed.

"This is not fair! Not fair at all!" he said, "The fact that my way of life may be considered reprehensible does not prove that my hypothesis is just guess work. To be frank, if we take up this issue as a moral question,

I must say we could not possibly survive unless we accepted the established order. Do you think that we would be spared?"

"You could have given up your profession. I did, didn't I?"

"You did because you were disgusted with the established order. But don't forget that you have lived your life as the wife of a reputable lawyer in this established order."

"My husband could have chosen another profession."

"What exactly could I have done? Grab a machine gun, go out and kill a number of capitalists? My argument will make them kneel. I confront them with reality, as the French say."

"How, please? By entrusting them with justice?"

"Well … well…" he said. It was as if his words proceeded with a speed his thoughts could not catch up with and left him out of breath. "It all boils down to this," he said eventually. "Once justice and everything else is in possession of uncrowned kings, people will realize that the Prime Minister and his gang whose sole concern is to appear on television have no longer any service to render, no function to perform, but are simply burdens. Thus, when their uselessness is understood, the prophesy of Marx the Great will have been fulfilled *ad absurdum*. He wrote that the infallible victory of the proletariat, i.e. of labor, has not been realized, but that they will put an end to capitalism…"

"And then?"

"The proletariat, once set free, will end the wildest and the most inhuman of established orders, capitalism. Sovereignty will be in the hands of labor and the ideal revolution will have been realized in the least expected country."

Can's effusive talk had carried Gül back thirty-three years, and she had before her the university student of old, and she empathized with him. But it did not take her long to recollect herself.

"What about the big bosses?" she inquired.

Can did not hesitate. "Since nearly all of the bosses will be foreigners and, therefore, outside the country, and since their representatives in this country will only be their vassals, there will hardly be any problem," he answered.

With a sudden movement, Gül rushed over to him and began kissing him. "Darling! Darling!" she declared, "You should have been a poet rather than a lawyer!"

Can hardly heard what she was saying. "In the meantime, I'll have Varol released."

Gül hugged her husband. "Sure, darling, sure," and tears began to run down her cheeks. "You certainly will."

"You do believe me, don't you?

"I certainly do, darling!" she said as if bewitched. She stared at her husband with admiration.

Can experienced the same feelings toward her that she felt toward him. He was looking at the beautiful eyes he found fascinating. He remembered suddenly the picture of Temel's mother. As if Marx's theory had been realized, he rose and crossed over to his jacket, took out the picture from a pocket, and handed it to Gül, saying, "This Temel's mother. Isn't she beautiful? Not to be compared with your beauty, of course."

"Not to be compared with my beauty? Come! Are you kidding? Never in my life have I seen such a beauty. There is something otherworldly, hardly to be qualified as beauty. She looks divine. We need to find another adjective for it.

Can took her in his arms and carried her to the bedroom where she undressed, and they began making love.

When their passion was satiated, she asked, "How could a mere newspaper article set off a chain reaction? Do you think that Cüneyt could write such an article? Suppose he doesn't? What if the editorial staff of *The Globe* turns his article down?"

Can replied, "Cüneyt said he could get it ready by tomorrow. I hope we'll read it then, and if not, the following day."

IV

CÜNEYT'S ARTICLE DID NOT APPEAR the following day; neither did it appear the third, the fourth, the fifth, or the sixth day after that. Before he wrote it he thought about the modernity, consistency, and usefulness of the scheme without neglecting to consider Temel himself. After nine days, he shut himself in his house and wrote his article in intense concentration. It was published the following day. To be frank, Temel's offer could not be declined. It stated that he was disposed to offer an apartment of nearly two thousand square feet overlooking the sea, consisting of a living room and three other rooms between the seventeenth and one hundredth floors of a skyscraper about to be completed at Maçka, for a sum to be obtained from the sale of "our reputable and esteemed writer's apartment of about half that size at Nişantaşı. However, it was difficult to guess if the reputable writer had written the said article, to which we could easily ascribe the attribute of "historical," under the influence of the generous offer in question or if he had already been thinking about it from the very beginning. Whatever lay behind it, the fact remained that his article had the effect of a bomb all over Turkey. The Turkey before publication and the Turkey afterwards was not the same Turkey. This article — which may not have been as seminal as Emile Zola's "J'accuse," written towards the end of the nineteenth century — gave the impression that its writer, before sitting in front of his computer, had obviously been inspired to a great extent by the translation of Zola's work executed seventy years earlier by an ordinary writer, now in the grave and long since forgotten. Nevertheless, it was evident that the article exerted considerable influence on Turkish public opinion, commensurable with the effect created by "J'accuse."

Did Cüneyt advance irrefutable arguments in the said article? No. Did he introduce anything new? No. He added nothing to what he heard Can say. However, the very fact that a feature article was given four times as much space as a regular column was a consequential event. To add to this, the long standing experience and reputation of the columnist enhanced the effect of exceptional coherence and cohesiveness. As a "veteran militant," he treated first the lack of cooperation between various organizations, which, in one way or another, had probably thwarted the realization of revolutions of greater or lesser scope, and second, dealt with justice as a state institution. Under the circumstances, he suggested that the only solution would be the privatization of justice, in other words putting an end to the state's ascendance, concluding that "Justice is a social institution important enough not to be entrusted to the state." The rationale for his argument followed. He said, "In the face of the privatization of universities, mines, communications, security, etc., and of the globalization process under way, justice could not possibly remain unprivatized."

According to him, state socialism was a perversion, the consequence of a totally wrong conception of society, while private enterprise as the most natural human condition when one considered that the contribution to the increase of population depended on the instinctual act of two individuals in a bed. On the other hand, globalization meant, in the first place, the sovereignty of private enterprises over nations without exception, relegating states to a subsidiary position. We were no longer in Montesquieu's world. This man had preached that kingship was based on the principle of honor, tyranny on the principle of fear, and a republic on virtue. Although Cüneyt's definition was not exactly correct, its principles were perhaps correct *per se*, but our world, in the meantime, had actually globalized. The world turned round the sun once every year and rotated 365 times on its own axis. Under the circumstances, in our age neither virtue, nor honor, nor fear could be qualified as basic principles. Who would instil fear in whom, whose virtue would prevail over whose virtue, whose honor would outweigh whose honor? In our land of milk and honey, the only criterion henceforth would be an objective of universal value, i.e. money. Under the circumstances, nobody could deny that fundamental self-criticism had become indispensable. The fact that the governments of the world, determined to keep justice as their exclusive prerogative, spoke without shame of "the separation of the legislative and the executive powers," manifestly showed thereby the absurdity of the traditional attitude toward justice. What we called separation was not a realized ideal, but an ideal to be realized. And the only way to achieve this ideal was the privatization of justice in conformity with the conditions prevailing in the market. Turkey's taking the first step in the realization of this sublime and indispensable ideal would earn our nation an important position as the pioneer and enhance our respectability. For the concept of privatization had the same connotation as "civilisation," and as everybody knows, the word *civil* had its origin in the Latin word *civicus*, meaning "civilian" in opposition to the military and the criminal as well as "civilized." Thus this radically new privatization would deliver a hard slap to self-complacent western nations who have always qualified us as an "underdeveloped," that is, an "uncivilized" community and would win us a privileged position among the nations of the world. At all events, postponing such a revolution would have a deleterious effect, whereas quickening it would be highly beneficial. Especially, if in a society where every citizen, feeling out of sorts, were to appeal to justice, this state of affairs would continue but many years. This would mean the end of the Turkish Republic. If we are among the poorer and underdeveloped nations, it was partly due to the fact that justice was in the hands of the state. In a nutshell, in this happy age of ours in which our world is incontestably globalized, the only way to immortalize the administration of the Turkish Republic would be to privatize justice.

Gül read this article in bed at 7:00 a.m., which meant one hour before her husband. At breakfast, having run an eye over the rest of the news, she threw the paper onto the coffee table saying, "I didn't expect such a lousy article."

Can tried to defend his friend. "You must take into consideration the level of our reading public," he said, which showed that *he* also had not found it satisfactory. All the same, "I warn!" had a dramatic effect and was immediately a subject of discussion.

That evening, nearly all the television stations in the Turkish Republic in their news programs summarized Cüneyt's "revolutionary proposal," followed by the views of the Prime Minister, the Minister of the Interior, the Minister of Justice, the head of the opposition party, and prominent columnists concerning this "interesting proposal." The views expressed were as interesting as the proposal itself. The Prime Minister, notorious for his reluctance to devote himself to reading, said, "I've gone over the headlines of all the papers this morning, and I've never come across such an article. As a matter of fact, I've encountered the name itself for the first time," justifying thus a widely accepted impression in important circles. The Minister of Justice explained that he could not spare the time to read the article, but\ based on reports from his friends, he found it interesting and coherent in its context, adding that he could, if need be, evaluate it and discuss it with his qualified friends, thus leaving the issue to be decided at an opportune moment in the future. The spokespersons for the opposition parties concluded similarly, shelving their decision to a later date and were disinclined to say 'yes' or 'no' to the idea. Since they had no personal views on any subject and weighed every issue according to its relative merits, as suited their ends, they merely stated that the idea deserved consideration and waited for an opinion to be issued from the powers that be before formulating their own. It is worth considering here — if the so-called *views* can be literally called *views*, of course — that the *views* of the prominent members of the same party differed considerably from each other. However, these contradictory *views* related to the authorship and the personality of Cüneyt rather than to the matter in hand. For instance, one of the vice-presidents of a formerly prominent political party said, "Whenever I read an article by Cüneyt Ender, I say 'there *are* philosophers in Turkey, after all.' Therefore, one should read this article as a philosophical treatise and assess it accordingly." Another said, "The proposal is interesting and vital. There's no doubt about that. We shall tackle the issue soon in all its dimensions." A third commented, "It's been almost a year that we have been discussing this subject in the meetings of our general board, and we expect to reach a decision very soon." A fourth said, "I never read that columnist!" and thus made an end of it. In short, they were all confused. A young member of parliament who had a Ph.D. in political science from M.I.T., a member of the party in power, whose name was often heard, declared, "Let the subject be widely debated on television in the first place, so that we may be enlightened," expressing in this way the opinion of the majority of the public. The first thing to do then was to watch television and benefit from whatever light it might shed on the issue. For in order that a subject be given due consideration, it had to be included first in the television broadcasts so that the viewers in schools, on the street, in the political parties, and in government circles might form an opinion and endorse it.

Nothing would be more natural. Columnists and academics who had opinions on every subject would provided sharp answers to questions from interviewers. Despite some minor diverging opinions, they concurred on the general principles with an air of triumph. For instance, Taylan Gökçek, one of the leading jurists of the time, had the following to say, "Our brother Cüneyt, while offending our dignity, has illuminated a subject that we, as jurists and specialists in political science, should have considered, and we should have struggled for its general acceptance. He has shown us the greatest flaw in contemporary democracies. If democracies will henceforth be inclined to endorse globalization, the nations of the world will owe it to our valuable thinker Cüneyt." On the other hand, İsmet Özgümrükçü from the University of Katılım identified Cüneyt as an unprecedented pioneer and stated that in case his notion were approved, it would mean that "our world is truly and completely globalized." Another doctor of law, associate professor Dr. Aleyna Şekure Köseibrahimefendioğlu from Sabancı University censured the famous writer and shouted rude remarks at him as if the issue of privatization had already been on the country's agenda for ages and was being discussed under his ægis. "What he says is perfect, no doubt!

But it is nothing to boast of. He happens to be behind the times!" Another academic, this one from the University of Yüceler, associate professor Dr. Numan Çakmak, said, "The powers that be in today's Turkey, having already experienced the problem before in many fields, are certainly capable of privatizing justice, for, and I'm saying this with special emphasis, Turkey has already reached this stage. Let no one doubt about it!" Speaking thus, he indirectly sent his compliments to the government in power.

What is still more extraordinary at this time were the big bosses (the number of little bosses was at an specially low ebb), who after vacillating for a few hours and having made a number of phone calls, came to the conclusion that Cüneyt's proposal suited their own interests and so decided to support it, therefore commissioning their spokespersons to find new justifications that would strongly support the scheme and make clear its indispensability. The brief speech made by the vice-chair of their reputable association — the membership of which had declined since the fourth quarter of the twentieth century, but the renown of which increased proportionately to the declining membership — was in the same vein. According to him this new scheme was the only solution for coping with all the judical drawbacks that resulted from capitalism. He attached special "meaningful value" to the fact that it had originated with "a reputable experienced columnist" who never made concessions out of mere generosity. Cüneyt's scheme received great acclaim as soon as "this belated proposal" was made public. No objection was expressed by the media.

As one would expect, the same attitude was observed in the press the following day. The positive reactions heard on the first day were succeeded by many other speeches in support, and in at least ninety-five per cent of the newspaper pages reserved for editorials, politics, economy, lifestyle, culture, and science, in short the whole magazine section, people commented on Cüneyt's article and, with slight differences, spoke, all of them, in favor of the privatization of justice. For instance, while one of our eminent woman writers said that the proposal put forth for privatization should not surprise us in a country where everything, including museums and forests that had formerly belonged to the state, had already been privatized and sold to the "public." Another author whose fame was not inferior to hers claimed that in a period of recovery brought about by privatization, the privatization of justice was a late comer. Another editorial writer who approved of the justification of justice drew attention to the fact that it might have disastrous consequences, while still another writer on the same page of the same newspaper contended that the sale of justice to a foreign concern should have "considerable benefits" since that was the only way to secure the independence of justice in this country. According to this article, it was a self-evident truth since a citizen would be liable to be led by the nose, while an outsider would remain objective, thanks to his experience and position. The blonde Didem Çiçek, the popular contributor to *The Illustrated Agenda*, announced that, based on the hypothesis that privatization is a kind of rejuvenation, "in the near future" we would have on the bench handsome young judges rather than white-haired, elderly gentlemen with sullen faces. On the same page of the same newspaper, yet another blonde, Ayça Oral, in her interview with another young blonde, suggested that the majority of the lady judges in privatized courts would certainly support the move. Men and women, an important majority of our columnists, were convinced that privatization would eventually liberate justice from all feudal elements, thus reinforcing another "pillar" of democracy. In this way, the separation of the legislative and the executive powers would finally materialize. The only dissenting opinion was expressed by Kısmet Güçlü, a middle-aged brunette movie critic, who contributed to the page reserved for culture. This foolish lady, just for the sake of taking issue with the majority opinion, claimed that the privatization of justice might corrupt the concept of law and lead to self-destruction. Therefore, she added that the separation of the legislative and the executive powers should at least be maintained, since otherwise this "so-called reform" would expose capitalism to danger, to which it was spiritually linked by "its umbilical chord."

The following day, another writer on the same page of the same paper, a theater critic named Yıldız Sarı, hurled invectives, claiming that the separation of powers was nonsense and declaring that since solidarity meant might, privatization would strengthen justice. This writer, with a foresight hardly to be expected from a theater critic, placed the privatization of justice on a capitalistic footing, noting that the sale concept converted justice into a "commodity." Some opinionated persons who could not free themselves form the yoke of outdated values made derogatory remarks, but when one considered the matter carefully, everything we received and gave, including affection and respect, were mere commodities. Formerly we obtained justice indirectly from the state through taxes, and we continued to do so even when we were outside the justice system. Henceforth we would be buying justice directly. In other words, justice would provide us with fairness at a cost. This happened to be the way of the world in the twenty-first century. Just as the idea of the state's operating bakeries made us laugh, so would the state's manipulation of justice involve a transition from the sublime to the ridiculous. On the other hand, according to Ms. Yıldız, bribery, which had been beyond control for ages, would disappear, since every citizen involved in a legal problem would have to pay for justice. Thus we would no longer need to bribe the grocer, the butcher, or the barber, or slip some money under the table for the prosecutor and the judge. Nor might it be necessary to engage lawyers. Despite the fact that this was merely a contribution from a theater critic, the concept of law as a commodity recurred in every article, speech, and forum, gaining an ever increasing respectability and importance, so much so that whenever the privatization of justice was mentioned, its untoward associations vanished, and people looked askance at those who remarked, "What? Can justice be privatized?"

Can's scheme had become socially acceptable within a couple of weeks. Nevertheless, on the other side of the fence, quietly voiced objections were on the way. As one can easily surmise, these crosscurrents did not originate with professors of law lecturing at universities. Even though these academics might be disposed to approve of the suggested change, they could not possibly run against the opinions of those from whom they received their appointments. On the other hand, in consideration of the fact that their own institutions happened to be within the boundaries of the private sector, opposition from law professors to the privatization of any organization could have endangered the legitimacy of the very organizations of which they were members, and even supposing they had their own views on the issue, they would, in all probability, have kept their views to themselves, either supporting the cause or remaining silent. Prosecutors and judges preferred to stay aloof from a battleground where the outcome was uncertain. Although a manifesto was published in a magazine with a small circulation, arguing that privatization would be the end of law and justice, this "heretical tendency" was due to the fanatical zeal of a handful of emeritus professors and had no repercussions. In a period of exuberance when the entire tabloid press and television highlighted the privatization, expecting these elderly men of modest income to find the opportunity to express their thoughts through the media would be too simplistic. As for two reputable judges from the past, namely Turgut Bayram and Arif Sönmez, neither they nor the associations with which they were associated were of any consequence anymore. These gentlemen were featured on television and tried to appear impartial, at least in matters not worthy of consideration. They published a laboriously prepared joint statement that appeared in a newspaper, but since they could not pass over in silence the disadvantages of privatization, all doors were closed to them. Their argument was compelling, however: "Can one say that the scales of justice operate fairly today?" This was followed by examples. Nobody emerged agreeing that the institution of justice functioned admirably already, thus necessitating any change superfluous. There was a pundit, a master of repartee in judicial arguments, who produced irrefutable counterarguments. This was Sabri, second in commend in the organization presided over by Can. One could not possibly expect him to oppose a scheme advanced by the organization for which he worked.

Thus the only commentator who could effectively challenge the scheme was Veysel Çakır, a columnist for *The Illustrated Agenda*. This elderly man, who was also a renowned poet, ended at least a third of his epigrammatic, humorous stories for the *Wednesday Supplement* with: "Given the fact that justice has remained since the beginning of history a nebulous concept and that it has been customary to commit injustice for the sake of this nebulous concept, to privatize justice would be tantamount to overburdening those in power with the responsibility of injustice, which in turn would eventually lead to revolution. If we believe that we are in fact a community that loves patronage, we must see to it that this sin remains God's and the state's responsibility." The majority of readers resented these remarks rather than thinking them amusing, and the majority of writers qualified them as "a continuous and insistent revolutionary and counter-revolutionary attempt," adding, "It is high time to silence such a dissenting voice or make it clear that the subject was too serious to be a subject for humor."

The spearheads of those promoting privatizing justice were Can and Cüneyt, whose pictures could be seen and statements read every other day in some newspaper. they appeared two or three times on television, sitting sometimes next to each other and sometimes facing each other, defending their cause. As one could easily guess from the available documents, their talks lacked variety. The programs were almost identical and were set up in the same fashion: the presenter gave the floor to Cüneyt, who explained the defects of the established order and outlined their scheme, and when it was time to discuss the legal aspects and revolutionary novelties that the new program would introduce, he pointed to Can and said, "The law embodied!" Can, after murmuring a few modest syllables, then began expatiating on the details of the scheme. The interesting thing was that, despite the uniformity of the contents of the talks, Can came up with new evidence that bewildered even himself. However, the example he cited most often was the case of Varol Korkmaz, who had been in jail for the last two years. He never cited the name of the persons involved, since he dealt with the instance abstractly, reducing it to its barest fundamentals. Yet his listeners understood perfectly who was involved and thus had no difficulty establishing a link between the abstract and the concrete.

Thus within a couple of weeks, faithful television viewers spoke of Can as "Mr. Law" as if he were a personal acquaintance. "Mr. Law will be speaking again in favor of the privatization of justice." However, when it came to facts, the leader was Cüneyt, who never failed to call television channels with suggestions for new interviews and forums, recommending his friends at universities and associations and new topics of discussions. He asked his colleagues from other newspapers to support the cause and reserved at least one of his five columns every week to the inevitability of the privatization of justice, all of which ended with these words: "This revolution, cherished readers, is a great revolution; to be precise, it is the last link in the revolutionary chain we are in the process of experiencing. Soon every citizen will *per force* endorse it, and the Turkish Republic will carry off the prize in the history of revolutions, and its well-earned position among the nations of the world will have officially been sanctioned." Although, at least in private, Can and Cüneyt's communist and anarchist pasts and their support of young communist and anarchist militants were now and then mentioned and false claims were made about the possibility of the utopian ideal as a leftist revolution, the great majority espoused the cause and said, "Since former communists and anarchists promote privatization, we should vote for it!" The short and the long of it was that even after five weeks from the day in which Cüneyt's article was published, there was no end to declarations, statements, speeches, and forums on the issue. This topic was not exclusively the media's but was "marketed" in schools, streets, coffee houses, trains, and airplanes.

There was a reaction from government circles. When Cüneyt's article on privatization of justice had created a bomb effect, some cabinet ministers responded with remarks that could be qualified as positive, even though on a minor scale. Quite a few pro-governmental columnists stated that the proposal "was worth dwelling on," but then, for some inexplicable reason, governmental circles had preferred to remain silent, and no comment, for or against, was made by any member of the party in power from the head of the smallest administrative district up to the Prime Minister himself. As one might expect, the attitude of other political parties had been negative. At the outset, assessing the issue on the positive or quasi-positive reactions of the political parties in power, they were mistrustful. "Turkey befooled again by spurious delusions?" "No such plan is on the agenda of Europe! What are we after anyway?" "Justice becomes a cheap commodity!" However, the euphoric interest of the media had induced them to change their attitude. Fifteen days after the publication of "I warn!," while the government remained silent on the issue, the opposition parties heartily supported it. The leader of the party, a self-styled leftist, made new statements every day, announcing that privatization — a process that could not be thwarted anymore — could no longer be called into question and recommended the powers that be should not delay returning what actually belonged to the public to its original owner, i.e. the public.

Finding that the opposition's support had been added to the positive stance taken by the press, Cüneyt began to see himself as a hero and think that he could lead the masses, which in turn made him think that he could start a revolution. One evening, when he, Can, and Temel were on the top floor of one of the newest skyscrapers and were sipping their whiskeys, while contemplating the beauty of the Bosphorus and the Sea of Marmara, the reticence of the government was discussed. Temel announced, "To my mind, these individuals must step down. We must put an end to special courts and the autocratic regime," and when he noticed Can's surprise, he added, "Your Varol is one of the victims of corruption." Lowering his voice, he said, "No need for any guns. If we can prevail upon thirty-five or forty members of parliament, the rest will automatically follow." He looked from Temel to Can and asked, "Are you with me?"

"I am for it!" said Temel urgently. "I can afford what it costs!"

Can said smiling, "Let's not imagine things! The year is 2073. Are we going to recruit a whole army on top of all the problems ahead?"

"As I've said, we have no need for an army. Once we have brought thirty-five or forty members of parliament over to our side, you may consider the affair settled."

Can, bending towards his friend, replied, "My dear Cüneyt, to hatch a plot in order to overthrow a government is not our way of handling things. What's more, if we acted that way, we would be cutting off the limb we're sitting on. Everybody would accuse us of doing away with democracy by force. Don't forget, the first thing to be considered should be the country's welfare."

"What's that got to do with the country or doing away with democracy?" rejoined Temel. "Our aim is to free the nation from conservative impostors."

"We're not going to use force," cut in Cüneyt. "We'll do it by stealth."

"Why not?" Temel rejoined. "Shall we let them get away with their spoils?"

Can made a wry expression. "The fact is that a frequent change in power would be detrimental to the country."

"Just because the policy has changed?"

"No. Because new power leads to the rise of the newly rich, which leads automatically to a decline in the number of honest people," said Can, which statement he followed with a detailed analysis of the political life of the country. He stated that every political party formulated a given policy according the circumstances of the day, defended a given set of principles, and brought change when it was deemed necessary. The only policy that remained in such a situation was the policy of the government in power. The party that came to power, regardless of whatever objectives it had declared, implemented the objectives of the outgoing party. In other words, the new party pursued the same policies of the old, adopting principles contrary to the public's benefit. It was a sacred duty to tag along with Europe and America and, last but not least, enrich its partisans, the principle objective. Focusing directly on his friends, he asked, "Am I wrong?"

"No matter what you do, you'll never be able to break with your past," answered Cüneyt. "Maybe you're right; however, if you stand aloof, the plan is doomed to fail," he added. "You can never tell, my proposal might make a mess of everything."

"We cannot interpret their silence as being antagonistic to our plans," said Can.

"Anything special beyond what I see?"

"No, but silence is meaningful."

"Which is?"

"Well, this reticence on the part of the ruling party may be due to indecision. Had they been categorically opposed, a surreptitious warning to the media would have sufficed, and the issue would have been erased from memory within a week or so. Who knows, perhaps they are waiting for an opportune moment."

Temel finished his drink of whiskey. "So am I!" he said. "I am waiting for an opportune moment for the house and the garden at Cihangir. I wish I had come to terms with someone else. The matter would have been settled by now."

Can frowned. "Oh, come on. I've told you over and over that even the thought of such an undertaking appals me. Don't forget that you are the founder of a city. Your name will be in history. We must see to it that it remains ever fresh. The Prime Minister will come around in the end."

Time proved Can to be right. "The ideal and perfect solution would be to submit the matter to a popular vote to determine whether justice should be privatized or not. Ninety percent of our population will vote for it, and the prominent members of the government in power will realize that for them to keep their jobs they will have to modify their views. After this the issue will be ratified by Mevlut Doğan, renowned for his allegiance to United States and for never failing to attend Friday services as well as for his recantation in the evening of what he said in the morning.

Less than two months later, on April 14th, 2073, Can was invited to Ankara "to discuss the judical issue." He appeared reluctant to accept the invitation, since he thought that it would be more effective not to go and so asked to be excused, claiming that he had not a minute to spare. Therefore, a representative from the government, the Minister of Justice, Veli Dökmeci, came to Istanbul. Sabri said, "Please Sir, don't meddle with this man. One should be wary of getting in the same boat with the devil. This affair could ruin you and the country, too." But Can persisted.

The interview took place at dinner in one of Temel's skyscrapers, on April 18th, 2073. Can took special care to be deferential towards this skilful diplomat with whom under different circumstances he would never have condescend to join over a cup of coffee.

The man was advanced in years and gave the impression of waking from a sound sleep. He kept asking Can to repeat what he had said, said nothing definite himself, and looked as if his mind were elsewhere. Further, he looked more inane than he did in his pictures. Nevertheless, Can was positive that he would be the best man to work with since he had been responsible for the government's delay in dealing with the proposal. In the last decade, three parties, each one the archenemy of the others, had come to power, and Veli Dökmeci had managed to keep his position as Minister of Justice with them all. Provided that his ideas, or to be precise, his interests were in line with the proposal, he would not fail to do his best with respect to the privatization of justice. Moreover, at the very start of their talk, he appeared to Can an attractive figure compared to other politicians, for he was quite direct. He did not wait to broach the subject and expressed his wish to hear Can's "progressive views" on the privatization of justice. He listened very carefully to Can's views and their grounds as if hearing them for the first time. He listened to their minutest details, a subject already vulgarized by the media *ad nauseam.* Whenever Can tried to convert his monologue into a dialogue with the Minister, Veli Dökmeci begged him to go on, perhaps because he preferred to keep silent while he was eating his meal or because he took care not to appear too enthusiastic about the idea. At the conclusion of Can's presentation, the Minister noted that the government was far from being satisfied with the functioning of justice, which had led to the sporadic creation of special courts. They considered privatization to be a radical solution, adding that, given the fact that even in the United States the dispensation of justice, our source of inspiration, had not yet been privatized, the government preferred to wait before doing anything. To this Can replied, "Sir, in America the states elect their own judges. This makes the privatization of justice unnecessary. Furthermore, would you and your party prefer to see our judges elected or would you rather entrust justice to private hands, an organization that would pay the government and in turn free you from the burden of allocating money for the courts, from which the salaries of judges, clerks, and others are paid? In addition the said organization would be paying tax." To a question from the Minister about the situation in European countries, Can said, "To the best of my knowledge, they are in no way better off. You know well that they advocate universal principles only to violate them themselves. They are not to be taken as examples. In point of fact, they will have to come around to our position as time will necessitate."

The Minister of Justice was taken aback. "Why should that happen?"

Can did not hesitate in answering. "For the reasons I've been giving, Sir," he said, repressing a laugh. "In a nutshell, because of globalization and the general privatization that follows."

Veli Dökmeci nodded assent. He stood up and laid his hand on Can's shoulder and with a benign smile hardly to be expected from a Minister, said quietly, "The fact is that Mevlut Doğan dislikes being identified as the author of the privatization of justice."

"But my dear Sir," rejoined Can, "how do you arrive at that conclusion, for God's sake? Consider the great number of previous prime ministers who did not refrain from indulging in the sale of lands and seas and who got away scot-free! And what's more, you're not going to sell justice but privatize it! There's a great difference between the two. On top of that you will be proud that you are the government that crowns privatization by privatizing justice."

Veli Dökmeci smiled. "You think so?" he commented. "Do you really believe in what you are saying? To put it another way, did you engage in this venture because you firmly believed that it's good for the country?"

"Most certainly. Had I not had this conviction, why should I have undertaken such a venture?" said Can. "Believe me, this will be highly beneficial in every respect. You will have unburdened yourself from a great headache. Let alone the fact that you will get rid of a great expenditure. Nobody will accuse you of being unfair. You'll say that justice is not your responsibility. Not only will you unburden yourself, but the political order of the country will be unified."

"True, nobody can deny that."

"Another point is the fact that your pioneering work in the privatization of justice will undoubtedly increase the respectability of your government in the world, and your name will go down in history as a torchbearer."

Veli Dökmeci nodded assent. "Indeed!" he remarked, "I see that you are a very clever, well-informed, and experienced man of law."

Can smiled. "If you say so, dear Minister."

"I say so!" replied the Minister. "This is my sincere conviction." After musing for a while, he sighed and said, "There is no denying that you are a very clever, well informed, and experienced man of law. Everybody in Turkey knows this, yet it seems to me that occasionally you let yourself be carried away by your enthusiasm to the detriment of your great ideal."

"What exactly do you mean? Can you give me a concrete example?"

"I can cite as a concrete example, as you say, the attitude you adopted during the Bıçakçılar case. You had difficulty keeping yourself from attacking the presiding judge, Cahit Güven. And what's more, you showed him in a bad light."

"But I was right."

"Maybe you were. But you should have known that the court involved had been established by order of the Prime Minister, who had himself appointed the judges, and he could not possibly be friendly towards lawyers that humiliated them. What you're after happens to depend on our Prime Minister, Mevlut Doğan."

Can reflected for some time before saying, "You're right, but the case in question had a special significance for me."

"I know. One of the prisoners happened to be your friend and was quite probably innocent. But the case in question had a special significance for the Prime Minister. His objective was to deal with a traitor, who had not shrunk from doing all the evil things he could, and reduce him to a state from which he could not recover. Yet one might consider perhaps a remedial measure."

"What sort of a remedial measure?"

"What sort of a remedial measure, you ask. Well, if one could bring the Prime Minister around, the accused might get away with a fine. He could escape with the payment of an insignificant sum of money, or he might be acquitted. That probability exists even now."

Can's sense of justice was rekindled.

"What about the others?" he inquired. "The innocent people detained along with Varol Korkmaz."

Veli Dökmeci smiled indulgingly. "They'll have to wait for their turns."

"Would this be fair?"

"Certainly not, but we're talking business now, aren't we? Do you want your friend released or not?"

"I do," he said, looking down. "But I do not quite understand. What business are we talking here?"

"You'll understand soon," he said. "I don't believe you'd imagine that we would be ready to give over the administration of justice to a private organization without reasonable payment in return."

"I am still at a loss, Sir," said Can.

The Minister of Justice said softly as if there were the likelihood of someone hearing what he said, "The proposal you have outlined is outstanding, no doubt about that. But just between you and me, don't you think that we must first come to terms?"

Staggered, Can stared Veli Dökmeci. "I still don't understand, Sir," he said.

Veli Dökmeci drew nearer. "Before proceeding you'll have to close a deal with our Prime Minister and with me," he said.

"That means... well, in other words..." Before he could finish his sentence, however, Veli Dökmeci said even more softly, "The Prime Minister and I must get our shares."

Can was astounded. "What sort of share?" he asked.

Veli Dökmeci laughed. "Nothing of consequence," he explained, "About three or four per cent, deductible from the sum payable to the government. Settled?"

Can was aghast. "My dear Sir, we're pursuing our plans on principle, not buying justice ourselves," he stammered.

Veli Dökmeci gave another laugh. "Come, don't invent things!" he retorted, then added, "I can understand now. I can read your mind. You want to preside over all the future judges, over justice. Let's not pretend honesty with each other! Right?"

Can went red, and Veli Dökmeci gave another laugh. "You prefer to keep silent. This is enough. I've understand. Agreed then! Keep going. Let Mr. Cüneyt continue writing his articles and forget that incident that has delayed your case. Understood?"

Can turned away, embarrassed. "Understood, Sir," he replied. "If you say so."

Two hours later, as they were watching the news on television, Cüneyt and Temel saw Veli Dökmeci announce with a winning smile to reporters — who circled him asking about the privatization of justice — that they were a powerful government and could, if they deemed it wise and appropriate, privatize even justice.

"This is it!" Can said. He began giving his friends the details of his talk with the Minister, and told them how he had said, "'Given the fact that our world is globalizing, the privatization of justice becomes indispensable!' Now how about that!?"

"Well done!" said Cüneyt. "You have used the magic word shared by all governments in power!"

Can fixed his gaze on his friend and smiled. "Yet what they call globalization may turn out to be the exact opposite of what I am aiming at," he said. "We, erstwhile leftists, can see this more clearly. With an end to private ownership, things will pass into the hands of monopolies. Privatization deprives the community and its individuals of their rights, and monopolies replace the state. If things go on this way, the justice systems of all the countries in the world will be under the control of one source, one single patron."

Cüneyt smiled. "One divine patron, a patron deity," he said.

"You said it!"

"And you'll find yourself in seventh heaven! But tell me, which side are you on, for God's sake?" Cüneyt asked. "You are not going to give up now for the sake of outdated theories just when we have reached the critical point, are you?"

"You've gone a bit too far," said Can. "We are aware of the world we live in and it is our aim to give it cohesion, coherence. We'll bring what we've undertaken to fruition, of course!"

Temel kept yawning. He cut in for the first time. "Deal with that house and garden in one way or another. That's all I want," he said.

Can was startled. In the beginning, this had been the mainspring. But now he seemed to have forgotten all about it. He felt once more that he was reddening and tried to smile. "It won't take long, you'll see, my dear Temel! Once privatization is achieved, everything will go well."

Temel sighed. "All right, but how? A protracted struggle and an uncertain finale. Supposing that your fancies have been realized, how about mine? And suppose they entrust justice to the hands of other people instead of ours? One can never trust Mevlut the Mud!"

74

Can acted as if he did not hear.

Cüneyt answered, "Those who pander to your desires are sure to give you the means to achieve your ends," he said. "But why do you call him 'Mud'?"

"Apparently, they used to call him that in school. But, look, if justice is appropriated by others, how are we going to get things done?"

Cüneyt smiled. "Don't worry. I'll launch a carefully orchestrated campaign. But I am of the opinion that the whole thing will be Can's eventually. Justice will be his private property. The campaign for change has considerable momentum."

Temel seemed to be in a bad mood. "We'll see," he said dejectedly, "whether it has momentum or not."

"Don't worry!" repeated Cüneyt.

The Minister's word in fact soon turned into action. His declaration that "we are in fact a powerful government and could, if we deemed it wise and appropriate, privatize even justice" was interpreted to mean that "We'll be privatizing justice any time now." Intellectuals from the think tanks, columnists, television commentators, and professors from private universities left aside the question of whether justice should be privatized or not and considered how privatization should be tackled, expressing their views on radio and television, in newspapers and in magazines. In the course of a week, all of the columnists in the country spoke their minds, and queries were received from people all over Turkey. Views were positive, romantic, idealized, and rosy, as well as jaundiced, negative, and pessimistic. In the meantime, Cüneyt sided with those who were of the opinion that the whole system of justice should be privatized. For instance, in the weekly *Commentary*, Naci Yavuz wrote, "Law is a whole. One cannot think of leaving part of it in the custody of the state while privatizing the other half. If a decision decreed by one is challenged by the other, the whole system will crumble. On the other hand, while private enterprise will pay judges high salaries, no judge would be willing to work for the government." In the meantime, while some writers considered the privatization of the Supreme Court and the

Council of State natural, they argued against the privatization of the Constitutional Court. In case justice were to be entrusted to the hands of foreign institutions, our pro-western authors, backed by western countries, were of the opinion that higher courts should be given into the custody of foreign legal institutions, and, therefore, they argued, "If we are intent on giving a radical footing to real justice, this is the only way." It would not be unfair to say that these people were people who silently cherished everything the origin of which was western and considered everything local disapprovingly. They looked down on the common man, yet they exerted considerable influence in certain circles. Moreover, even assuming that they were sincere in their convictions as had been pointed out in some of Cüneyt's articles, inevitably the problem of language would crop up. These foreigners could not be expected to assess sentences pronounced in a tongue they did not understand, made according to laws of which they had no inkling, and concerned with organizations and individuals in a community with which they were not acquainted. How would these foreigners decide? By tossing a coin? Despite his inveterate admiration for America, the person who resented these pro-westerners was Temel. "They have a talent for searching out such stupid things! Do they intend to mess things up and persuade the government to capitulate? Haven't we already waited long enough?" he grumbled.

Can smiled, saying, "Don't worry. Progress can't be stopped with criticisms from scoundrels. You'll see, everything will turn out to be just as we wished, in due time."

The "due time" was long to come. Five days after Can's meeting with Veli Dökmeci, at 3:30 p.m. on April 22nd, 2073, İnci, in great haste and without knocking, rushed in and informed Can that there was a call waiting for him from the private secretary of the Prime Minister. Can picked up the receiver and, after waiting exactly two minutes, learned from Mevlut Doğan's private secretary that he would be waiting for Can tomorrow at 4 p.m. at a place to be designated in the morning. Can did not wait to communicate the good news to Sabri, Cüneyt, and, last but not least, Temel. Cüneyt and Temel were overjoyed, while Sabri was impassive.

V.

CAN, PREOCCUPIED WITH HIS UPCOMING TALK with the Prime Minister, left his law office two hours earlier than usual. He was the author and the promoter of the project. Night and day he was obsessed by it. He spoke of nothing else but the project. He listened to nothing but the project, and he could expatiate on it for hours on end. As he knew the Prime Minister's mental capacity, he didn't have to make any preparations for the interview. All the same, it would be better to go into his visit with a relaxed mind. When he opened the door of his house, Gül told him that he had a visitor. Having been told that it was Rıza, he frowned. Not because he had any objection to receiving Rıza, but because he had dropped in unannounced, unceremoniously, and quite probably he would talk his head off as it had been quite some time since he had visited him.

"You know, dear, once he starts talking there is no end," he said, "I have already been the target of Sabri's tedious talk."

"Hush," said his wife, "he might hear you."

"Let him hear me!" he rejoined. "Tomorrow I'll go to the Prime Minister. I don't want to have to discuss old business."

At this moment, the door from the small living room opened and in came Rıza, with his curly hair, round face, thick eyebrows, bluish grey eyes, and snub nose. His smile gave the impression he was going to give important news. His high spirits affected Can, who forgot all his recent negative feelings. They embraced fervently.

With glasses of whiskey, they sat at a small round table. Rıza's pervasive high spirits were shared by Can. He said, "What you said a while back is wrong. I'm not dealing with things from the past."

"What happened? Don't tell me that you're obsessed with the future now."

Rıza didn't answer. Holding his glass, he became silent for a while, then said, "Whether it's today or tomorrow, they'll sink into oblivion, into the darkness of prehistoric times."

Ever since he was a young man, whenever the past was mentioned, Can's response, frowning, was, "Forget the past. What matters is the present." Can stare for quite a while at Rıza, then ventured, "You've mentioned 'prehistoric times'? You also have undergone a change, it seems? Obsessed by prehistoric times?"

"No, I'm not obsessed by prehistoric times," he casually replied. "But prehistoric times have re-emerged in Turkey."

"How do you mean?"

Rıza sighed again. "Nothing to wonder at!" he said. "While you nourish yourselves with things you grow in greenhouses, most of our population in mountains and plains are wandering around starved, trying to satisfy their hunger, and eating bark from trees, herbs, worms, crickets, frogs, tortoises, whatever they find edible, and drinking whatever water they find. Is this not a prehistoric lifestyle?"

"Don't talk nonsense, Rıza; don't exercise your wit on me. You happen to be on the 107th floor of a skyscraper and the liquor you're drinking is twelve years old. Presently you'll be treated to a great meal. Now stop poking fun at me and speak!"

Rıza fixed his bluish grey eyes on his friend's and said, frowning, "Haven't you heard of 'castaways'? Are you so absorbed in that privatization fancy of yours? I know there is a ban on the press to speak or write about it. But I should have expected that a communist like you, a well-informed man, interested in the life of the masses must have heard of this? Are you serious that you've never heard of them?"

Can was watching his friend intently and could not decide whether he was joking or not. "Gül dear, please come here," he called. "Listen to what he says. Apparently there are people like herds of horses that range at will, people who roam the fields and mountains naked and eat herbs, worms, frogs, crickets, whatever they find in order not to starve, in the year of our Lord, 2073."

Gül burst into laughter. "You must know Rıza," she said. "He does not just write poetry. He is a born poet, creating things out of nothing. He must have concocted this story. We must expect him to write a book about it soon."

"Looks like it," said Can, somewhat relieved. "The book must be in the genre 'fiction.'"

Rıza banged on the table with his fist, scattering his glass and dishes of hors d'oeuvres.

"No doubt you are on the 127th floor of Temel's sky scraper. Domiciled in heaven, you shuttle between your office and your home In other words you are not in this country," he said, but from Gül's look he realized that he had gone too far. He conclude, "I apologize, but you know nothing, indeed, nothing at all!"

As Gül cleaned the mess on the floor, Can, apparently to ease things, got up and opened the window. "My dear Rıza, living on the 127th floor of a skyscraper has its advantages," he remarked. "Come, have a look at the landscape before you. The moon seems to have married the sea and the sky. You loved the sea as I recall."

Rıza did not move. "Even the sea has become repulsive to me," he said, "ever since it was monopolized by that Yankee crook..."

"But the fact it is in the hands of a Yankee does not diminish its beauty..."

"It transforms its contents, which is worse. When you think that all the waterways of the country are in the hands of an American idiot, and that their natural course has been altered into vast fish farms. No sooner do you approach these places than colossal guards with guns and night sticks threaten you."

Can drew the curtain with a laugh. "Turkey is a free country, a heaven of democracy," he said. "It can sell anything it wants. Even jeans."

"I wish that instead of selling those jeans, it threw them to the castaways. It would have done some good."

"How so?"

"Because the castaways attach great value to clothes."

Gül had wiped off the coffee table and replaced the glasses, adding one for herself.

"They'd prefer selling. They are unprecedented in this, but Rıza is right. These Yankees have also altered the very nature of fish," he commented. "Take any fish. They all have the same taste, which is none at all. It's nauseating." He gazed at the armchair and seemed to be obsessed by a problem even worse than tasteless fish and the fact that the waterways of the country had been for the last fifteen years in the possession of an American company. He poured some more whiskey into his glass, adding ice cubes, and gave it to him. Facing him, he asked, "How about saying just what you mean?"

Rıza took a sip from his glass and began with a slight frown, "I am not trying! I *am* telling it. I even wrote a book about it, *Herds of Castaways,* published by Kaçak Publishers. Walking is not your custom, so you can't have run across it. The next time I visit, if I'm allowed, I'll bring a copy. Humans are roaming around the country in distant places, a host of people, the elderly and the young, male and female, adults and children, an army of the starving, deprived of all clothing, wallowing in dirt, wandering in hills and valleys like primitive tribes. They eat whatever they can find, earthworms, frogs, wild herbs, bark, and algae. They even fight over a dead crow. They are forbidden access to farms guarded by human monsters armed with machine guns. What they shoot is not considered dead, just the living that is not living..."

Both Gül and her husband, shocked, stood aghast, although they could hardly believe what they heard. They thought that the man must be telling them something he dreamt.

Can put his hand on his friend's shoulder. "I see you have abandoned your cause, the social struggle for poetry, and you're giving us a picture of place inhabited by ogres, a figment of your imagination."

"Not true! I have seen these people with my own eyes and lived for two weeks among them," he said, his voice rising and his hands, feet, and lips trembling.

"You're imagining things," said Can, "You are overwrought and the victim of your own fears. How about staying with us for a couple of days and pulling yourself together. We could send for a doctor."

Rıza flew into a rage and stomped on the floor like an angry child.

"I tell you. I've lived these things!"

"But why?" asked Gül. "What was wrong with these people? What caused them to abandon their villages and take to the mountains?"

Rıza shook his head as to dismiss the question. "Who said they chose to do this? These are castaways turned loose to range at will. Horses, donkeys, mules that had once been part and parcel of human life, once they grow old and have to be dispensed with are exiled to the wasteland far from the villages, and so are the castaways. The flock together and roam at will. Animals like horses and donkeys are almost extinct. Now it's the humans' turn. Those who can't work and are doomed to remain jobless are cast away. They go to the countryside with young people and children. It is sad to note, on the other hand, that nature is no longer the way it was. The strange thing is that human beings, the toughest of the species, can survive under the hard conditions to which they are subjected, and yet they reproduce..."

"I can understand the elderly, but the young generation and the children, why?" asked Gül. "Why do they get rid of them?"

"Well, because they are worthless and they would eat what others would like, and because they would be unpleasant in our pristine cities and towns and cities. The citizens don't want the ugly sight of bodies lying around. Moreover, they are not forced to leave their usual homes anyway, since more often than not they are the ones who would go in search of food elsewhere."

Both Can and Gül, shuddering, listened to him intently but incredulously.

"Why on earth can't they find jobs?" Can, asked. "The economy is thriving as everybody knows. Istanbul is being demolished to be rebuilt!"

"That's it!" said Rıza. "Machines have replaced men. Those employed will sooner or later lose their jobs and those gnats that suck the blood of the population — the foreigners you have a particular attraction to — will pack their luggage complete with their dirty laundry and dirty money and go away." He stopped to take a deep breath and went on: "Among those roaming the wasteland, I've seen plenty of architects, engineers and teachers."

"There are about a 150 men I employ," Can said.

Rıza was unconvinced. "150 employees next to Istanbul's two million."

"Two million? How do you get that number?" asked Gül.

"Two million, maybe less..." replied Rıza. "Of the inhabitants of this city..."

Can interrupted him: "How come we do not know all this?" he asked. "Are *we* deaf and blind?"

Rıza took a picture from his pocket and threw it on the coffee table. "Take a good look!" he replied "It is a photograph of a place near Bergama, taken two months ago. Ninety-five per cent of the trees are dried up, leafless, rotten to the core. They could be pushed over by a seven year old kid. They don't just fall down but become shit-colored powder."

Can felt as if he were being drawn into a nightmare and tried to resist.

"Answer me first!" he insisted. "How come we don't know all these things? Are we so stupid?"

After a few minutes, Rıza sighed.

"It seems that this privatization passion has made you forget almost everything. "Now you live in this country, you are a celebrated lawyer, and so is your wife. You are both lawyers and former militants. You must know what's going on around you. Yet you seem to have forgotten that the concept that everybody, without exception, reveres is the concept of prohibition. You are besieged with prohibitions. Prohibition teams have been organized, so that you need a pass to gain access to whatever you want. Unless you have a pilot's licence, they don't generally allow people like you and me to leave the city, and that's true not only in Bitlis and Sivas but also in Bursa, Balıkesir, and İzmir. There are places the entry into which is strictly forbidden. The fact that roads between cities have been erased from the map facilitates the work of those who love prohibitions. And when you look down from high places you can't possibly see the swarming herds of castaways. In short, it's no easy job to spot these new creatures, not to mention the fact that it's extremely dangerous, for once you're among them you can't easily escape."

"If such is the true state of affairs, they are still natives of this country in spite of everything."

"Not quite. Most of them are not officially married, and their children are not officially registered. They are treated like snakes and frogs. These things stretch back many years into the past, fifteen years perhaps."

Can, his eyes riveted on the ceiling, said, "Just the other day I was flying to Ankara, and I can't say I saw anything like what you're describing."

Rıza smiled. "I've just told you, you can't see them from the sky." After thinking a few minutes, he continued, "I don't think they would like to be spotted. If you flew close to the ground, you could see them perhaps. I'm not sure." He added, "If you don't deem it too risky, why not try flying low enough to see the dry and barren land, the ash colored mountains and hills. They'll delight you, I'm sure."

Can said, "I'm not going to ask you how you came to know all this. I know that you are inquisitive, and you recall everything before anyone else does. I'm still at a loss to believe all you've said."

Gül, who had been following them closely, agreed. "So am I."

"I wish you'd read my book first. We could see eye to eye then. One thing is certain. I'm no poet. I've written a non-fiction book. Only the illustrations are missing. If your husband would like to give me a hand, my intention is to publish my book with illustrations."

Can laughed. "You want money then?"

Rıza was furious. "Not for your utopian privatization. An important page is being turned. Maybe it's the end of history. Don't tell me that you're not interested in your money. I wouldn't be surprised to see you develop a new theory just to change the subject."

"What theory?"

"Oh, I don't know! We have been hearing lately from idiots that once life on our planet became extinct, Turkish culture could be transported to another planet. And you tell me, 'I can spare no money for the enemies of the established order.'"

"Thanks! This might be exactly what would suit my purpose!" said Can with a wry smile. He stared long at his friend's face, then felt tears coming to his eyes. "Fool! You fool!" he said, "Did I ever refuse to give you money? What makes me treat the matter as I do is that you might get into trouble again. Don't forget, you're no longer young. Prison is not the place for you anymore."

Gül rejoined, "Don't worry, Can. What he's describing is just a figment of his imagination."

"Well, if you say so, so be it, Gül," said Rıza. "You arrange all your affairs, and when you feel tired, you fly off to Paris, London, and Florence. Of course, you can see nothing that way. But these castaways swarm all over the country. In a sense, we are part of their species."

A shudder ran down Gül's spine. "No," he declared fervently. "I am not one of them! Such creatures do not exist!" He put his arm around his wife's shoulder and drew her close. "Whether they exist or not, let's forget about it. Let's not discuss this privatization issue either. Let's think back to our experiences in the past like three old comrades and talk about the good old days."

Rıza burst out laughing. "Like old bourgeoisie," he remarked. "Let's overlook what's right under our noses and ignore realities. But this home is your home, and it all belongs to you. Let's go back to the good old days and turn a blind eye to what we're going through now."

"As if we knew nothing of these castaways!"

"Correct."

And correct it was. They began to relive their past experiences. When Gül consulted her watch, it was already quarter to four.

"Time for bed," her husband said.

However, the next day, when he got into his private spaceshuttle to meet the Prime Minister, Doğan, in his mind he was still in the past, twenty-six years ago, hand in hand with Gül Aşkın. As he was leaving home, she had said, "I wish you wouldn't talk to that man anymore!" But his businessman instinct prevailed. At exactly 3:50, he got out from his spaceshuttle and made his way to the door of a white two-storied country mansion. The image of the Prime Minister came to mind, and he repeated his name quietly, "Doğan, Doğan" Keeping in mind that such a man as that could be the Prime Minister, you knew that you could never fully understand the nation that elected him.

VI.

AT EXACTLY 3:59 ON APRIL 23ʀᴅ, 2073, at the sumptuous entrance of the country mansion, a middle-aged man with a moustache stood in front of a half dozen security guards, giving the impression that it his custom to meet his guest everyday at the same spot. "Welcome, Sir," he said. "The Prime Minister is waiting for you." He led the way up a flight of seven or eight steps into a spacious parlor containing a round table and several red armchairs. Can's dramatic reception disarmed him, and he had the sudden impression that he had been the victim of a nasty trick. There was no trace of the Prime Minister. But soon Mr. Hasan Berberoğlu, a sandy haired gentleman in a navy blue outfit with affected manners and a radiant smile appeared and said, "Welcome, Sir, the Prime Minister is praying. It won't be long. He'll be here in five minutes. Can was directed to a chair next to a larger one that must certainly be reserved for the Prime Minister. The sandy haired gentleman told him it was an honor to meet such a valued businessman and thinker. When he began expatiating on Can's successes as a lawyer, Can replied that he did not deserve such praise, adding that all his virtue, if that was what it was, had been to give everything its due, nothing in short to be proud of. The private secretary, for that is what he was, insisted that it was "a thing to be proud of, most certainly!" adding, "I have studied law myself, and I know what one should be proud of. The Prime Minister Doğan shares this opinion."

This gave Can a sense of *esprit de corps*, but he wondered, "Why does he tell me all this?" It called up in him a sensation he often experienced: people who surrounded important and celebrated individuals were even more affectionate and comely than the individuals themselves, and Hasan Berberoğlu was no expectation to the rule. "Yet I wonder why he has to respect the name of the Prime Minister," he thought. He wondered if he might have been mistaken about the man. At all events, he had to wait for some time yet until the Prime Minister had completed his prayers. He leaned toward secretary and said, "Hasan, allow me to ask you something confidential," and, without waiting for a reaction, he bluntly asked, "Do you like the Prime Minister?"

The private secretary was visibly upset. "Why do you ask?"

After a moment, Can said: "I just thought that your impressions might shed some light on what to expect. Do you like him?"

The private secretary answered with a cheerful smile, "Certainly, Sir, certainly. I am devoted to him. What about you?"

"Oh I don't know. This is the first time I'll see him, but I have a feeling that I'll like him."

No sooner had he said this than the Prime Minister entered the room. As the private secretary backed away, the Prime Minister advanced with his customary look of impassivity, and Can stepped forward with a faint smile. He was amazed to see that his own hand had momentarily vanished in the Prime Minister's huge grip. The hands were incredibly big.

The Prime Minister asked, "What have you been talking about?"

"Your private secretary was telling me how much he admires you."

Doğan broke into a laugh.

"He does, I'm sure. God bless him. He is unstinting in his praise, entirely loyal to me."

He walked resolutely to his chair, and pointed to the one in which Can had been sitting. "Please be seated," he said, adding, "I am so sorry to have troubled you by asking you here. I always receive my guests here when I have important things to discuss. This is a place where security reigns supreme. The surroundings are regularly sprinkled with most effective sprays. The place is a kind of a greenhouse. No ticks, birds, flies, microbes and viruses can survive here. You can wander in the garden in absolute security. If I were to invite a man of your calibre and he were to die within the week, I'd be the one they'd blame. I am particular about having my guests safe and sound." After these preliminary remarks, he tackled the subject at hand without further delay. However, like many civil servants, he filled in the background first. He spoke of his passion for privatization, which he saw as a 'life jacket, a safety valve, and mentioned the fact that some eighty or ninety years earlier, the loyal subjects of this state, the devout people in love with their God, had launched a fundamental privatization campaign. He added that if they had failed to do this, "we would be far behind where we are today.' Then he pressed a button, and to the attendant who instantly appeared, he ordered a couple of Cokes. Then, as if he had run short of energy, he was silent behind his impassive expression.

Once he imbibed his soda, however, he pulled himself together and managed to smile. "You know what, Temel, you have opened a new vista for me. You know why? You assume that everything has been privatized at present. You deplore the fact that you can no longer make any contribution to your country, since it seems that nothing remains to be privatized, and you despair. Major countries snub you, and the citizens of your own country are disappointed. You can't get great pleasure from your position as Prime Minister, and then suddenly there appears an intelligent man like yourself, who declares, 'Wait! That's not the end of the world! There are still things to be considered!' Thus you realize suddenly that there are still things to be done and, you feel relieved. Indeed! An intelligent statesman always finds something to sell, for there is always something left unsold." Having said this, he took a sip of his soda, pointing at the same time to Can's. He laid his hand on Can's. "But," he said, "not even the devil would have thought of such a feat. The privatization of justice has so far been done nowhere else in the world. One must be quite sharp to invent such a theory." Having congratulated his guest on his achievement in shaping public opinion within a couple of weeks, infusing the public with an awareness of the necessity of such a reform, he got up and came towards Can saying, "Come, let me congratulate you." Taking Can's hand, he drew him to his feet, embraced him, and said, "I heartily thank you for this. Indeed I do!" And he again indicated, that his guest take his seat.

Can suddenly felt affectionate towards the man who stood in front of him with his square face with big greedy eyes, giving the impression that it had been carved out of a hard wood with a jack knife. As they had been watching each other for some time, an idea flashed through his mind, "I think I've seen these hands and this face before. Long long ago … so familiar this face and these hands. Definitely! It can't be coincidental."

They resumed their seats.

Doğan explained why he had agreed with the privatization of justice as soon as he had read Cüneyt's seminal article and how everybody from the aged president of the Republic to Doğan's private secretary had opposed the idea. He expatiated in the minutest detail how he had countered their criticisms. Can listened to the flow of words. While he studied the Prime Minister's features — his eyes, his nose, his chin, his forehead, his hair and shoulders — trying without success to remember where he could have seen this face, this body, these hands, these eyes and these gestures. At long last, during the Prime Minister's narration of his umpteenth encounter with the president and just as he was saying, "I said, Sir, my name is Mevlut Doğan! And banged on the table with my fist," Can made a sudden jerk and had difficulty keeping himself from shouting, "Smerdyakov!" As Doğan continued talking, dumbfounded as Can was, he thought to himself, "I'd thought that only in *The Brothers Karamazov*, would there be a face like that, not that one day we'd be sitting opposite each other." Focusing on the Prime Minister's appearance, he had failed to concentrate on what the Prime Minister was saying. He recalled his younger years when he and Gül read and discussed Dostoyevsky. He remembered that Smerdyakov had obsessed him. He was haunted in his dreams by this face as if carved in wood, with a sly glance and enormous hands and jerky gestures. Once again, he concentrated and looked straight at the Prime Minister. "It's him!" he said to himself. "It's him!" Smerdyakov had appeared in his dreams in the form of a thick wood the likes of which apparently could not be seen in the world, yet after so many years, here he was. The only difference was that the Prime Minister's garrulousness, babbling on and every now and then repeating his name 'I'm Mevlut Doğan!" as if to deny his similarity to Smerdyakov.

Can stopped a second to study the Prime Minister's moustache, for he was not certain whether Smerdyakov had a moustache or not. He felt momentarily detached from where he was and focused on Semerdyakov's appearance as he remembered him from his youth. Can kept silently repeating, "Did he have a moustache or not?" without reaching a conclusion. It occurred to him to call to his wife, but then he realized that this might be seen as a delusion due to lack of sleep. He tried to forget Smerdyakov and give his attention to Doğan, who had by now concluded his passion for privatization of justice and had begun expatiating on his own achievements in order that they might be approved by Can. In this, he was successful. He ended his sentences by declaring again, "My name is Mevlut Doğan." Apparently this refrain was not simply to corroborate his infallibility, but also to point out his other outstanding merits. Can listened to him intently, now that he had identified him with Smerdyakov. When the Prime Minister said yet again, "My name is Mevut Doğan!" Can ceased his internal monologue, though with difficulty, and kept from saying, "This does not prevent your being Smerdiyakov, too." Instead, thanks to his instinct as a lawyer, he blurted out, "Is there anyone who does not know you, Sir!" Towards the end of the Prime Minister's speech, just when Doğan repeated once again his identity, Can recalled Smerdyakov and said in a whisper, "A Smerdyakov with a moustache," adding, "Yes, Sir, your name is indeed Mevlut Doğan." The Prime Minister saw no irony in this remark but felt somewhat upset, although he kept himself from showing it.

"Anyway, let's get back to our subject," he said.

"As you wish," said Can.

Can saw him vacillate. He stared at him, the same old Smerdyakov with a moustache, yet there was a change in his complexion. He was no longer that proud, condescending and conceited type Can was accustomed to seeing on television. Neither was he the man of a short while ago who enumerated his achievements, repeating periodically, "My name is Mevlut Doğan!" Can maintained the air of a businessman speaking with another businessman but one far richer than he. Although he said, "Let's get back to our subject," otherwise the Prime Minister remained silent. Can feared that Doğan might have changed his mind.

"Anything wrong?" he finally asked. "You seem to have something on your mind."

The Prime Minister laughed. "I was just thinking. A Prime Minister's mind is always busy and engrossed in an untold number of problems, even though they may be minor. I had been thinking …"

"Minor?" Can thought, astounded. "But Smerdyakov hardly ever thinks. He just observes the world and human beings, but he never thinks. So does Feodor Pavlov imagine him. If the Prime Minister were subject now to an epileptic fit and began having convulsions, Can would not be surprised in the least.

"What had you been thinking, Sir?" he asked

"Last week marked our second year in power," Doğan replied.

Can was still watching Smerdyakov. He, too, had double personality, just like Doğan. "Is that so? Splendid! My heartfelt congratulations, Sir," he said.

The Prime Minister added with a frown, "I am being harassed by difficult problems that keep me from sleeping."

Can thought that he was fishing for compliments. "A successful two years! What could ever prevent you from a good night's sleep, Sir?"

"The elections are looming, less than a year away."

"But you'll certainly be elected for a second term!"

"That is not certain! You know why? Because from the beginning of this century until now, no party has won a second term. No Prime Minister has been re-elected. In other words, we are doomed to lose. We'll be faced with difficult problems."

"What sort of problems, Sir?"

The Prime Minister's face expressed despair. A Smerdyakov cheated of his last hope!

"Once you fall, servile flatterers and self-promoters will try to dominate you and accuse you of the most trivial offences, of unheard crimes, of embezzlement, and so forth. The number of such people is so large that you would be at a loss to address any. And if you fail to be elected a member of parliament you're done for. You'll be driven from one thing to another and spend your life in prison or under legal restraints."

The figure of the criminal Smerdyakov surged in front of Can, and he smiled and cleared his throat as if he were going to pronounce a universal truth.

"You are right, Sir," he said, "great men, great worries."

This provoked a cough from the Prime Minister. "In truth, I don't think we shall lose the election, for we are not like our predecessors," he said. "In one way or another, I intend to do something about your privatization project. This is important not only for the country and me but also for my friends. It may play a part in my being elected for a second term."

"Do you think that enacting the law might take some time?"

"No, that's not the point. Once the idea is ripe, it's a matter of a couple of days. But first, we must, you and I, I mean, put it on a firm footing. My name is Mevlut Doğan. I protect myself and my friends against all possible risks."

"It's a matter of duty to assist you however the law permits." He stopped. Smerdyakov was suddenly transformed back into the Prime Minister he was accustomed to see on television.

This was soon confirmed. "My name is Mevlut Doğan, my dear Can. I leave nothing to chance, and laws do not provide me with enough protection," he said. "We'll make a contract, the two of us. There will be no witness. A written contract it shall be. I will sign it and give a copy to you, and you will countersign it and give me a copy. Only in duplicate. There'll be no other copy. Understood?"

Can was petrified. "Are we to sign it right now?" he asked.

Doğan spoke with calm and confidence. Every now and then he banged his fist on the table and repeated his motto, "My name is Mevlut

Doğan! There is no hurry! We still have time," he said, "We shall first force the bill through the parliament. Once we succeed, we'll draw up a contract, a sales or transfer agreement, leaving all the courts of the country to your care. While a representative from your firm will sign it together with my Minister of Justice, we'll be in another room where we can sign and exchange our own confidential agreement, it being understood, of course, that everything is between you and me only."

Can was confused.

"We've got a whole week to think over the stipulations," said Doğan, "You must call me. Dial my direct number, all right?"

Can brooded over this. He was dumbfounded but tried to appear resolute although he was aware that his concern had not gone unnoticed. "I originated the project, and you are now directing it. If I were to change anything, I'd lose the confidence of my colleagues," he said. "I'd like to know what the stipulations will be?"

The Prime Minister laughed under his breath and said, "That's why I called you here. You'll know shortly. However, you need not be afraid. My stipulations are not so exacting. You'll see to it that actions brought to court against us, which is to say me and my party and government, will be dismissed, and actions brought to court by us against certain persons and institutions will be dealt with according to instructions we'll give." He stopped suddenly, looking intently at Can, then continued, "You frown. You don't like our stipulations?"

Can swallowed a few times and considered leaving the room immediately. But upon reflection, he thought that such a departure would be unwise. "Such a policy would endanger the respectability of us both. It might harm the people's sense of justice and terminate their confidence in you," he said. "I think that we should not be so categorical about it and rely on our judges' common sense."

Doğan laughed. "You're right. I think I've gone a bit too far. But you'll admit, I hope, that justice must always be on the side of the powers that be. It has always been so."

Can thought again. "You're certainly right, Sir, but it would be advisable not to forget that overstepping limits might end those powers sooner." After hesitating a moment, he continued, "If you want my humble opinion, certain actions brought to court by you could turn out to be counterproductive. For instance, a friend of mine who was involved in one of your initiatives has been in prison for the last two years, serving a sentence not yet determined. We are still in the dark about the nature of accusation against him. Such cases will certainly have negative effect on the public opinion."

"Is that so?" said the Prime Minister with a laugh. "What was his name, your friend's name?"

"Varol Korkmaz, Sir,"

"I see, Varol Korkmaz, eh? Varol Korkmaz," said Doğan. "I remember now that during his trial you were held in contempt by our chief-justice Cahit Güven." He rose from his seat and approached Can, laying his hand on his shoulder. "Can," he said, "you're a great lawyer, but believe me, upon my honor you can release him once justice is privatized." After a moment, added, "No! why defer it, after all. Let's make an exception to the rule. Let's see to it that before the next session. The court will set him free. Whether we agree or not, let them release him! Take my word for it." In fear of being overheard, he lowered his voice, "I'll do you one more favor. You can arrange the sentence as you want but not for a year."

"Why not for a year, Sir?"

Doğan laughed. "All right then," he said, "six months. We have already taken care of them all. They won't be any more trouble. You can proceed in this way. In the first session you can continue to hold the one in charge and let the directors and the specialists go. And during the following session, you can arrange his release, too. You'll do it in a clever way, I'm sure."

Can almost said, "Sir you have already privatized justice," but gave up the idea. "Thank you, Prime Minister," he said instead. "I'm grateful to you."

"My name is Mevlut Doğan. I'll do anything for friends," he said. "This is not the only case in court. You can also arrange the other cases according to my wishes. Moreover, you don't have to make a special effort. All the cases we consider important are within the jurisdiction of judges loyal to us. It's enough if you don't remove them from office."

When he learned of the imminent release of his friend, Can was in heaven. He chose not to reply and thought about the situation. Then he proceeded, "Prime Minister, you know well that such attachments hardly ever last beyond the lives of those in power. We must change them when the time comes and replace them with people even more authoritative. This policy will be not only for us but for you as well. We're not going to remove them all of course. It's a matter of proportion."

Doğan smiled. "No sooner had I seen your face than I had understood you. You are an intelligent man. I'll think it over." He continued to smile at his guest. "However," he went on, "this is not all. I'd like to have two large apartments in one of the new skyscrapers to be erected at Maçka and to have it registered in the name of my sister-in-law but to be used by my political party."

Can heaved a sigh of relief. Now that they were bargaining, justice had nothing to do with it. "Temel will consider it an honor, Sir."

"Not to mention of course one billion lira for my party, under the counter."

Can riveted his eyes on the ceiling and considered the Prime Minister's stipulation for a while. "This is an enormous sum, Sir, I don't think we can afford it at present," he said

"Let us say then half a billion, to be deducted from the income from privatization."

"Even that is too much,"

"All right, two hundred-and-fifty billion. Will that be all right?"

"Still astronomical."

"A hundred and fifty, perhaps?"

Can had not expected this. After thinking about it for a while he asked, "Will it also be deductible from privatization?"

"Only half of it," said Doğan, and seeing that Can nodded assent, he heaved a sigh and said, "Now, let's have some Turkish coffee and part until we meet again. Soon. Right?"

"Right, Sir."

"In the meantime, while we're waiting for the coffee, you can tell me if you have anything special to ask. Anything in particular?"

"Not for myself, Sir," said Can and took a deep breath, "Temel is encountering certain problems, though."

"What sort of problems?"

He thought first of the house and the garden at Cihangir, but instead replied, "The municipality creates enormous difficulties for him related to his construction projects at Cihangir, Taksim, Sultanahmet, and Fatih. Some say, 'I won't have my road changed.' Others say, 'I won't have my trees cut down.' All sorts of such impediments that hinder the progress of his work and involve expenses more than the actual worth of the property."

"All right, let him send the file to my private secretary, succinctly explaining the matter."

"Thank you very much, Sir. Temel has another problem as well. It is his ruling passion to erect a Statue of Liberty like the one in New York, the cost to be entirely met by himself. He says that it will be the symbol of Istanbul and of our love for America. This may require reclaiming land from water, taking a modest part of the palace's garden, and building an access road, but the Preservation Committee…"

"I understand. I hope Temel has considered everything. I'm sure our American friends will be delighted. As for us, although we are religious, we are not against beautiful statues."

"But the Preservation Committee won't hear of it, Sir."

The Prime Minister suppressed a laugh and said, "My dear friend, my name is Mevlut Doğan. If I choose, I can disband that committee instantly and form a new one in five minutes. So you may add the Statue of Liberty also to the file."

In the meantime, coffee was ready to be served. After drinking, the two men stood up. Doğan clasped Can's much smaller hand and pressed it warmly. Just before they parted, Can remembered what Rıza had said. "Have you heard about the crowds of castaways scattered around the country, Sir?" he asked.

"Who do you think I am!" said the Prime Minister, "Even a fly cannot fly without my knowing it! I have heard of them. Not only have I heard about them. but actually I have seen them. They wander all over the country. This is an old story. They were there before I came to power."

"Any idea of their number?"

"Two and a half or three or at most four million."

"It makes one shudder."

"Don't exaggerate; the number in Africa is still greater. Apparently they often raid and sack towns and cities."

"But, Sir, nobody speaks of them. They are not in the news. No paper writes anything about them."

"Well, there is a tacit agreement on both the national and the international level. Any mention of them might upset the economy."

"Do you have a solution for them, Sir?"

After thinking some time, the Prime Minister, "My name is Mevut Doğan, I said. I did not say I was God. What solution can I consider? This state of affairs goes far back before I came to power. They proliferate at an incredible rate. It's true that they eat whatever they can get hold of, the bark of trees, worms, bears, wolves, foxes, and so forth. The number of those animals has been falling steadily and they shall soon disappear. These people are a sturdy species, though, much like your species and mine." He laughed. Seeing Can's grave expression, he added, "However, their condition has improved slightly during our term in office. Our municipalities dump their refuse at spots where there are many of them. I'm told that there are also municipalities that arrange collections of second-hand clothing for them. Don't think that we neglect them."

Dumbfounded, his mouth and eyes wide open, Can stared at the Prime Minister, who laughed at his guest's attitude and put his hand on his shoulder. "The other night I could not sleep. I took a history book from the shelf and began turning over the pages. I read that during the second half of the past century, less than a hundred years ago, the slogan of a conservative party was 'A Turkey of one hundred million.' I could not help laughing. Can, can you imagine a Turkey of one hundred million! Once they had almost neared this figure. We are doing our utmost to reduce our population to the level it had when the Republic was founded."

Can looked even more flabbergasted than he had before.

"Well, I don't know, Sir. You know, Sir, every age has its own criteria, its principles, and ideals."

Prime Minister gave another laugh.

"Yes, but as Mevlut Doğan, I find such an ideal ridiculous. Am I wrong?"

"You're not, Sir. You live in the year 2073."

Doğan lapsed into silence.

They walked to the doorway. In the parking lot, they shook hands like two friends. Just before they parted, the Prime Minister said, "Can, you know what? I like you. People spoke to me about you as an 'unreliable communist,' yet I've had the opportunity to listen to you speak a couple of times on television, and I said to myself 'Here is a clever man!' I saw today that I was not mistaken."

They looked at each other, smiling, before Doğan asked him *sotto voce*, "Are you a communist?"

Can replied in the same tone of voice, "As much as you are, Sir!"

They burst out laughing.

Doğan embraced him.

"See you," he said fixing his looks on Can's spaceshuttle. "My my!" he said, "Your shuttle is better then mine. Nice! This is an indication of the fact that the dispensation of justice by you will be fitting."

As Can boarded his shuttle and ordered his pilot to take off, he murmured, "Funny man, unaffected, but not without worldly wisdom. His powers of observation are remarkable, but he doesn't exaggerate. He says that no party has ever won elections twice, without indicating that the party in power continues to reign. There are no changes in the principles that are followed, while standards in the administration of justice degenerate. The castaways are the result of this party, one hundred and fifty year old." He had difficulty keeping himself from spitting. "Such is he man whom I am doing business with and concluding confidential agreements."

The sun had already set when the spaceshuttle landed a half an hour later on the top of skyscraper No B-164. Humans below on the pavements were in their mini-cars, driving back from work. They proceeded resolutely, not at all suspicious of what was going on. They were not aware that they were but ordinary members of an abstract and immutable order. Can said to himself, "What of those above? Of the powers there? Are they better informed than the rest of the population?" The image of Smerdyakov confronted him again with his moustache, hair combed straight, self-complacent, and perfectly happy. "How about them? Do they know what to expect? Do I? Suppose I do, so what?" he said to himself. "They are swept along by passions, the whole mass of them, each one no different than the others, just like robots. Every one of us is a robot in this order, every one of us. Myself, Doğan, Cüneyt, Varol, even Rıza, all of us. But what about Gül?" he thought. He put his head between his hands. "I wonder if it does not occur to her to get a divorce? If she doesn't, I'll wonder why. If she does, why on earth does she keep silent. As soon as I am home, I'll ask."

He did not do that, however, since as soon as he saw her, he clasped her in his arms and kissed her passionately, and nostalgically he took a few steps back to look at her, thinking how much he loved her.

"Tell me, dear, did Smerdyakov have a moustache or not?" he asked.

Gül was astonished by her husband's frenzied behavior, and she asked the reason for his strange question, "What does Smerdyakov have to do with anything?"

Can took a deep breath. "The man, I mean Mevlut Doğan, is a perfect copy of him!"

Gül tried to smile. "He has a moustache," she said.

"Didn't Smerdyakov have a moustache?"

"I don't know, maybe he did. We must read the novel again, but you know well that Dostoyevsky is concerned with the inner world of his heroes and heroines rather than the way they look. All the same we must read it again. It might take us back to our youth," she said, standing in front of her husband without moving. "Did he also feel an intense hatred towards Russia?"

"No doubt he disliked Turkey, but I don't know about Russia."

"His own motherland, the very ground in which he flourished, just like Smerdyakov," said Gül, putting her husband's arm in hers and leading him to his chair. "Come on, sit down and I'll get you a glass of water. It'll do you good." She waited until he drank it. Then she took his hands in hers saying, "Your small hands have always been a source of wonder for me," she said.

"They are small, indeed! Not like Smerdyakov's."

Gül saw that her husband was coming round and so asked him a few questions about his meeting with Doğan. She added that Rıza was still sleeping at the guest room. "If you listen, you can hear him snoring." Can listened. Gül said she was afraid that he might not be well.

"Rıza is his name, and he hardly ever gets sick, but this is his way, you know, sleeping for forty-eight hours straight after staying up for the previous forty-eight hours."

Gül was surprised. "Do you mean that he will be snoring like this tomorrow also?"

"No, I'll wake him up presently." He got up and went to the guest room. He opened the door and saw Rıza, sound asleep on the bed wearing his jacket and boots with no sign he might wake. "You fool!" said

Can. "You will end up some day in a street corner or dead in a cheap hotel wearing your lousy jacket and muddy boots. Wake up," he said in a loud voice. "Time to get up! You've slept all day! Come on, time to get up!"

Rıza rubbed his eyes before opening them and smiled at Can, then straightened up. "Here I am!" he said. "How did it go?"

"Settled already," he answered, "just like all business I undertake."

Rıza was not expecting this: "Oh, no!" he said, astonished, "Not this nonsense, Even that blockhead could not do anything so stupid."

"Not only have I arranged it, but I've prevailed upon that blockhead, as you call him."

Rıza shook his head in despair. "It's hideous! It's the end of justice!"

"No, this is evolution and a revolution, a bloodless one. The return to the essence of justice, the redemption of justice in the twenty-first century!"

Rıza suddenly sat up and gave his friend a hostile look.

"I'd rather have a bloody revolution, rather than a bloodless one," he said angrily. "Fuck your moneyed revolution and justice by the strongest!"

Can rose to his feet, saying, "I see that you've forgotten everything I told you last night. Come on. Let's go and eat something."

"I'll be with you in five minutes," Rıza said.

He appeared ten minutes later but seemed unaware of where he was. His eyes were fixed on a photograph, and he saw nothing but what was in the picture. Finally he placed it before Gül.

"I found it on the coffee table there and I was stupefied. 'No,' I said, 'it can't be true. At least, personally I haven't seen such a beauty.' Aren't I right? This divineness, this harmony, this looks, this smile. The Mona Lisa could hardly compete with it. I think … I think that this face …"

"Yes, "said Can, "You think that face …"

"It might have belonged to Eve. I took it with me when I went to my room and fell asleep."

Can and Gül were moved.

"You're right," said Gül, "exquisitely beautiful!"

Gül looked at her husband with a smile and, bending toward Rıza, she whispered as if revealing a secret. "She is Nokta Diker, Temel's mother. She died fifty-five years ago."

A shudder ran down Rıza's spine, followed by a strange, radiant smile.

"There can be no better instance of the absurdity of life and the height of nonsense. A woman so beautiful giving birth to a ruffian like Temel! Nonsense! The height of nonsense."

"Aren't you exaggerating a bit!" Can remarked, putting his hand on Rıza's shoulder. "Temel intends to refashion the face of the Statue of Liberty he wants to erect on Seraglio Point with his mother's."

Rıza sank into the nearest armchair. "No! That's impossible!" he murmured. "This face on that statue? One should kill him! The fool!"

"Don't you like the idea? The man is building Istanbul anew."

"Indeed!" said Rıza, making a face. "Poor Istanbul, a guinea pig in the hands of the rabble, some from Aydın, some from Trabzon, and some from Urfa. All of them wanting to re-build the city according to their ideas of ideal beauty. There is no end to absurdities in this country."

"You, Turkey's last communist, taking Eve for the most beautiful woman!" said Can, holding him by the arm and leading him to the table.

The discussion about Nokta and the Statue of Liberty lasted until the end of their third drink. Then Can gingerly tackled the subject of his interview for which Gül had been waiting impatiently. He had not expected that his story would cause much laughter, but as he recited the details, and especially the Prime Minister's frequent transfiguration into Smerdyakov, his audience was quite amused. When he mimicked Doğan's manners, repeating, "My name is Mevlut Doğan," Rıza and Gül laughed. Nevertheless, all three felt something had gone wrong. They felt misgivings. Concluding his story, Can said, "This is what happened. Who deceived whom and who will win in the end is a mystery to me."

Rıza asked, "This Smerdyakov of yours, does he know anything about the castaways?"

"He does."

"Has he any plan to relieve their situation?"

"Indeed, he has. He plans to ignore them and have municipalities dump their refuse where they live."

"What a clever idea! I wouldn't exchange one Smerdyakov for a hundred Doğans."

Gül glanced back and forth from her husband to her guest, settling finally on her husband. "One hundred Doğans, eh?" she said. "I wish you had nothing to do with these people," she added harshly.

Can shrugged. "Business is business. I'm doing this for my client, in a sense," he said.

"Smerdyakov, did he also pop up on behalf of your client in your dreams?" asked Rıza.

Was he trying to change the tone of the discussion or subtly making a joke? Neither Can nor his wife seemed to pay any attention.

"Your greatest mistake was to have that man as a client," said Gül and, after thinking for a moment, she added, "All I know is that all this privatization business for an insignificant property consisting of a house and a garden is simply ridiculous."

Can flushed. "Don't speak nonsense! I am a lawyer, and Temel is my best client. Moreover, I have repeatedly told you that this is for the country's benefit, and I believe we will succeed in snatching justice from their hands. Whatever the cost, my efforts have begun to show results. Varol will be released in a couple of weeks. Both of us know well what I've done for him. On the other hand …"

"On the other hand," said Rıza, interrupting him, "this has nothing to do with justice as such. This is only venality, selfishness, nepotism …"

"What was I supposed to do? Should I ignore him, leaving him to rot in jail for years? Self-complacency or my own benefit has no part in this. The principal aim is the freedom of my friend. I don't want to be a show off, but I'd have done the same thing for you."

"I can't deny that. But now you are certainly in the wrong path," said Rıza. Your concerns are off the mark, subjective"

Can saw his wife nod to Rıza.

"Both of you are blind!" he roared. "Don't you see that I am trying to rescue justice from the hands of an administration that keeps an innocent man like Varol detained without producing any evidence to justify it and that sells whatever this country possesses to foreigners, confidence men. Just yesterday evening I was telling you this, but let me finish where I left off."

Rıza simply smiled. He did not seem to be affected. He turned towards Gül and said, "A funny sort of fellow your husband has become. He is instrumental in having those men add another evil practice to their list of horrible crimes, and by having justice privatized, he intends to immerse them in the worst of all possible wickedness. He greases their palms and wants us to praise him for this."

"My finances are so modest I wouldn't be likely to share it with others."

"Yes, but your client should not be underestimated."

"What client?"

"Temel, of course, Temel. The odd fish that has converted Istanbul into a forest of phalluses."

Can felt uneasy. "My dear friend," he said, "you're misguided. You are not looking at things with the eyes of the present. The man has devoted his entire life to Istanbul, trying to give it integrity and identity, a contemporary unity, wholeness."

Rıza burst into laughter.

"Dear Can, you are poking fun at us!" he said. "Don't you realize that he pulls down whatever exists above the ground? He throws away everything from the foundation up. Heaps of debris reach higher than the city itself. Antique buildings, monuments, and roadways are turned into rubble to be re-born. You cannot be blind to this. If he could, he would not hesitate for a instant moment to demolish Haghia Sophia or Topkapı Palace. Skyscrapers galore! He does not just pierce the sky but the earth, even history!"

"You're being ridiculous, Rıza. Temel is doing exactly the opposite of what you are saying. He pulls down the unseemly stuff, patchwork architecture, and replaces it with harmonious buildings of uniform design that give the city a healthy and strong look. You don't try to see it," Can went on, smiling mysteriously. "The reason you do not understand is that you are ignorant of the concepts of synchrony and diachrony."

"Excuse me? Marx doesn't talk about such things."

"Correct. He does not." Can began to describe how cities elsewhere can be seen in their historical evolution, but not Istanbul, which had lost this aspect long ago except for a few historical buildings. Greedy people in the course of the preceding century had made a mess of it, turning it into a heap of monstrosities, a scene of chaos. Therefore, the thing to do was to rebuild the city, designing it with buildings, roads, and streets uniform in appearance and embellish the whole with contemporary means of access and construction. After a deep sigh, he continued, "This is what Temel is after. He might not be able to explain this properly, but everybody could see that his intention was to re-build Istanbul as a homogenous space. He had devoted himself to this ideal and done everything in his power to make it happen."

Rıza turned to Gül and said, "This is your husband. Whenever he feels he has reached a dead end, he makes up a theory and believes it himself."

Gül said with a smile, "I know this very well. He does invent theories, and more often than not, they make sense."

Can sighed. "I can't say what I mean. No more about skyscrapers, justice, and the Prime Minister. Better speak of other things."

"All right, let's do so," said Rıza.

Gül nodded. They went back to their memories of the past. Then much later Rıza took Can by the arm and said, "I forgot to ask you. Did you fly low on your way to the Prime Minister or on your way back or take a look at the mountains?"

"No," said Can, "On my way there I was preoccupied with the up-coming interview, and on my way back, I was thinking about what we had discussed."

"Pity! Try to do it next time!" said Rıza. "You'll be amazed at the beauty of the bare mountains. They'll give you a sense of the cosmos as if it were being re-created, or … as if it were assuming the face of Nokta …"

VII.

"I WISH I HAD A DAUGHTER EXACTLY LIKE HER, beautiful, good humored, and attractive," said Can, looking at his secretary, İnci, as she approached him. As if she understood what he was thinking, she put a finger to her lips, telling him in a whisper that Temel had been waiting for him for about half an hour. "Damn it!" said Can quietly. His eyes fixed on İnci's, he waited a moment before opening the door and found Temel, who was clearly in his best mood.

"I see you are in good spirits, Temel," he said. "Inaugurating a new skyscraper?"

Temel laughed. "You don't know anything about what's going on," he answered. "From now on, we will arrange a single ceremony to inaugurate the building of ten skyscrapers."

Can seemed astounded. "New potential customers from Europe?"

This time it was Temel's turn to appear confused. "Are you kidding? You know nothing about the latest news?"

"No. What happened?"

Temel drew his chair towards Can's until their knees almost touched. "I would have thought you had also been informed," Temel said. "Yesterday evening, they called me from the municipality, telling me of the permission issued for the construction of forty-two skyscrapers plus the erection of the Statue of Liberty. All they require is a letter."

"Great!" shouted Can, "We must celebrate this, this very evening! Can you imagine, it's not yet 29th of the month? Three cheers for Mevlut Doğan! He's kept his promise!"

"Indeed!" confirmed Temel, although he did not seem to be entirely gratified. "What about the other issue?" he asked.

Can was taken aback. "What other issue?" he asked.

"The house and the garden of that obstinate teacher! Have you forgotten it already?"

"Forgot? How could I? But, I couldn't mention such a relatively trivial thing to the Prime Minister."

"You call it 'trivial.' You know perfectly well, it has great significance for me. The very project of privatization was an outcome of this 'trivial' issue. So many months have gone by and yet nothing concrete has happened. I was relying on you. Had it not been for my confidence in you, I'd have settled it long ago."

Can got up and paced up and down the room before resuming his seat.

"Take care," he said, "not to become involved in illegal activities. See that no shadow falls over the elegance of your skyscrapers! You know, before long we'll have dominion over the entire judicial system. The matter will doubtless be fixed then. Don't overestimate the importance of such, to repeat, a trivial affair!"

"You say 'trivial,' yet, it is of the greatest importance to me!"

"A little more patience. You saw that the permission for the erection of the Statute of Liberty has been granted. That lousy site, is it of greater importance than erecting your Statue of Liberty at the Seraglio Point?"

"It is at least as important. Moreover, now that the Statue of Liberty has been sanctioned, the significance of that piece of land is even greater."

"What for?"

"Well, you know it's been my cherished goal to erect a skyscraper on the site in question. Years have gone by and my goal is no less important. Tears come to my eyes whenever I think about it. It is my custom once a week to pass by and look at the site, then turning my gaze to Seraglio Point and thinking how glorious the panorama and the Statue of Liberty could be seen from that angle. Haven't I told you about this before?"

"You have, more than once."

"That house will be the end of me. If I ever have the chance of erecting a skyscraper on that spot, I'll move in as soon as it is finished. And don't forget: one of the apartments is yours!"

"You're getting sentimental" Can said, "You'll see, in due course, that it will happen. That's a promise!"

"It should have been the first one done," said Temel with a sigh. "You have chosen a long and arduous route."

"That was not altogether a personal choice. The idea began with me, it's true, but it was approved by everybody, including you."

"Yes, you began it, and we went along blindly."

Can became angry. "What do you mean? Do you mean to say that I have been misleading people? Tell us frankly what you mean, so that we can know where we stand and get it out of the way. If you are against it, say so. You can hire another lawyer, if you want. I won't object."

"The fact that you spoke to him about everything except this bothers me, but I'm not a fool who would dismiss a lawyer with your abilities." He took a deep breath and said, "We are friends. Never forget that. I'm not so stupid as to leave you in the lurch."

"Well, then?"

"I expected that you'd speak to him about this matter, making room for a skyscraper and not forgetting to add that money was no issue. It just didn't cross your mind. So be it."

"He had sent for me to discuss a definite issue. In spite of that, I managed to speak of other things, too. And we've seen the result. But for a trivial ..."

"You did manage to mention your friend in jail, though."

Can grew angry again. "Two different things. Varol is my closest friend. You can't compare him to a piece of land."

Temel suggested that it wasn't important but was reluctant to say more. "All right!" he said. "See to it that this privatization business is realized as soon as possible so that our 'trivial' matter can be taken care of at last. Don't forget, I'm always ready to provide support."

"How could I forget!" said Can with a smile. "You're my biggest partner. Did I say 'partner'? You're the boss."

"Yes 'boss', just as we said," repeated Temel, standing up and getting ready to leave, but as he headed to the door, he stopped and came back to shake Can's hand warmly.

"I just thought," he said, "that you might perhaps take me to him. Not to discuss your issue. No, I have no say in that matter, but he happens to come from my part of the country. Who knows, perhaps he could do a favor."

Can made a crooked smile. "Just give me time, we'll find a way out for that, too," he said, taking him by the arm and directing him to the door.

As he left, Can fixed his eyes on a black and white picture hanging on the wall. "What an idea!" he murmured. "To compare a piece of land with Varol! Temel may be right, though. That house with its small garden was where this all began. I have been trying unconsciously to forget it. Perhaps I don't want to see that house demolished. It may well be that I launched the privatization project to put that off. Oh, I don't know! I'm so confused!" He continued to look at the picture on the wall. "Strange," he said, "the artist painted the human beings in the shape of storks, and the storks in the shape of humans. They seem to be escaping from each other or from something else." He felt as if it were time to leave, disregarding the possible dangers that might await him on his way home. He wanted to live for a while, like Rıza, among the castaways. Then he pressed a button and asked İnci to send Sabri in. He went to the men's room, and when he came back, he found Sabri waiting in front of the desk. "Here's an intelligent man," he said to himself.

"Sabri, I've got news for you: I received a phone call from Veli Dökmeci yesterday evening. Apparently, soon, perhaps before six months have passed, justice in Turkey will finally be in our hand. The government seems to be certain. Great, isn't it?" he said and looked at his assistant sarcastically.

Sabri, after hesitating, said, "You know what I think about it, Sir? This is madness. I have already told you. It will upset both our lives and the life of the country. Our function is to assist the law. As a private organization, we cannot possibly pass judgment in the name of …"

Can, with a winning smile, interrupted. "In the name of the Turkish nation. In this country nearly everybody speaks in the name of the Turkish nation. Why should we not act likewise?"

"We are lawyers, Sir."

Can smiled again. He felt a strange serenity as he recognized his assistant's concerns.

"My dear Sabri! We are not going to grow wings to wander around the country passing judgments," he said. "We'll get organized and find decent judges. We'll train them or dismiss them. We'll raise the level of justice in this country and reduce injustice to a minimum. Just think, the present judges, sometimes without recognizing the actual state of things and sometimes on purpose, pronounce unjust sentences! Why do they still keep Varol in prison? To prevent injustice? I know we are not one hundred per cent perfect, but one thing is certain, we'll be better advised and more honest than the present judicial system. We shall pronounce our sentences in the name of the glorious Turkish nation."

"After having purchased justice, Sir?"

Can responded quickly. "They have purchased universities and given them with the label of 'T.C.' — that is, identified them as belonging to the Turkish Republic. The biggest and the oldest university in Turkey bears today the name T.C. Şaban Kekikli University." He drew a deep breath. "Everything has a value and a logic of its own. Today's logic is not a logic we are familiar with. It's the capitalist's logic. If we accept the fact that it is the private sector that rules this community. Accordingly we must agree to the privatization of justice. On the other hand, be it private or public, there are different ways of dealing with justice. We, as true lovers of the people, are prepared to pay the cost involved in order to operate a privatized justice system as impeccably as we can." It was Can's custom to continue expatiating upon a subject once he had begun, but Sabri interrupted him

"Do you really believe in all that you are saying, Sir?"

This unexpected response troubled him. "What did you say? Will you please say it again?"

Sabri turned red in the face, but did not retract his words. "I asked whether you were definitely convinced that you'd be able to rescue justice, Sir."

"I certainly am," Can said, "That is, not a hundred per cent,"

"Oh?"

"Fifty-Fifty, let's say!"

"Can fifty per cent be considered grounds for a conviction?"

"Why not? In our age, not only fifty per cent but even five per cent can lead to a conviction. For instance, our the Prime Minister is thoroughly convinced of the existence of God, but to my mind, I'd say his belief cannot be more than five per cent."

Sabri smiled. "To hear such words from the mouth of a celebrated lawyer is confusing," he stammered. "You must be joking!"

Can lowered his head and, after thinking for a while, said, "To believe or not to believe are outdated concepts; no one believes today in anything. The man of today looks at things from the viewpoint that suits him best, what he does in fact is to rationalize, in which he easily reconciles the things most irreconcilable."

"All right, Sir, aren't we doing the same thing that in trying to reconcile two conflicting attitudes?" asked Sabri.

Can replied immediately. "We are, in fact!" he said. "I am aware of the fact that at the outset, our objective was to obtain the release of Varol and then put Temel off with trumped-up excuses, in other words, do it just for the fun of it. However, henceforth after all the outcry, it is undeniable that our institution, and we ourselves, expect to derive a certain benefit from the whole thing in addition to anticipating the honor of dispensing justice in the best manner possible. The benefit and the honor in question are of such a nature that they do not clash with the idea of justice, since honesty and logic do not have anything to do with it. You may remember that I had told you that in a community where everything has been privatized, the dispensation of justice by the state should be considered self-contradictory. In point of fact, this chain of reasoning may take us far. The state itself becomes a paradoxical. Taken in this context, the privatization of justice becomes inevitable. At all events, after my interview with Doğan, I firmly believe in this. Justice should no longer rest in the hands of these people."

"Yet I don't think that your ingenious arguments can lead you to their logical conclusion," insisted Sabri, "if Montesquieu's point of view is correct — in other words, if laws conform to the regime in power, if every government will pass only such laws that suit their own purpose, whether justice is privatized or otherwise — nothing will change anyway. What I fear is the likelihood of our being playthings in the hands of these people. We can certainly not assert that working is a virtue for them."

Can was re-experiencing the enthusiasm of his school years. He paced to and fro for some time before suddenly stopping in front of his assistant.

"Montesquieu was wrong. To be precise, his eighteenth century logic does not fit our twenty-first century logic. The conformity of laws to the government in power is quite evident. The fact that royalty is based on honor, tyranny on fear, and the republic on virtue, is evident, but if there is something called justice, everything must follow from an immutable universal law. Otherwise, in a capitalist society, the conformity of law to capitalism would be tantamount to the absence of law. I believe that when Marx said that the proletarian revolution would be the end of the state, he must have meant that only then would universal justice lie in the future. This will be our aim."

Sabri did not seem convinced. "You're back again to Marx," he said. "The establishment of Marx's utopia in a community that Marx himself had said was doomed to collapse is a contradiction. Your initial idea in starting your movement to solve Temel's problem — a motive unlikely to be expected to receive Marx's approval — is hardly compatible with the idea of privatization of justice."

Can remained silent for a while. He thought that Sabri's position was sounder than his own, yet he did not give in. "You may be right, Sabri, but only in terms of formal logic. Yet if you consider the issue from the point of view of concrete facts, don't you think that Temel also may be justified in his own way? The fellow keeps erecting skyscrapers all over the city. People line up in front of his house to persuade him to erect some for them as well or hire middlemen to do this for them. People pulled down their lovely houses and bulldozed their gardens. Almost the entire city was for it. Yet an elderly gentleman, an old Don Quixote, strayed from the usual path and preferred to stick to his ancestral home and garden! Who knows whether Montesquieu might not have found Temel justified. In a nutshell, in the established order in which everything is privatized and backed with money, an exception couldn't be made for justice. Am I wrong?"

Sabri took a deep breath. "I don't know. Maybe you're right," he noted. "Just as you said, fifty-fifty."

Can felt almost sorry that his assistant, in whose logic he had profound confidence, should agree. "Yes, dear Sabri," he said, "we live in an age which makes it impossible for us to remain attached to morals we only encounter in old books. If we stick to our old honesty, integrity, and respectability, we find ourselves beset by all sorts of impediments and interdictions. Under the circumstances, you've got to survive and try not to be among the oppressed. You have no other alternative. All that you can do is to mitigate the effects of the disaster and try not to step on anyone's toes."

"In other words, we shall be neither completely honest, nor a fraud through and through."

"Yes, once again, optimistically put, fifty-fifty."

Sabri made a gesture of assent. "I believe you are right, Sir," he said.

Can sighed and lost himself in thought. He seemed to be disappointed in his assistant's submissiveness. "All these things make me miserable. On top of everything, Gül's objections frustrate me," he complained. "The first thing you should do now is to prepare the bill to be brought before the parliament. I could assist you in case you need me."

"What bill, Sir?" Sabri said, astonished. "Oh, I see. Are *we* going to prepare it, Sir?"

"Yes, I gave my word to the Prime Minister. We've got to get it ready within a couple of weeks," said Can. "A judicious one, one that the other people who devoted themselves to this job have failed to do …"

Sabri was confused. "We are near the end of April. Do you mean to say that the proposal will be voted on this term and not the next year?"

"It's the expectation and anticipation of the Prime Minister that it should be put to a vote this term," he said with a smile.

At that moment, İnci entered without knocking.

"Sorry, Sir. I've just received a call from Yıldız. She said that Varol has been released. Apparently he is at his home now. Yıldız …"

"Hurrah!" cried Can without listening further to what İnci had to say. He said to Sabri that he was going out and that they'd talk about the bill tomorrow.

On his way to Varol's place, he swore whenever he had to stop at traffic lights. He felt as if he should get out and walk. It would be quicker, but there was far to go. He imagined the joy felt by of Yıldız and the children. "Two years! Two years exactly! Easy to say!" he kept muttering. "They must be out of their minds with joy.

However, no sooner had he stepped into his friend's apartment than he was disappointed to see the whole family in despair, all of them in tears, with red eyes. He was immediately frightened that something had gone wrong. "What's the matter?" he asked. "Where is he?" There was no reply. He scrutinized each of them and repeated his question, "Where is he now? Wasn't he released, as I was told?"

Yıldız, dissolved in tears, pointed to the door to the left. "Released, yes. He came home at exactly 12:15 but remained with us just long enough to exchange a few words no longer than prisoners are allowed to talk with their family. Then he ran into that room and locked the door. He says he won't come out unless the others are also released. He says he'll not even come here," she said, crying. "Ali and Zeynep have been here for an hour now. He didn't even want to see them and his grandson. He says he might come out but only when we're not around."

"Why?"

"He says he is innocent, but so are the others still in jail. He says it's unfair to let him go while the others are there. He says that if he starts living like the rest of us, he would be collaborating with injustice. He says he will disobey, defying what the authorities want."

Can, stupefied, said, "He's mad! This has nothing to do with injustice."

Yıldız wiped away her tears. "He heard that *you* were responsible for his release. Apparently you prevailed over the Prime Minister to get him pardoned, and he is angry with you," she added.

"Absurd! The height of nonsense," he vociferated, trembling. The family asked him to take a seat, but he acted as if did not hear them. "I know how to get him out of there," he muttered and walked towards the door that Varol had locked from the inside. After rattling the door a couple of times, he shouted, "Varol, open the door!" But there was no answer. He began banging on the door and, when there was no response, began kicking it as if in a trance, shouting, "Open the door! Come on!" The child cried while the others, horrified, watched. One last time, he repeated his words and threatened to break in the door. No sooner had he said this than he backed away and ran at the door, trying to force it, but without success. He tried a second time.

Then suddenly the door opened and Varol appeared. When Can saw him, he staggered, thinking that some trick must have been played on him. The man standing on the doorway did not look like the friend he had seen just a few weeks ago. He looked miserable, emaciated, his face pale and drawn, his eyes sunken in their sockets. Only his voice seemed to be the same, although strained, and he sank into the nearest chair he could find.

"They've released only me, and the rest of us, thirteen comrades, are still in jail, all of them as innocent as me," Varol said, pointing to his grandson. "Selim, one of our older members, sixty-eight years old, is suffering from cancer of the liver and racked with pain. They give him no remedy except aspirin. Had you been in my place, wouldn't you be upset to leave them there and get out of that place free?"

"You're back home," said Can. "You're among your family. You are free, as free as other innocent people."

"Don't expect me to feel innocent when my friends are inside."

"But you haven't escaped. You are out by judicial decree. You didn't have to incriminate any of your friends, and you didn't have to beg for your freedom."

"Judicial decree, huh?" he said. "Through an unlawful and devious strategy. Had you been in my place, wouldn't you feel resentment?"

Can remained quiet for a second or two. "Those who have detained you and your friends, knowing that you were all innocent and have turned you into a scare-crows have reason to be ashamed, not you," he said. "Honesty does not pay, at least in our day."

"I don't care about our day. I've decided," he said, fixing his eyes on his friend and, pushing him aside, making a dash for the door. Can stood still for some time before turning back to the others in the room. He saw Yıldız carrying a television. With a puzzled look he asked, "What's that?"

"'At least take this television with you,' I told him. There was no television in the prison! We thought perhaps he would listen to you." Her words were broken with sobs.

Can made no reply but went for the door as if walking in his sleep.

VIII.

EVER SINCE WAKING, Can kept hearing Yıldız saying over and over, "At least take this television with you," followed by, "There was no television in the prison!" Her words continued to haunt him during breakfast with Gül, then as he was about to leave the apartment, as he boarded his spaceshuttle, and as he entered the his law office. Without even casting a glance at İnci or saying "good morning," he headed to his armchair and sank into it, his eyes resting above. Yıldız's words obsessed him. It seemed as if they had become integral to his existence, of his body and soul. "What can I to do?" he muttered. He looked at Sabri, who had entered the office, as if seeing him for the first time. Can said nothing, and Sabri was at a loss, not knowing whether to speak to his boss or leave him alone. Just he was about to leave, he saw Can, indicating him to sit in his usual chair.

Saying "Thank you," Sabri took his seat. "Is anything the matter, Sir?"

Can continued to watch him but did not speak, did not reply, and did not move. Sabri grew anxious and was about to go into a panic, when Can straightened up, rose from his chair, and, approaching him with a sorrowful look, said, "You have always been critical of my taking on this business, and that's caused me to view it sceptically. But yesterday after I left you, I decided that no justice could be worse than the one determined now by the brutes in charge."

As Sabri watched, expecting him to elaborate, Can pull up the chair to the table where he sat when working. With a calm voice, he said, "Come on, we must begin! There's no time to lose!"

"I'll never understand this man," Sabri said to himself. "There must be more than one person under that skin." He was certain he was correct. Only yesterday, Can had asked him to prepare the bill himself. As if no such conversation had taken place; he now began to enumerate the general principles of the new law as if he were reading from a prepared text.

"One second please, Sir," Sabri said, "Let me get pen and paper and turn on the recorder and the printer."

Can waited. His assistant came back with pens and a pad of writing paper and sat opposite him.

"You never get rid of this schoolboy custom," Can said. "Since the recorder and the printer commit everything we say to paper, why would we need these pens? Just listen to what I'm going to say and interrupt me if you detect any inconsistency or error." He began the preamble to the bill, and Sabri used neither pen nor paper and did not interrupt.

When Can had finished, Sabri took a deep breath as if he himself had been the speaker. "Excellent!" he said. "A draft could not be any better."

"I'd like you to examine it carefully, and don't spare any criticism."

"Right!" he said nervously. He left and read through the document on his computer but made no change in the text and then returned to his boss. "Sir," he said, "you have made clear and explicit every item. It is so comprehensive that a single correction might cause the whole edifice to crumble."

Can smiled. "Aren't you exaggerating a bit?"

Sabri seemed slightly offended. "I'm not exaggerating, Sir. You know very well that exaggeration is not my habit, and under ordinary circumstances, I'd never hesitate to refute your arguments, if there were any I disagreed with."

"I suggest that you go over it once again. Infallibility should never be taken for granted. It sometimes leads to extremes, or inadvertently creates hostility."

"I realize once more that I'll never be able to understand you, Sir,"

It took Can and his assistants a whole week to prepare a draft of the bill of thirty-five pages based on the preamble stating the reason and the intent of the law. The motion was submitted to the approval of the Minister of Justice and his team before it was submitted to the Grand Assembly on May 16th, 2073. It was carried by a 76% majority with great applause, and having been duly ratified by the President, it took effect following its publication in the *Official Gazette* on May 27th, 2073.

Except for two Istanbul papers with small circulations, the press in general acclaimed this law as Turkey's first and foremost victory. Television channels and the press that claimed to be ostensibly independent agreed with the pro-government media in calling this a legal reform of great scope and hailed Doğan and Veli Dökmeci, the Minister of Justice, as pioneers of a great revolution, while pointing to Can and Cüneyt as the chief authors of this great reform. It appeared that for the last hundred and fifty years, no reform of such scope had been realized, and the words "reform" and "revolution" had never been used so often or carried such magical meanings. In the meantime, many columnists were of the opinion that this act involved returning what once had belonged to the public back to the public. Even among those who still mourned the dismantling of the European Union without having accepted Turkey as the thirtieth and final member, there were voices that argued that with this revolutionary achievement, Turkey, perhaps for the first time in its history, had given the European nations a meaningful lesson in globalization. Writers of a more sober inclination and commentators on television expressed the view that this revolutionary law was but a compendium of a larger work that depended on the institution that would assume the responsibility for its execution, the Turkish Basic Law Partnership Corporation, or the TBLPC as it was called, that Can and his team were about to incorporate.

As for Can, in these jubilant days he shunned newspaper correspondents and television reporters, and when he could not do so, he made the following prudent statement. "We are prepared to assume responsibility for this sacred duty, and we believe ourselves to be worthy of this function. However, there are organizations that are as desirous and capable as are we of assuming this task. It's up to the government to decide." Despite the insistent queries of news correspondents, he added nothing to this short statement. Was this because he had become suspicious of the administration of justice turned over to him within such a short time? No. He had already come to an agreement with Doğan, according to which Temel would register at the registry of deeds three large apartments in three different skyscrapers in the name of the first lady and her sister. The formalities had already been completed and were ready to be signed. The problem now was to find one hundred and fifty million dollars "in hard currency." On the other hand, the Turkish Basic Law Partnership Corporation was ready to take on its task.

The Articles of Association of the Corporation had already been drawn up, despite fierce opposition from Sabri, who argued that "this risks being a moot point." It was decided to refer to the leading commercial and industrial establishments for contributions to the cause, and although the CEOs of these concerns expressed reluctance to make investments in a field that was not in their line of business and was far from being lucrative, they agreed to do so, thinking that if upon the conclusion of a ten day waiting period, they decided that they didn't want to participate, there was certain to be tension between them and the powerful organization in whose hands justice would very soon be entrusted. In turn this would have negative effects on their legal affairs. If they sanctioned the corporation, their cases would be dealt with more swiftly. What was even more interesting was that these the prospective partners, not willing to take a back seat, saw to it that their contributions were considerable. With the addition of an extremely generous contribution from Temel, the Turkish Basic Law Partnership Corporation, the TFLPC, became one of the leading organizations in the Turkish Republic. Although in the beginning, a leading Anglo-American organization in cooperation with a couple of American and English universities set up a law office in an attempt to usurp the administration and dispensation of justice in the Turkish Republic. it seemed that the system would be entrusted to Can and Temel's group, following "intelligence" that most of the "qualified staff" be Turkish citizens, conversant with the Turkish language. On the other hand, three or four local organizations, formed by certain rich lawyers and their 'clients,' looked as if they were waiting for a disagreement between the President and the Prime Minister.

Doğan's capitulation to an injunction from the President of the United States and the British Prime Minister was not out of the question nor was the possibility at the last moment of siding with local or foreign concerns that promised a more lucrative offer. Although Can did not expect that the Prime Minister would recant, he did not want to give the impression that everything had been foreordained, and to the questions directed at him by newspaper correspondents who asked why he was silent on this issue, he simply answered, "Justice is a serious affair."

As soon as the date of bidding for the legal system was made known, he, along with the other three organizations, filed an application.

At the spacious meeting hall on the ground floor of the ministry of justice at 3:30 on June 24th, 2073, the prominent members of the four applicants prepared themselves for a display of the nature and resources of their respective organizations. Meanwhile Doğan and Can, the founding chairperson of the Turkish Basic Law Partnership Corporation, in a room on the twenty-first floor especially reserved for it, conversed at a round table as old friends, exchanging in a jovial spirit anecdotes and jokes as they followed the negotiations on an enormous monitor.

According to Doğan, the negotiations took exactly three hours and eight minutes, at the end of which a decision was reached to transfer the entire judiciary system to the TBLPC. This was followed by signing a contract that delegated the responsibility of Turkish justice to the private sector. Veli Dökmeci, Minister of Justice, signed it on behalf of the government and by Sabri, secretary general, on behalf of the TBLPC.

At about the same time, a bottle of champagne and two glasses on a silver tray carried by an attendant in uniform was brought into the room on the twenty-first floor. However, the Prime Minister ordered him to leave and return fifteen minutes later. Then Doğan took out of his briefcase two documents, each consisting of a single page, and set them in front of Can. The latter, leaning back in his chair, perused them and affirmed that they reflected the stipulations expressed at the Prime Minister's residence. The parties signed and exchanged copies. All of these procedures were completed within fifteen minutes as foreseen by the

Prime Minister. At exactly the sixteenth minute, champagne was served, and the parties toasted each other's health. The Prime Minister took his first sip sitting on the arm of his chair, an old habit of his, while Can, as was his custom, sniffed his before drinking. Not ten minutes had passed before the Prime Minister put his document into his briefcase, and laying his hand on Can's shoulder, said, "It has been a pleasure to know you. You're a nice fellow. Whenever you are in a difficulty, come and see me. I wish you success in everything you undertake"

The two men embraced like brothers.

The next day there was nothing in the press, on the radio, or on television about this affair, the exchange of documents, and the toast that followed. Instead, the media gave ample space to the privatization matter in its minutest details. *The Globe,* the leading daily, gave it a headline reading, "Our Pioneering Work sanctioned by the Assembly," while *The Universe* announced it as "Two signatures for a First." The *Illustrated Agenda* began by saying, "Turkey, Leader among Firsts," thus considering the triumph as an achievement of the entire nation. *Tomorrow,* under the headline "The Most Arduous and Indispensable Privatization in History," recorded the myriad aspects of the incident. *Belief,* referring to the antagonism between Europe and Turkey, announced that Turkey had given Europe a lesson, while *Motherland* made a rather funny remark ascribing 'Self-punishment' to the event, interpreting what had been granted to Can as a privilege that should, in fact, be considered granted to every Turkish citizen. Among comments, one of the leading columnists claimed that history would soon be noting the fact that justice had not been entrusted to a foreign organizations, either French, German or Italian, and this was a great error, a deplorably missed opportunity. Even columnists who could not help reminding their readers from time to time of their leftist past stated that the ministry of justice had indeed done the right thing by entrusting Turkish justice to a private organization presided over by a reputable jurist, i.e., Can, but were puzzled that the prosecutor's office remained outside the functions of new establishment, while other writers praised Can as "the new patron of Turkish justice" and made laudatory comments accompanied by illustrations, speaking of his merits as a thinker, lawyer, and jurist. There were also authors like, for instance, Talip Tahir Uçar, a member of the *Motherland* staff, who suggested that May 25th, the date on which the bill had been voted, or June 24th, the date of the effective transfer of justice to the private sector, should become a national holiday. In short, the general belief of the Turkish media was that Turkey after June 24th, 2073, would not be the Turkey that existed prior to the said date, since this "brand new" Turkey had the honor of being the first country to be awarded the laurel wreath of democracy in "our highly globalized world." In the column reserved for him in the *Universe.* the reputable writer Sharman Altan, whose attitude towards the event was ambiguous, stated that this "great step" was but a beginning rather than an end and said that "the said great step" might soon inspire the idea of making justice an international matter, emphasizing that this was not "a breakthrough." To those who might claim that his opinion was paradoxical, he answered that from now on as long as the position of the United States was not considered a paradox, his observations should not constitute a paradox either. As for Cüneyt, who had been struggling for months to attain this "happy ending," gave in his essay "At Last" — written after he had read all the other articles on the subject — a "summary" of the great efforts that had been made to bring about the desired end. He stressed the fact that justice was a natural consequence of the directions being pursued at this time, adding that he thought irrelevant the views expressed by certain authors who regretted the fact that justice had not been entrusted partly or wholly to foreign establishments, since, he noted, nearly all of those associated with the Turkish Basic Law Corporation, the TBLPC, were actually partners in the world-wide, illustrious, and leading concerns of the United States, Britain, Italy, Germany, and Sweden. He concluded, "I address you as a spokesman for the Corporation and wish you all to be peaceful at heart and have no moral worries. Do not forget that the TBLPC has anticipated everything that should be anticipated."

In spite of all these positive reactions, there was one person who seemed to have qualms: the man who had laid the foundations for the TBLPC. As he listened to the unwelcome criticisms from certain professionals, Sabri among them, Can realized that quite possibly he had tarnished his reputation and wealth for the sake of an ideal that he might fail to realize. In three months, when the courts came under the jurisdiction of the TBLPC — in other words, when the TBLPC had reorganized the entire judicial system — the project might come to nothing even before it was put into action. The salaries for thousands of employees, the cost of maintaining thousands of buildings, and the money necessary to keep the system functioning seemed already too great a burden. The government had assessed the cost of the privatization of justice at a certain level and arranged to pay for it in instalments for five years. He did not worry about that. The problem remained, however, of coping with the heavy burden of which the government had rid itself whether there would really be enough money to pay for it. Would it be possible to raise the standard of living for the judges as had been promised? Advisors were generally optimistic, though there were pessimists among them. The shareholders' contributions should not be underestimated, and that could cover salaries for the judges and other staff for two years. There was no doubt, on the other hand, that every new case to be brought to court meant a flow of money into the coffers of the TBLPC. Moreover, the fees in question could be raised if need be. As a matter of fact, this had been done for various reasons in recent years. The precedent had been set, so it could be done again without needing to ask permission from any authority. But there had been a steady decline in the number of legal appeals, because of their ever increasing cost. Can could not forget the words of a young researcher who had told him, "Anyone who turns to the court to pursue a debt is expected to deposit ten thousand lira in advance. To pursue a case involving defamation costs as much as a small automobile. Under the circumstances, people prefer to resign themselves to fate or look for other means to settle their problems. What I am driving at is the probable decrease in the number of people likely to appeal for justice."

Can reported this to Gül that evening. She was in a good mood and listened to what he said. But before going to bed she asked, "Well, how did you respond?"

"I said, 'OK, but how on earth has this escaped my notice?'"

"What did he say?" asked Gül.

"He said, 'You are the head of a great concern, Sir. You don't have to meddle with such trifles.'"

Gül stroked her husband's hair as if he were a child. "What he says is correct, but you should have realized this before. Sabri kept warning you, but you paid no attention," she said. "Try to get some sleep now, dear."

Can slid into bed, took off his glasses, and laid them on the night stand. He felt like smoking and imagined the smell of a cigarette. "Should I start smoking again?" he said to himself. "I wish I had let Temel appeal to the Mafia to take care of this."

In the meantime, Gül had put on her nightgown and sat on the edge of the bed. He drew her close. "Thank God, Sabri has been in Ankara for quite some time. Were he here, he'd keep saying, 'Didn't I tell you so?' Enough to drive me off a skyscraper."

When the next morning, he entered his office an hour and a half late and saw Sabri waiting for him, he hesitated. With his right hand, he leaned on his desk before sitting down. He drank the glass of water İnci brought him. Sabri asked if he were all right, to which he replied, "I'm perfectly all right!" He tried to tell him his impressions of the researchers who said that the prospects for the company looked very dismal. Sabri smiled, which he interpreted as a sardonic response.

"What do you mean, Sabri, by your sardonic look?"

"Sardonic? What makes you say that, Sir?" said Sabri. "Is there nothing to laugh at?"

"Do you mean to say that we're in trouble?"

"I mean nothing of the kind."

"After all that I've told you?"

"Yes, but something else, something important seems to have escaped your notice. You and your associates seem to have overlooked the text of the law you prepared yourself. We are not obliged to maintain the old system. We are establishing a new order in which we shall see to it that everything functions smoothly and properly."

"All right, until when? Don't you share the opinion of our research team?"

"As a matter of fact, I don't."

Can lapsed into silence, then responded, "Up until yesterday, you were opposed to the project. Now you seem to have changed your opinion."

Sabri smiled. "I was opposed to the very idea behind it, the privatization of justice, but theory and practice are two different things. I suggest that you do not get tangled up in such trivial questions," he said, adding that the urgent thing now was to convene a shareholders' meeting. Given the fact that the people on whom Turkey's production and trade depended were among the TBLPC shareholders, they would likely shed light on pressing issues and reduce their own responsibilities."

"Good heavens!" said Can, "Why on earth didn't I think of that?"

"You did think of it, Sir! This was the necessary conclusion to be drawn from the draft you yourself prepared. The matter is still in the incubation period, and we are tired. We're are about to assume a heavy burden. Now we must set a date for the shareholders' meeting."

At 4 p.m. on July 5th, 2073, as Can headed to the lectern from which he would deliver his inaugural address in the hall donated to the TBLPC by Temel the week before, he was quite nervous but remembered his father's maxim: "The foot heads forward while the heel goes backward." However, no sooner had he stepped onto the platform than there was loud and long applause. He stood immobile for some time before greeting the audience with a wave of his hand. He picked up the roses in the vase before him and threw them toward the guests. The speech was interrupted with frequent applause. It seemed that the shareholders were more optimistic than he as was corroborated by the speeches from various members that followed.

The speaker who followed was Tolga Caymaz, the renowned aggressive CEO of a chain of supermarkets. His protruding belly preceded him onto the platform. He waved his hand, greeting the audience as if he were a rock star and waited for the applause to end before a began speaking in his provincial accent already fallen into disuse by others but to which he was faithfully attached. He drew attention first to the fact that a very intelligent man by name of Can had been sent among them as a quasi-prophet, thanks to whom justice would be redeemed for its original owner, that is to say the Turkish people, for which God should be thanked, and then he began to expatiate on the fact that ever since the beginning of creation "everything, without a single exception" had been a commodity, a system in which exchanging goods or work for other goods or work was the norm. Therefore, what we designate by the term "justice" could not possibly be left outside the confines of the universal order and no matter what we did we could not change this order of things. He added that given the fact that now that justice had been privatized, it was necessary to make plain what privatization meant and that its execution should take place "in due conformity with its tenets." He stated that all of the associate members should feel proud of having a share in this achievement, making it clear that private law should be applied with due consideration to the universal rule of trade, which meant that the justice would be administered more fairly than that when dispensed by the state, and in turn, justice should be maintained at a high level, which would eventually benefit the shareholders. Having enumerated many complicated examples and arguments, he underlined the fact that both the defendant and the plaintiff should be assumed to be "clients" and that the judge and the prosecutors be considered sales people. Further, he observed that the success of the new system could be achieved by inducing the citizens to appeal to justice at every turn, thus making it instinctual to turn to the courts, which in turn meant an increase in the number of courts. He concluded his speech by saying,

"Once again I repeat dear brothers, the court is a supermarket. It's at our disposal, ready to serve us, and we must never forget this!" When he finished, Can inclined towards Sabri, who was sitting next to him, and said "We're done for!" Yet, at the same moment he saw Temel, the greatest supporter of the cause, applaud warmly the CEO of the chair of supermarkets, and this boosted his morale.

The next person to speak was Ergin Çıpa, known to be the "number one subcontractor" in Europe and America in the assembly and sale of airplanes, one of the prominent tycoons who held eighty per cent of the shares of the airlines in Turkey. Pot bellied with wavy, white, well-trimmed hair falling over his shoulders and with his collar open exposing his hairy chest, he spoke with a stentorian voice that endeared him to his listeners and put them at their ease. His speech considerably allayed Can's fears. He announced, "Dear friends, you seem to be on edge. You think that we are henceforth responsible for the dispensation of justice in Turkey. Please do not exaggerate. Believe me, justice in this country has never been on the shoulders of the state, nor will it be on ours. Think of the age we live in. Consider the fact that monopoly has failed to dominate the economy, considering the fact that there are competitors competing with me for instance in the number of flights as well as aircraft manufacture and sales. How can we shoulder the burden of justice while barring access to others. This was not possible yesterday; it is not possible today. The difference is that just as we are the cream of business life, so shall we be the cream of justice. We shall apply ourselves and derive what's due to us." He interrupted his speech and scrutinized the audience before resuming. "Some of our friends, especially the jurists, seem astonished by my words. But believe me there is nothing to justify your perplexed faces. We cannot deny that the justice meted out by the state was expensive, the result of the old way our modern economy was ruled. We should expect that it will be more costly after privatization. However, one should not forget that even in 2073 not every citizen can afford a private spaceshuttle. It is also true that not everybody can travel by air. Under the circumstances, we cannot expect that every citizen will seek full justice. In other words, he or she is not obliged to appeal to the law every time. Therefore, some will have to settle their own affairs at the police station or through private means. Others, having fulfilled the requirements will find justice in the TBLPC. He paused with a smile. His smile received applause as did his words. A shareholder in one of the rear rows shouted in a loud voice, "Long live Çıpa!" to which he responded: "I will, and together we all will!" This received even greater applause. He reminded his audience in detail that state socialism had formerly made appeals to justice that there were courts in almost every part of town. As if this were not enough, the state had given people with modest incomes the right to hire lawyers for free, which accordingly had increased the number of disputes and the number of appeals to courts, creating thereby an ever increasing burden for the justice system. "We are, all of us, aware of the fact that justice has a prestigious, even sacred character. And it will remain so. On the assumption that justice has this sacred quality, it must be a domain wherein only cases conforming to its prestigious and sacred character are settled. This is the *raison d'etre* for the privatization of justice. Therefore, as a logical consequence, it is necessary that, benefiting from the powers that the law grants us, we must reduce the number of courts to twenty, no, to thirty per cent of their current number and redress, enabling them to serve the capitalistic system." So saying, he went into such detail that even the jurists present had difficulty following his train of thought. He crowned his speech with the words, "To cut a long story short, the aim should be to raise the level of the economy by preventing justice from being detoured by trifles." His talk was applauded by part of the audience, while the rest was at a loss how best to express their resentment.

Gül was among the latter group. "The man is a downright fascist," she muttered. "He wants the entire justice system to be given over to the command of bosses, namely the capitalists, and operated exclusively for them." As Ergin Çıpa returned to his seat among cheers of 'Long live! Hurrah!" she leaned toward Can and whispered, "This man considers everybody, except the bosses, as a common herd."

But Can either did not understand her or was engrossed in his own thoughts, for he had a happy smile. "Strange!" he said, thinking of what the speaker had said. "This did not occur to me. Now I see that we'll make it work!"

Gül did not understand what he meant. Her face was blank, and she was not alone in feeling the way she did. The handsome young businessman beside her leaned over, saying, "Ergin never changes. He takes himself to be a sociologist, psychologist, linguist, jurist, and professor of history. Once he starts speaking there is no way to stop him."

Gül didn't have a chance to reply, for a third speaker had taken the floor. It was the CEO of the chain of stores called "The Flag," which sold high-end clothes. He produced and represented world famous brands. He had once dabbled in politics but had changed his profession due to his squeaky voice and his manic behavior. In his talk, he focused on the formation of security units, the responsibility for which now belonged to the TBLPC. He dwelt on the power and effect of justice and the effect on people who were not to be trusted. He proposed that the staff be selected from young men of thirty-one or thirty-two who were taller than six feet and were trained as commandos They should wear uniforms and be equipped with weapons throughout Turkey. Having said this, he said that the audience was about to see three models wearing uniforms designed and manufactured in his own establishment. He added that the said uniforms would be made available to the TBLPC shortly at a reasonable price. Having been heartily cheered, he asked the board to promise that these uniforms could be used.

Sabri, General Secretary of the TBLPC, was then granted permission by the chairman to speak. He mounted the platform while being applauded and said, "The suggested personnel will soon be recruited and dressed in the uniforms proposed by our valued member. Let no one doubt this! I must add, however, that we had also decided to engage women as security officers whose were no less than five feet, six inches tall." This statement was also applauded, although not as much as the other speakers had been.

Twelve other speakers took the floor following Sabri, but they did not receive the same warm reaction. The issues on which they elaborated were confined to items tackled earlier, and the audience had begun to grow weary. In the meantime, a couple of interesting ideas that might have shed some light on the workings of the TBLPC remained unspoken.

At the conclusion of the meeting, Can took the floor to thank the members for their attention and added that he would be at their disposal for whatever they might suggest. He would consider their suggestions as "orders." Further everything would be done to realize Ergin Çipa's proposal. At the conclusion, he asked the members to specify four candidates to be elected to the board to take part in the first General Meeting. Nominations were made, and since fifty were nominated and fifty were present, it could deduced that each member had voted for himself. However, in the end, the winners were Ergin Çıpa, Tolga Caymaz, and Hasan Sayar, all of whom were former member of the Supreme Court of Appeals. General Secretary Sabri, having announced the results, invited the shareholders to proceed to the adjacent hall where refreshments would served.

Just as Can, with his wife on his right and the General Secretary on his left, were about to enter the hall, he felt a hand on his shoulder. Startled, he turned around. Temel stood there, fury in his eyes. Can tried to smile, but Temel's anger froze him into silence. Temel complained about the indifference of the audience in regard to his problem and wanted to know why all this trouble for so-called privatization had been undertaken if the house he wanted could not be obtained. "You know what, I have become suspicious of the whole thing. To the best of my knowledge, the reason this whole business was begun was to get that house, wasn't it?"

Can remained still. Temel, the CEO of the TBLPC, was being criticized by one who seemed ready for a major blow-up despite their friendship. Although Can considered ending this confrontation forcefully, he changed his opinion and took Temel by the arm, leading him away from the crowd and, with a smile, putting his hand on his shoulder.

"You're right. When you look at things from that angle, it's as if the mountain had given birth to a mouse or a mouse to the mountain," he said and, lowering his voice, added, "This is not so bad after all. If we try to consider the whole thing all together, your share in the project isn't just that house and its minuscule garden. You should have a firm guarantee."

Temel continued to look sullen.

"Can you tell me when we will have the pleasure of witnessing the demolition of that rotten house?"

At this, Can grew angry himself and, turning to Gül, said:, "Do you realize, this man is about to have a fight with me! He's in the grip of an obsession and will not listen to reason. I could understand him better if we had already taken over the administration of justice. There are three months to go. Am I supposed to take an axe and demolish the house?" He turned to Temel and calmly began to deliver his conclusion. "I am aware of the fact that you're not entirely wrong. We happen to have taken a tortuous path. We've kept you waiting for a long time and caused you great expenses, but I had no other choice. Once we have everything as we wish, I'm sure we'll be in a position to find out a legal solution. On the other hand, don't forget that you and I have carried out a revolution that history will record. This alone is itself tantamount to building a skyscraper. You have been patient up until now. Please try to be patient a little longer. Don't expect that we'll be through with everything once we have settled the issue of the house. As I say, a little more patience."

"How long will we have to wait?"

"Not very long. Let's wait until the armed guards are selected, and Göktürk Tekbayrak has their uniforms ready."

Temel submitted as if he were a docile boy. "All right, let's wait," he said simply and headed for the exit without even shaking hands with Can's wife.

"Hey, boss, where are you going? Don't you want to see the guards' uniforms?" Can called after him.

Temel made a hand gesture that signified his indifference.

In the adjacent hall, the majority of shareholders had circled around the three security guards and, drinks in their hands, were lost in admiration as if they were viewing statues in an exhibition. Gazing as if bewitched at the models, gigantic in their headgear with collars and cuffs embroidered with silver thread. Some could not resist touching the hands, the arms, even the chins of the guards, probably to make sure that they were real.

"They are like children," commented Gül.

Can reached for a drink from the waiter. "Temel was a real child," he said.

"Maybe," she said "but in fact you were toying with him as if he were a child. You keep putting off what he wants most. You seem to turn a deaf ear to his repeated request."

Can turned red. "It's true," he said. "It may seem funny to you, but I don't want to see that house demolished, at least while the old man there is still alive."

"Why?"

"I don't know, dear, truly I don't. Actually I never saw him, but the way he has put up a bold front and has turned down all the attractive offers affects me."

"You forget all that has been done, the promises you made to Temel and the huge sums he has already spent …"

"I am well aware of that, but my principal driving force was never the house."

"What was it then?"

"I don't know. I really don't. It may have been a deep passion for power, or a desire to fashion beautiful houses. It may well have been to secure freedom for Varol and Rıza, or simply to challenge the powers that be, or pursue some legal consistency, a game, or … or … to save that house from deteriorating."

Gül was stuck dumb, but after a while she smiled. "Dear, there are times when I don't understand you at all! The only thing I can say is that I love you very much."

Can, in turn, gazed at his wife as if he could find its secret. "I don't know what to say, "These days, I must add, I don't recognize myself. Why? I don't know. Perhaps because we are all changing. As the philosopher said, everything changes but change."

"And monotony. I don't believe life or people are so erratic," she remarked. "On the other hand, I don't know that yours is a genuine change. You claim for yourself more than one personality, five in fact, in the course of the day. I can see this. But the one that seems to prevail is the revolutionary who snatched a gun from the belt of the policeman, your cherished image of yourself. I like you that way. As a matter fact, I think there is no difference between your privatization efforts and snatching the gun and directing it at the policeman himself."

Can put his arm around his wife and pulled her to him. "You're being dramatic! Actually, we are like herds, the castaways, living on the margins of life. We are not sure of what we do and actually want. Perhaps they have driven away what we call imagination and cemented it in hard facts. They don't dabble in theories, and they know about economics.

Gül embraced her husband. "How about Marx?" she asked. "Didn't he know about economics?"

"He certainly did," replied Can. He stared at the floor for a while before answering. "He knew better than anyone. Yet he had not drawn it away from its context. He created links between economics and people."

Gül sighed. "You are right, dear," she said. "He defined capital not as an individual's power but as a collective one. But enough of theories now. I'm not in the mood for new theories."

IX.

THE GENERAL MEETING WAS NOT OPEN TO THE PRESS, yet democracy reigned in the country, and the speeches delivered and the decisions reached were revealed in their minutest detail by all the television channels and newspapers. Moreover, the CEO, Can, and the General Secretary, Sabri, in the statements that followed showed how the decisions were to be implemented. They revealed as well that in about three months' time, they — that is, the TBLPC —would have the entire responsibility for the administration of justice, in other words the entire judicial system, with the exception of the Constitutional Court and the Supreme Court of Appeals. They revealed also how they would carry into effect the work to whose execution they would dedicate themselves. However, the subject that particularly concerned the public and, consequently, the press, was the way in which the proposal made by the celebrated businessman Ergin Çipa and unanimously adopted by the participants would be put into practice, that is, how they would handle the layoff of the current personnel, i.e. the judges, employees, and clerks. Sabri said, "As they say, 'great minds think alike.' Both our board of directors and our esteemed CEO opted for regional courts." He then went into details. According to this scheme, the city courts in Ankara and Istanbul would be closed and only the provincial courts would be left intact. Meanwhile, at least twenty and at most twenty-five regional courts would be set up. Under the circumstances, not even great provinces like Kayseri, Erzincan, and Van would have courts of their own. For instance, the Çukurova regional court would have jurisdiction over cases from Adana, Mersin, Gaziantep, Hatay, and Kahramanmaraş. All of the western provinces from Balıkesir to Muğla would come under the jurisdiction of the İzmir province, and in certain major towns there would be a judge charged with guiding the citizens to the path they should take in legal matters, while preparing, if need be, their files for the regional court.

However, in every province, and if need be in every town, there would be a judge. The result would be a tremendous reduction in the number of judges and juridical advisers with raises to be effected in the salaries of the rest. Sabri quoted now and then approximate figures that puzzled the newspaper reporters, who asked such questions as "What has led you to do this?" or "How will justice be dispensed?" or "Will cases be finalized within the lifetime of the complainant?" or "Will citizens be required to testify something of no consequence if they have to travel from Muğla to İzmir or from Elbistan to Adana? Laughing quietly, he said, "Let us not forget that private enterprise will doubtless act speedily and effectively in this. Moreover, as evidenced by laws that entrust justice to the private sector, the Turkish community will be developed and become one of the foremost civilized communities in the world. Conflicts among our citizens are expected to be reduced to a minimum partly thanks to us. One should also take into consideration that communications between provinces have been facilitated and generally operated by airlines. Last but not least, these new conditions will help to promote the country's tourism and enhance the citizen's knowledge and view of life."

The superiority of this system followed the design of the whole structure, of which the public was ignorant. The TBLPC had acquired hundreds of courts of justice whose sites were of incomparable value, which meant the accumulation of great wealth. It was evident that the organization would derive considerable benefit from the sale or rental of these buildings, some of which were of great historical value. On the other hand, as stated by Temel, the major shareholder of the organization, the skyscrapers to be erected on the former sites of law courts and buildings associated with them in Istanbul, Ankara, İzmir, and some other big cities would bring in great sums of money while catering to the requirements of the organization. Thus not only considerable monetary contribution would have made its way into the organization's budget, but the improvement and betterment of cities would be fostered. Ergin Çıpa, who had recently become the prominent spokesman for the organization, pointed to another source of income. Doubling the fees to be charged to litigants would secure a smoother functioning of the mechanism of justice and reduce the number of irrelevant cases, which wasted much valuable time. His reply to citizens who would object that some might not be able to pay the required sum was that there were a great number of the mentally ill who, petition in hand, spent half of their lives before the judiciary. This sort of men, who expected to be immediately received and heard by the courts, should be barred from having access to them. The respect for law would be one result. Sabri asked, "Is it the responsibility of tribunals to try offenders who have murdered and injured others? The perpetrators of such crimes are quite often impoverished. What shall we do about them? Shall we send them away?" To this, Ergin Çıpa replied with his peculiar smile, "Certainly not. We might not charge them anything. This may be considered as an indication of the great generosity of our private organization."

A few people applauded this. Can raised his voice saying, "It seems that law has become for Ergin a personal matter. The TBLPC should be proud of having groomed him to be a jurist." To this remark, not only the members, but Ergin Çıpa himself laughed.

As they laughed, judges throughout the country brooded over their bleak future. The point that concerned them especially was that there would soon be an army of them out of work. Therefore, a considerable number preferred to withdraw from active duty rather than believe vague promises about the imminent improvement in their lives. About nine out of ten of the members of the Supreme Court filed petitions asking to retire, and other judges followed suit. A considerable number of judges and prosecutors who had not yet reached the age for retirement preferred to withdraw from office to become lawyers. In such an atmosphere when Can had a few free minutes, he called Halis, the judge in Temel's desire to have the teacher's house expropriated, asking about his health like an old friend and asking him not to act as other judges and prosecutors who preferred to withdraw from active service but to keep working. In particular, he should pursue Temel's case, about which nothing had been done for the last year and a half. Halis was a learned judge who had not dismissed Temel's case, because it had been brought to court by one of the prominent lawyers of the country. On the other hand, he had heard that the source of the privatization project was related to this case. He was clever enough to understand the meaning of the call from the man destined to rule over justice in Turkey. This man desired that Temel's case be finalized before Can took over the justice system, so that he might not be accused of malfeasance. At a time in which the future of eighty-five per cent of the country's judges looked bleak, taking into consideration the fact that due to the excessive increase in court fees it would be almost impossible for a lawyer to make a decent living. Halis thought that, under the circumstances and the money he needed for his private life, it would not be too great an offence to declare a mistrial. "My dear Sir, I have lately been considering how I could settle Temel's case. I think I found a way out a couple of days ago. You may consider the case settled."

Can felt the hand with which he held the receiver tremble. He wanted to ask Halis which "way out" he had discovered. Failing to find the right words, he simply said, "Thank you, Halis, thanks a lot. Frankly, I could not think of a way out myself!"

Whether he placed the receiver on the desk or let it drop, he could not have said. His nervousness continued. He realized that many things in his mind were changing and assuming unexpected meanings. Until the telephone call, everything had gone as it should, even better than he had anticipated. Now Halis communicated to him that he had found a solution to the problem and even without having been asked for it. He was facing a dilemma. Quite unexpectedly he found himself gauging his actions. Suddenly he saw Sabri on the doorway with a happy face and notebook in hand. Can realized that he, too, was smiling. "You have quite a smile in your face, Sir. Good news, I hope?" Sabri asked.

He told Sabri about his conversation with Halis. "What do you think of it?"

"Good news, I should say. This saves us a lot of trouble. You know, Temel is obsessed with it," he said, reaching for the telephone, "Let me inform Temel of this news. It will cheer him up."

"Wait," said Can, agitated. "Let's not rush. You can never tell. Something amiss could crop up. Let's not tell him for the moment. This is Turkey. Everything could change."

Sabri, puzzled, studied the CEO's face as if there a secret he was trying to conceal.

Can realized that he was being scrutinized but simply smiled at him. "You know what, Sabri, I think I have been experiencing a funny sort of feeling these days, things I can't account for. Things for which we have spent so much effort end up appearing strange. The proposals that our colleagues make, for example, puzzle me. I don't understand the reason for some of their measures and for the increase expected in court fees. What do you say to that?"

"We talked this over, Sir. There is nothing to be surprised at," said Sabri. "They have become our associates, and it was quite natural for these business-minded people to look at this venture as commercially lucrative."

"But we are going right now through the initiation phase."

"So much the better, Sir. We are in Turkey, and the most compelling decisions are made in our community during transition periods. The worst changes are contrived during these periods."

"But I have not set up this venture for lucrative ends. I cannot deny the mercenary concerns behind the scheme, but you remember how often we discussed it. The principles far outweighed other concerns."

"You know best, Sir. Every enterprise is based on principles, but we cannot expect that every principle should remain in the end. Furthermore, they need not remain unaltered."

"All right. But why should it be so costly?"

"You think so, since you haven't lately been wading through the minor details of the company, figures outside your area of interest. The costliness of justice is nothing new. As a matter of fact, it has been prohibitively expensive lately."

"But why?"

"You should know, Sir. Because justice concentrates on solving the problems of the wealthy. The solution of great problems involved great expenses. Can you guess why we have been flourishing lately, why we have become such a profitable firm?"

"Because we perform our work correctly."

"It's always been our, or rather your, custom to act in this way. Money has always been secondary as you told us. It's quite natural now to set the costs for justice rather high."

"All right, if the objective is to make as much money as one would wish, how do you account for Ergin Çıpa's proposal being accepted with such enthusiasm? Don't you think that reducing the number of courts, while making justice a costly affair, is paradoxical? How do you reconcile the *laissez faire* principle with this state of affairs?"

This caused Sabri to reflect. "The doctrine of *laissez faire* of Vincent De Gournoy has become obsolete. It never proved applicable anyway; for, as you yourself said, capitalism means, above all, exclusivity, and accordingly we are appropriating justice, all of it. Now that we enjoy this privilege, there is no sense in enlarging the system. I told you that many courts were superfluous. Governments insisted on not reducing the number of courts at the beginning of the century in proportion to the decreasing population and went on paying salaries to judges. Nevertheless, the number of citizens appealing to the courts declined considerably. Eventually, appeals to the court are now generally made by a single class of people: the very rich."

"But why?"

"Why? Because contrary to expectations, at the beginning of the century the population began declining at a tremendous rate. Justice became a costly affair, and the income of people markedly decreased. Thus ordinary people began settling their disputes through other means."

"Such as?"

"Illicit means."

"I see. Under the circumstances our task as jurists is relieved of a considerable burden, and …"

"Not quite, Sir. Had this been the case everything would be all right, but there is something that has escaped our notice when we were making our plans. The unsettled cases date back to several years — some ten, some twenty, some forty years back and some dating back to the twentieth century, tens of thousands of cases. They are waiting to go to trial and at little cost. We missed this point during our deliberations."

Can shuddered. "It follows that we have undertaken something beyond our abilities. Well then, how are we going to cope with this problem? We have inadvertently reduced the number of courts to thirty-one. Weren't you aware of this fact?"

"I was," said Sabri with a winning smile, "Not while we drafted the initial proposal, but later on."

"Why didn't you object to the decrease in courts?"

"As a matter of fact, I asked Ergin to do so."

"Why?"

"Because this was the only way out, Sir."

"But how?"

"We are not going to waste our time with these protracted cases. We'll not devote all our time to them. We'll be handling them now and then as long as the restricted means at our disposition will permit. There is no doubt that the cases will drag on, but our expenditures will not rise considerably. If the litigants are still intent on having their cases settled so much the worse for them. Since they have waited so long, they must be accustomed to waiting. Let them wait a little more."

Can scrutinized the general secretary for a while without speaking. "You are a true philosopher, aren't you? Not only a philosopher but a child of the devil!"

Sabri laughed. "I don't think that I deserve such an honor, Sir," he said. "I am but a worker trying to protect the interests of my boss."

"But will there be no end to these long-drawn-out cases?" Can asked after some deliberation."

"Not exactly, Sir. Litigants will gradually give up their causes," said Sabri. "This is evident if we carefully consider the tendencies we find in the country and in the world at large."

"How so?"

"You should know it better than anyone else, Sir!"

"The funny thing is that I don't."

"I mean as a good Marxist."

"What has this to do with Marxism?"

Sabri stared at him for quite a while before he said with some hesitation, "I believe you have been told about castaways?"

"More than once! I even spoke about them with the Prime Minister. What's more, Rıza wrote a booklet about them. He is going to have an edition published with illustrations before long. Yet I don't think that these people really exist. Sometimes I say maybe they are, but then I deny what is claimed for them. They are exaggerations. They are like the UFOs of the past century, sheer hallucinations!"

"But so-called castaways do exist, Sir. If you believe that they are real, everything will be so much easier for you."

"I see, or rather I think I understand," replied Can. "Yet I'd like to have your opinion of them."

"It's a matter of opinion, Sir!" said Sabri, "There is not a single species of castaways. One should speak rather of categories of castaways, or of a stratification among them. Some understand from this term the herds of human beings living in a state of starvation on the outskirts of towns and cities much like old horses turned loose to range at will. On the other hand, we know that literacy in our country is much lower than it was in the mid-twentieth century, down by almost fifty per cent. For the majority of people, to send their children to school has become almost impossible. The education of one single child costs twice a worker's income. All public schools envy the income made by private schools, and the principals of private schools want to make as much money as possible with the least possible effort. A worker can feed his children all right, but he or she has not the means to send them to school. You must have heard of the fact that a section of the population organized themselves, trying to educate their children outside the schools. They teach them writing and reading themselves. This does not qualify them for finding a job. Even the simplest job requires basic training, not to mention a diploma. Men try to manage on their own and strain to do something, but finding that they can't, they emigrate. Under the circumstances, they have hardly any time to spare for old legal cases."

Can was staring at his assistant with admiration and envy. "Emigrate, you said?" he asked, "Do they imagine that they can find jobs elsewhere in Europe ?"

"Emigration has changed direction, Sir. Europe is no longer an attractive place to go. The poor prefer to go to the east to Afghanistan, Pakistan, and Russia. It appears that even though they may not find jobs there, at least the vegetation is lush. There are also people trying to survive among us, but they lead a marginal life."

Can seemed to be listening to somebody telling a nightmare he had the night before. "How?" he inquired.

"You know this better than I," continued Sabri. "The remaining category of the poor consists of people living at the expense of their brethren, the retired people who have a meagre allowance, parents, brothers, or sisters."

"Aren't you exaggerating? Newspapers, televisions never mention the existence of such creatures."

"True, the powers that be prefer to ignore them. The newspapers are no longer the newspapers of our youth, Sir."

"On the other hand, just look around. We are in an age of peace and plenty. The sky swarms with spaceshuttles. Temel erects skyscrapers to vie with those in New York and sells them with little effort."

"Yes, but there are other human beings, jobless. Most of them see no way out."

"Why can they not find jobs with all the affluence around us?"

Sabri drew a deep breath. "As an old Marxist, you surprising me, Sir. The proliferation of sophisticated machines has made workers redundant. Fewer and fewer men are needed to operate these sophisticated machines."

"Why?"

"Even the most ordinary janitor requires some know-how. Most trivial occupations require more than one electronic gadget. The janitor, the canteen boy, our staff, everybody has a diploma. For instance, some of the guards we have engaged are law school graduates. Some are civil engineers, and most of them are graduates of the High Security School."

"Those who have no diplomas find homes outside the city, I presume."

Sabri waited for a minute before answering. "There are many among them who have diplomas, but the worst of it is that nature itself is becoming increasingly barren. It becomes difficult to find food for them all. The contemporary man produces excessive waste. In recent years, the heaps of refuse have grown. They've become massive as Temel's skyscrapers result in new piles of rubble. These new geographic formations are now taller than our mountains."

"You should have been a poet," Can said. "What can we do to stop this? Any solution you think of?"

Sabri smiled ironically. "Yes, Sir. To do what has been done in the case of our courts."

"You mean?"

"To make a reduction."

"In other words, birth control?"

"No. If we cannot even control men employed by us, how can we manage family planning? No, that won't do. It's a long range affair, let alone the fact that the newborn may be considered untouchable. Communities today are impatient. They want speedy solutions. We need short-cuts. The natural resources in America are comparatively richer than ours, yet we are hearing that certain clandestine ways of dealing with these people have been initiated even there. It is said that America is applying the policy it implemented in Vietnam, Iraq, Iran, Syria, and Libya and on its own continent, of course not visibly. They can make this happen perhaps better, since they are experienced. The native Americans were the first victims."

"How so?"

"By lynching even the least offender, for instance someone who stole a loaf of bread."

"Sabri, you must be joking. How did you come to this conclusion? How come I have no idea about these things or Gül for that matter or Temel?"

"Because you and Gül spend your time reading fictions and Temel is engrossed in his pet hate, the old man who won't move."

"All right, but we watch television and read the newspapers every day."

"Just as I have told you, Sir. These issues are not allowed to be discussed. Yet the problem does exist, the greatest problem of our day. A solution must be found for them."

"What you are saying is a frightening. Even imagining a likely solution is horrible."

"I am not to blame, Sir," he said. "If I could, I would have prevented it. But might is right, as they say. In order to survive they find this essential."

"All right, what about nature, mother nature? Would the solution lie there?

"Nature has dried up and been turned into a wasteland. The earth is covered with a thick crust of refuse. Bringing it back would be extremely difficult, we're told."

"Technology and science have made prodigious advances. I should think that there would be a way out."

"They say that it's too late, Sir. Yesterday my father told me how they had once been swimming in the sea. My cousin thought that it must have been a joke."

"You're right, in our youth. I remember references were made to swimming in the sea now and then. Strange, but true! How come that our world dried up in less than a century?"

"The capitalists went too far. They put the burden on the archenemies of nature, machines. They removed themselves from nature and humanity."

"I didn't know this side of you. You speak like Rıza."

"Rıza's point of departure is Marx, while you choose that option after trying other things. Personally I try to observe my surroundings from wherever I happen to be. However, they all boil down to the same thing. None of us can resist this problem. Our position is, in fact, quite the reverse, since all that we can do is contribute to it."

"In what way?"

"Let me give you an example. We are complaining about the drying up of nature, yet we continue to support Temel."

"Now, just a minute! Temel is a separate case. He stands for harmony, consistency, unity, and uniformity. He is above all a lover of order."

"I don't deny it, Sir. He has a passion for order, in his own way. This is why he cannot support nature as such. He is loath to see a flower or a tree anywhere in the city."

"Don't you don't find him praiseworthy?"

"Not quite, Sir. We read in books that the residents of Istanbul have transformed the city into something unrecognizable, yet I'd rather have them than him. What they did was contribute to a gradual decline and did not raze the city virtually to the ground."

Can smiled. "You're right there. Our master builder is unlike his predecessors. Temel has neither a past nor a future in his view. His is a continuum, a perpetually continuous present, a present that can provide man with a sense of immortality, an impression of unchangeableness, a stasis. It must be interesting to be able to come to a standstill after the ravages of time. "

"This is your point of view, Sir?"

"No, his. But the fact is that Temel is a philosopher who expresses his ideas not through words but acts."

"They say that he is an admirer of New York, and he himself does not deny it. But New York is also a relatively old city, Sir, in a sense much older than this city of ours. If you ask my opinion, even New York shows similarities …"

"New York is for Temel merely a point of departure. What he is after is an Istanbul anchored in change."

"A frightful change. He razes to the ground all vegetation …"

"In the meantime, he exterminates viruses and bacteria. You remember what he says? Razing to the ground old buildings to be replaced with skyscrapers where vast spaces will make room for large greenhouses, enabling people to have access to better sanitary and hygienic conditions. According to him, the higher one soars from the surface of the infected earth, the more secure one will be. He is right in this," said Can. He remained lost in his reflections. After a while, he said, smiling, "It's a matter of opinion. What do you think about me? Don't you have a positive impression of me? Come on, say it, frankly, what sort of an impression do I make on you?"

"On me, Sir? Frankly there's hardly any difference between the impression I make on my own self and the impression you make on me."

"Don't you think it humiliating to be employed by Temel's proponent?"

"No Sir, certainly not!"

"Why?"

"To begin with, I know you, your past, and your true philosophy of life. Then, if we find a job at present we've got to stick with it firmly. Were you to dismiss me now, there is no reason why I'd not join the herd of castaways. I might not find a job anywhere. To get jobs nowadays has become unusual. I can't imagine how many judges will swell the ranks of the employed and become part of the herd in the aftermath of our privatization."

"What about truth?"

"I think that truth is interpreted differently in every age. What is actually true for our age is sheer egoism."

"You should write a book."

"Another grim reality of our age is the free expression of basic realities. Under the circumstances, every one of us is trying to save his own skin. They say that among the castaways there are people that do not bury their dead. Everybody is on his own, *apres moi le déluge* as they used to say."

"I don't think we have reached that point yet. Furthermore, I do not think that human beings would degenerate to that extent. Considering that human existence has a long story, that there lived once upon a time a Socrates, a Marx, and a Dostoyevsky, the world cannot deteriorate to that extent," said Can, although he himself was not quite convinced of what he was saying.

"I think, Sir, it is not a question of deterioration, but a metamorphosis. There is a great difference between the two," said Sabri, looking at Can. It seemed that he still had something at the back of his mind which he hesitated to reveal. He finally asked, "I wonder, Sir, whether you'll be able to spare some time to examine the applications we have received from Anatolia?"

Can was taken aback. "What applications?" he asked.

Sabri replied with some surprise, "Applications for the formation of the regional courts."

Can flushed with embarrassment. "Your astounding views and accounts have driven me away from everything to the point of making me forget the civic duties with which we are burdened. All right, let's tackle them right now."

Sabri got up and went out, returning with a rather thick file under his arm. He began reading the summaries they had tagged in each application. According to these reports, nearly all of the applicants, both individuals and organizations, claimed to be capable and in possession of the qualifications required. They said that they would perform their duties with the utmost objectivity and in the best manner possible and that they would considerably increase the assets of the TBLPC, adding that they were ready to give a sizeable payment in advance. The strange thing was that it seemed that all of these applications appeared to have a common origin.

Can, wearied to distraction, become nervous and edgy.

"That's enough for today," he said. "Sabri, I suggest that you form a committee with yourself as chair to screen these applications. It seems that these applicants have worked with each other. They all take justice for a commodity. This is not correct."

"But, everything *is* a commodity, Sir," said Sabri. "However, there is something in this beyond the issue of mere commodities. What sort of committee would you consider, Sir?"

"Well, a committee formed by our learned friends that will carefully go over the applications and decide on their sincerity, honesty, and efficiency."

"Would this be sufficient?"

"Wouldn't it?"

"I think not, Sir. To my mind, the applicants must be screened at their homes. It seems to me that some of these expect either to finalize longstanding hostilities and disputes among them or to expect that once in possession of the administration of justice they will be in a position to oppress people under them. They intend to settle their petty affairs with us backing them. Had their intention been otherwise, they would not be so extravagant in their estimation of themselves."

Can burst out laughing. "Sabri, you have a quick and insightful mind, no doubt about that, but you seem to have over reached even yourself in this matter of privatized justice. What are you thinking now?"

There was no change in Sabri's face. "I happen to be the general secretary of the corporation, Sir, and I am being paid for this."

Can laughed again. "Now that everybody has turned out to be greedy, your salary should be doubled." Then suddenly his expression changed. "Shouldn't we go back to the beginning? Have your ideas changed since then?"

"What was happened has happened," said Sabri smiling. "A least, we have not done anything outrageous. What we have done so far has been to convert judges into lawyers and lawyers into judges. We can call this a minor revolution."

"This was a consequence of change. It wasn't our express intention. Do you think this has been a bad thing?"

Sabri laughed again. "No Sir. However, it's evident that there will be certain irregularities in the way the mechanism functions. For instance, simply from habit, the judge may be inclined to side with one of the parties, and the new lawyer may try to be impartial. But this also is a novelty, isn't it?"

Can laughed again. "Who knows, this may give rise to some wholesome results." Then suddenly he remembered that while talking with the Prime Minister's secretary, he had heard him say that those who advised important people were, in general, one step ahead of their superiors. It occurred to Can that this might be true as well for him and Sabri. He felt tired but asked, "Is there anything we should work on now?"

Sabri considered the state of affairs and said, "Not quite, Sir. However, private security remains an issue we have to discuss. The minimum requirements for the personnel we are going to hire are as follows: regarding the male personnel, some fifty or sixty men no shorter than six feet and not older than thirty-two. As for the women to be hired, there should be twelve not shorter than five feet ten inches. We have not decided yet about their wages but will try to keep this as low as possible."

"All right, but let's not be so parsimonious," said Can, but the security issue had made him even more depressed than he had been. He drew a deep breath. "Once we used to argue with security personnel. Now we are building our own."

Sabri smiled. "This is life, Sir. I have listened to the stories of good old days from many seniors. There must have been promising days back then."

"There were, indeed!" he said. "We were young then."

"Another point demanding our attention is the control of our buildings on the European and Asian sections of the city, Sir."

"Please arrange another committee to take care of this. Ask Temel's advice also. We can discuss the results later."

"Right, Sir, I wish you a very good day."

"A very good day to you, Sabri."

Can gazed after him until he disappeared from view. "What am I doing?" he said to himself.

In the evening, he had to tell Gül all that he and Sabri said. She was worried to see him weary and despondent. She had never been positive about privatization. Although she occasionally agreed with certain arguments, she could not help feeling irritated, so she asked her husband whether he could develop a theory that might help to relieve him of his worries.

Can sighed and said, "I used to base my theories on the public needs. All those theories led up to the same end, but according to Sabri only capitalists and tycoons remain to be served. They had discarded the fundamental element, the general public, which was either eliminated or had undergone some transformation. We cannot think of castaways as the public in the proper sense of the word and eventually, a new theory that does not have the public as its *raison d'etre* cannot be called a workable theory."

"Theories that leave the public out of consideration seem to come under Sabri's special field of expertise," Gül remarked.

"Sabri does not develop theories. What he does is to show us the points that have escaped our notice. I think we have come to a point where no theories can be formulated anymore. Anyway, I feel tired and I have become confused."

Gül smiled. "Maybe because you can no longer devise theories," she said.

"Maybe so, but I really feel worn-out. A funny sort of weariness. Call it despondency, if you like. I had been so enthusiastic at the beginning.

Now I am scared. I feel as if my brain has been emptied of its contents. I think that this general feeling of depression came over me after I learned about the existence of those castaways. Ever since I was told of their existence I began feeling myself to be a stranger on an unknown planet, in another world. I feel transformed into another man. One bearded philosopher complained about the conversion of children's blood into capital. Today, they do not even do this. They merely cast them away, as they are considered surplus …"

"What about my existence, my face, my words, do they not drive away your worries? Given the fact that your wife is the same old wife you've always had, how can you be different?"

"I don't know. But then you also have become a stranger. The worst of it is that I can't forget the sort of human I was in the past. It's sort of a break in my personality."

Gül found her husband's explanation unfounded, exaggerated, affected."

"I expect you have already solved the problem of Temel at least. Has he finally acquired his cherished site?"

"No, I haven't even mentioned my talk with the judge to him."

"You forgot to mention it to him?"

"No, I haven't forgotten. I can't bring myself to speak to him about it. This may be one of the reasons I'm depressed. It seems to me that complying with Temel's wish would be tantamount to denying all my professional ideals."

"But you are not a judge. You're a lawyer. Just do what you should and then forget it."

Can straitened himself up and looked at his wife:

"You're telling me to do this?" Then he lowered his head. "I can't," he said. "Maybe because I am no longer a lawyer. I feel tied up. Had it not been for Sabri, everything would have ended with a fiasco."

"Wasn't he against this privatization project?"

"In the beginning, he was. We are living in such a queer age that to be opposed to a project does not preclude being in favor of it. He is the one now who spares no effort to see it realized. Much as he may not believe in it, his thinking is far apart from what he does."

"How about you?"

"I can't act like him. Especially since the day I had a conversation with that judge. Thank God, Sabri was there to help me," said Can, staring at the floor.

Gül was going to ask her husband why he had not asked Sabri to take care of that as well, but she didn't, not wanting to put her husband in an uncomfortable position. He looked crestfallen but then suddenly felt a wave of affection for his wife as he had in the old days, which led him to put his arms around her shoulders and press his cheek to hers.

"There is no going back," she said. "Like it or not, you'll have to keep things moving along. What you're experiencing now will pass. Still, it might be a good idea to consult a doctor."

Gül's suggestion seemed to justify her fears. Her husband had been obsessed by that house. The situation involving Varol Korkmaz had made things worse. Nor had he told Temel about the telephone conversation he had with the judge Halis.

However, back in his office the following morning at 9:45 a.m., he insisted, "I'll be damned if I do not settle this house business by tonight." Before he had time to reach a decision about Varol, he saw Sabri in the doorway and smiled at him, as if resolved. "Do come in, Sabri. Take a seat," he said.

"I've come to take you somewhere, Sir. Don't worry, it won't take more than half an hour."

"Where are we going?"

"Allow me to keep it as a secret for the moment, Sir."

Can acquiesced without further questions and rose from his seat submissively. They took the elevator, which stopped at the floor used as a gym. "Please," said Sabri showing the way to Can, who was rather puzzled.

"What are we supposed to do here?" he inquired.

Sabri did not answer the question. "You'll see presently, Sir," he said simply. Suiting word to action, he opened the door of the G hall.

No sooner they crossed the threshold than a booming voice was heard. "AT-TEN-TION!"

Before them were three rows of about sixty male and fifteen female guards in dark blue uniforms reminiscent of heroes in science fiction films. The uniforms had violet badges indicating rank and bright gold buttons. Each person had guns in his holster. A man clad in the same apparel and as tall as the guards clicked his heels and announced, "The Legal Security Guard is ready for your inspection, Sir!"

It took some time before Can understood what was happening. "In such a short time!" he murmured. He remembered his days in the army, saluted the guards, then marched forward, shaking hands with each. He approached Sabri, saying, "Within such a short time? Incredible!"

"Nothing was easier, Sir," was the reply. "A single notice sufficed. Had we wanted, we could have found thousands." Sabri asked then whether Can had any suggestion regarding the guards and other members of the staff. Learning that he had none, he dismissed the guards, gazing after them proudly and smiling. "Twenty-one civil engineers, sixteen jurists, four medical doctors, three philosophers, all of them graduates of the Private Security High School," he said.

Can had begun to relax, though still bewildered. . A sentence from Cüneyt's article on privatization came to mind: 'Privatized justice is civil justice.' He smiled but did not tell his secretary why. "Excellent!" he commented instead, "both the uniforms and the guards. People will think that peace and security and justice are firmly established in the country. Bu why are the guards so tall?"

"You must have forgotten. It was the General Meeting's decision."

Can put his hand on Sabri's shoulder. "That's true," he confirmed. "It reminds me of our demonstrations in that past. When we saw tall police officers behind us we felt relieved since they could never catch us. The inability of the tall to catch up with the short may sound false, but it's true."

"I had not thought about that, Sir," said Sabri.

Can patted him on the shoulder. "Now you can!" he replied, with a sudden laugh. "Any way, now that we have our security unit, we can say we have at our disposal a sign of our conception of justice."

When he was back in his office, his mind was still full of memories of his student years. It must be this that led him to kiss İnci, pressing the index finger of his right hand on the pointed nipple of her left breast as he warmly said, "Get me Temel please."

X.

TEMEL HUNG UP THE PHONE. His eyes remained fixed on the date displayed on his desk calendar, August 17th, 2073. He repeated the date several times in loud voice. Then as if he had failed to find what he had been looking for, he took a deep breath. Leaning on his chin, he closed his eyes and, without moving, brooded for a half an hour or so. His conversation with Can about a meeting with Şirin, the retired teacher whose resistance to moving had caused so much trouble, bothered him. "A clever fellow, Can!" he said. "As a lawyer he has no peer! But when the subject is that old idiot's house and garden, he beats around the bush, dodging the issue as if he were *his* lawyer rather than mine. Now he wants me to go and speak with him. 'Go and tell him in a persuasive tone the reason you're interested in his property and invite him to make some kind of sensible arrangement,' he tells me, and adds, 'Tell him that this is the best way to deal with the problem, the road to success.' We're apparently from the same province. As if this meant anything in 2073! If this had been the best way to handle the affair, why have we waited so long? He should have known it. Why on earth had he to keep it from me?" He opened his eyes wide. "What am I to say to him, to that damned fool?"

No sooner had he said this than the telephone rang. His secretary informed him that she had at last got in touch with the person in question. He straightened up. "Hello, Temel speaking, am I addressing Şirin?" Having ascertained that it was, he took a deep breath. "I wonder if you remember me. I'm the one who brought a court action against you. Some call me the Skyscraper, some Temel. I was just thinking that we might perhaps sit and talk somewhere for half an hour, or, perhaps you would be kind enough to let me visit you. I happen to be nearby, and it would take only a minute! All right, all right, I'm on my way. We'll talk it over when I'm there," he said and hung up.

He was confused to see the old man's favorable reaction and ready acceptance of his suggestion. This suggested the possibility that Can had discussed the issue with him earlier. Who knows, they might also have fixed the amount of compensation. "Well!" he said, "I don't care why the old man is going to give in at the end." This was Turkey, and he was accustomed to see one pay twice or three times the usual price for anything, even for the purchase of a sumptuous apartment in a skyscraper, depending on the importance of the buyer. His answer to his critics who taxed him with being extravagant was "I have one aim in life: to re-build the city of Istanbul. Money means nothing!"

He happened to be in a jovial mood today. He had never been nearer to his objective than at the moment. He had reached the Cihangir district, where his car went without any serious obstacle other than occasional joltings. There were neither cars nor pedestrians in sight, since he had purchased all of the houses and apartment buildings and had razed most of them. Cihangir had been a desolate area for about a year now. Although he often visited here, Temel felt a great burden bearing down on him. He preferred to close his eyes and not to see the unpleasant scene. But when Şirin, with a broad smile, opened the gate of his garden to welcome him, he felt relieved. He entered the house and, having taken off his shoes as a courtesy to his host, was led into the small drawing room. On the wall hung a bear skin. Small framed family photographs turning yellow were placed here and there. A thick black woollen blanket on the couch, a dinner table littered with books, and a threadbare carpet decorated the room. The room had a fusty smell from the old furniture, a smell he had long forgotten. He felt he had gone back in time and despite all his modern notions he experienced a sort of inexpressible happiness. He stared at the little white haired man with a white moustache facing him. Şirin seemed like an old acquaintance.

"I believe we are both from the same region," he said.

Şirin showed no reaction. "Which region you mean?"

"Well, Trabzon, Garson, Serene, Rise, Catelli," said Temel.

159

"Right! However, this is not difficult to guess, as our noses testify." He pointed to a photograph on the wall. It showed a young woman seated with young boys staring at a point far ahead. Both were smiling radiantly. After a careful examination, "Yes," said Temel, "they are like us." Then suddenly a shiver ran down his spine. "But ... but ... she looks exactly like my mother," he stammered.

Şirin smiled. "Just like the boys, who resemble you."

Temel appeared not to have heard what he said. "A remarkable resemblance," he said, adding, "However, my mother was more beautiful."

Şirin was not particularly impressed by this remark. "It depends on the way you see her."

Temel took out his mother's photograph from his wallet and handed it to Şirin The latter took it and examined it carefully. As he returned it, his hand was shaking ...

"You're right, your mother *is* more beautiful, a paragon of beauty!" Then he added, "Before we proceed, what would you like to have? Tea, coffee, or something cold perhaps?"

"Thank you, nothing," said Temel, but thinking that a refusal might be misinterpreted, he added, "A glass of water, perhaps. I hope you won't mind if ..."

But before he could finish his words, he jumped up, a deathly pallor on his face. "A cat!" he stammered. "You've got a cat in your house!"

Şirin looked at him sardonically. "Indeed," he said, "not just one cat, but nine in all."

"But ... but ... ," Temel stammered. "I thought that cats had become extinct in Turkey!"

"Well, not in this house, anyway. It's true, however, their number has declined. From the seventeen I had three years ago, only nine are left."

Temel hardly paid attention to what Şirin said. "An army of cats! And you're not afraid?"

"Thank God, we have not been detected all these years," he said. "If we ever get caught, well, we would have to resign to our fate. If those who banned them had the courage to …"

"I didn't mean that," interrupted Temel. "All the germs that cats might carry! Doesn't this scare you?"

Şirin answered with a laugh. "No, Sir, it does not. My cats are cleaner than many people. Moreover, personally I am immune to infections." After hesitating a moment, he added, "However, if you are apprehensive, I can shut them up in their room."

"Truly, I'm scared of cats. I'd be glad if you did so." Then, changing the topic, he said, "It's hot in here. Would you mind if I took off my jacket?"

"Please, Sir, make yourself at home!" he answered. "I'll be back in a couple of minutes." He went out of the room calling, "Kitty! Kitty!"

Temel saw the cats forming a circle around the old man: four tabby cats, three tawny cats, and two white ones raised their heads and looked at him. The sight horrified Temel. He saw them go towards the door after Şirin. As the last cat vanished, Temel felt relieved. "The Pied Piper of Hamelin," he said to himself smiling.

His heart was throbbing. It seemed to him that he had been torn out of the present when he crossed the threshold of this house. Later in the garden, he saw a plastic tray with green and red designs with two glasses of water and a decanter. As he sat opposite his aged countryman, not only did he forget about the cats but also the reason for his visit. He studied the colorful pansies at the foot of a high wall, the pine tree in the shade of which he was sitting, the hazelnut tree opposite him, and the pomegranate tree on his left. All this gave him an air of serenity he had never tasted.

"You're right, professor, it's cool out here," he said.

"Yes, my garden is always cool, even in the hottest days," replied Şirin.

They lapsed into silence for a few minutes. Had it not been for a couple of sparrows making love breaking the silence, the two men would have dozed off. When the chattering ceased and the sparrows flew away, Şirin noticed that his guest was looking at the pomegranate on the tree. "The only produce this year," he said. "In the past there were times when it gave us three, five, or even eight pomegranates. This year, only one. Must be getting old, like me."

"I doubt it," said Temel. "It doesn't seem old."

"But it is a fact. This coming May it will be thirty-six. Its fruit is delicious though."

Temel nodded and said, "One can see that."

"It must be ripe already. Would you like to taste it?" said Şirin, rising from his seat.

"Taste what?" he asked. He saw nothing edible in sight, and when Şirin replied, "Why, the pomegranate naturally," he shook his head vigorously. "Oh, no, please! Please, professor, do sit down!"

Şirin resumed his seat, and a deep silence followed for the next five minutes. Two sparrows, a male and a female, perched on the hazelnut tree. Şirin wondered if they were the same sparrows that were there before. He watched them for a while. "They are all alike," he said. He realized that he had actually forgotten about his guest. He tried to smile. "The hazelnut tree is exactly nineteen years old," he said, "yet, ever since the day the day it was planted, it has produced nothing. It must not have found this place up to its standards."

Temel remembered suddenly the reason for his visit. "My dear professor, I've got something to tell you." Temel seemed to be looking for something to say. "How about the best and most beautiful hazel grove in Giresun, where, if you like, I could build a palace-like residence for you, or if you'd prefer, move this house there."

"But why?" asked Şirin with a smile. We've just met today."

"You know why, professor," he said.

"I certainly do. Your want to have this house pulled down, and you want to pull up those trees."

"True. This place is very important for me. As you know, I have already purchased all the apartment buildings, parcels of land, and roads around here with the exception of your property. Unless you sell it to me, everything will remain as it is. But if you do sell, the biggest and the most splendid skyscraper in Istanbul will be built here. Cihangir's aspect will change and the district will become the most beautiful in the city. Your house is the best place for my project."

Şirin looked at his guest as if he were seeing him for the first time, and sighed. "I am sorry, Temel," he said. "You have been building a series of skyscrapers in Istanbul. This house has been the only place I can afford. I sold the house I inherited from my father and had this house built on the site of one that had belonged my brother. When the time came to construct the windows and the roof I was hard up, and I had to sell off the two fields I had inherited. My two sons were born in this house. My wife died here. I am far advanced in age and can no longer live elsewhere. All my memories are here. All my belongings are here. I consider myself happy in the company of my old trees, and I am determined to die here. So long as I live I won't have my house pulled down. Further, changing the look of Cihangir does not seem a good idea to me. If it still has any particular look at all, of course.

Temel took Şirin's hands and held them tight. "Look, Sir, in a couple of years, I promise to give you the best apartment in the skyscraper I am going to build here. I can even build the exact replica of this house on top of it. I'm not joking, an exact replica of it up under the sky. I can even bring up there your trees and garden. It's a promise! Just think, the house and the garden up in the sky and made new again. Your cats will be safe there. How about that?" He took a deep breath. "Just press one of the buttons in the elevator and almost instantly you'll be in your new home. You will have a view of the world from above. Believe me, I am devoted to order. I'd do nothing of the sort for anyone else. As far as money is concerned, I am prepared to pay any sum."

Şirin stared at his visitor, thinking he must be out of his mind, but began to feel uneasy. Suddenly and unexpectedly, he withdrew his hands. "May I ask you why you have to spend such a lot of money?" he asked. "Sites in Istanbul for skyscrapers are plentiful. To waste such huge sums for ..."

"Just a moment," interrupted Temel. He was short of breath as if he had climbed to top of his imagined skyscraper. When he had recovered, he continued, "Look, money is no problem. I am building, I mean trying to build, a new city, all by myself, a city of skyscrapers, all of them alike except for their street numbers and colors. Just imagine, wherever you turn your gaze you'll have the same great view, everything perfect, including the roads. Not even in America can you see this. Istanbul will excel New York and become *the* city of the age. This will be realized sooner or later, but my decision is to realize it as soon as possible, before I die." His forehead was covered with beads of sweat. He was elated and seemed ready to continue.

"One moment," said the professor, "You say that everywhere will look alike, so why do you insist so much on my house? Why not go ahead first with other skyscrapers."

"Everywhere will look the same, but this spot is different. The statue I will erect will look better from here."

Şirin's was stunned and saw his fellow countryman in a new light, as a lunatic rather than at a city founder. "What statue, Temel?" he asked with some concern.

"Why, the Statue of Liberty of Istanbul, of course, the greatest monument in the world."

Şirin remembered having read something in the newspapers about a statue. "I sympathize with you. I understand your situation. But try to understand me. I want to die here, in this house, not up in the sky, but close the ground. I must tell you, the picture of Istanbul in your imagination does not appeal to me. You say that this spot is different for you, and so is it for me. This is *my* place!"

"Is this your final word?" asked Temel.

"Yes, Temel, as long as I live. After I am gone, I don't know what will happen," said Şirin with a sigh. "I can't decide on behalf of my son," he added.

Temel thought he must be mad. "You said you had two sons?"

"Yes, but one died long ago?"

"The other?"

"The other followed him, but, well, not exactly. He did not die, to the best of my knowledge. He went to America. He even changed his name. It's been ten years since I last saw him."

"I see," said Temel, as if speaking to himself. He lapsed into silence, during which he kept looking at the old man. He wanted to be angry but could not bring himself to do so. He wanted to leave without saying anything more, but somehow he felt tied to the spot. Sympathy had developed between him and the old man, who seemed venerable, as if he had known him for ages. "He is like me, obsessive," he thought. "Funny! I'd never have thought that doing nothing could be a passion." He stood up. "I'm afraid I must leave, Professor," he said.

Şirin stood up more nimbly than one might expect from a man his age. As he shook hands with his guest, he asked what he was thinking.

Temel smiled and put his hand on the old man's shoulder.

"I don't know. I really don't know," he said. "I like you very much. I am as mad as you are. That's certain, but there is something else that is certain, too: I am prepared to do everything in order to realize my project."

Şirin did not seem to be surprised. All that he did was frown. "Could you kill a man?" he asked.

Temel did not hesitate. "I think I could," he said. "I could kill a man. That's what's different between you and me."

Şirin warmly shook the hand stretched out by his guest. "We're not much different, though," he said. "You know what? I. too, can kill."

"I understand. I must be off now," Temel said, turning suddenly and heading for the garden gate.

He was excited when he was back in his car and told his chauffeur to drive on. His sight seemed to be dimming and his fists were clenched. "I am scratchy, jittery, and excited. Why, I don't know. Have I become angry at Şirin? No. At Can? No. At Sabri? No." He was simply angry for no particular reason. It must have been his fate at which he was angry. His cursed the fate that had led him to this situation by putting obstacles in his path: such a house, such a garden, and such a congenial yet obstinate man! When he dashed into Can's office without asking İnci to tell her boss that he had arrived, he sank, short of breath, into an armchair.

Can realized that Temel had come to quarrel. "What happened?" he said. "I hope you have not argued with the old man?"

Temel, his eyes fixed on his hands, hesitated whether he should speak or keep silent. He finally opted for the second.

Can rose and approached him, saying, "Come on! How was the interview? What did the old man say?"

Temel's expression was grim. "No way! There's no way to bring him around." His face hardened, and he looked as if he had sunk in to the depths of despair.

"Don't worry," Can said. "A little patience. You'll see that it will be settled before we take over the administration of justice. Believe me, that's how it will be."

Temel looked into the lawyer's face for the first time since he arrived. "When?" he asked. "The press is still saying it might be deferred."

Can shrugged. "The date is prescribed by law. Don't worry about what the papers write. It's their usual approach, as if they had nothing else to do," he said.

The press did in fact comment on every contingency. *Tomorrow*, notorious for stirring up problems as was the television station of the same name, complained about where the administration was to be located. It dwelt on whether the administration of justice should be located in the capital of the Turkish Republic or in Istanbul, which was only one of the 115 provinces. In case of the latter, could it be because rich people happened to live there? Under such circumstances, would the authorities feel at home in such a situation. While the latter remained silent, the media with the highest ratings, especially *The Globe*, were openly pro-Istanbul. The TBLPC was a big organization whose importance was beyond dispute, and it had the support of the rich and powerful. It was a national entity whose functions were incontestable, so it was clear that its central offices should be where the majority of its shareholders lived, which is to say Istanbul. The headquarters for the Supreme Court also should be in Istanbul in order that things worked smoothly. One of the columnists of *The Globe,* Şarman Pekman, went further and argued that it was ridiculous that the TBLPC move to Ankara. At last, Sabri, as the TBLPC's General Secretary, who had lately made a name for himself with his coherent statements and affability, put an end to the deliberations with a brief statement: "We have taken over this sacred duty as an organization whose central office is to be in Istanbul, the greatest of our provinces. Should we be compelled to move that office to another province, we shall not hesitate to return what has been entrusted to us to its former proprietor." The announcement by Mevlut Doğan, the Prime Minister, put an end to speculations by announcing the day, September 1st, 2073, and location, Istanbul, of the inaugural ceremonies.

In the great hall, on the 124th floor of the skyscraper B-214, dubbed the "Justice Tower" by the anglophile media, which had been built only three weeks earlier and in which ten floors had been reserved by Temel for the TBLPC, a group of fifteen or twenty judges was seen in their tricolored gowns created by "Flag New Fashion" and black caps with green tassels. The guests made their way first towards them to have a closer look, including smartly dressed ladies, famous celebrities, government ministers, and writers. Imposing officials ushered the guests to their seats informing them that the ceremony was about to begin. The national anthem was followed by a "concise" speech from the CEO. At the conclusion, the Prime Minister, wearing a cap and gown, marched resolutely to the rostrum. Every phrase he pronounced was loudly applauded. The general enthusiasm encouraged him to expatiate on topics unrelated to the business of the day. He said that the privatization of justice was a good thing just like privatization in all other fields, and he was confident that "our great nation already understood this." He ended by thanking Can and his group on behalf of the great Turkish nation before stepping down amid rousing cheers. Gül, inclining toward her husband, said. "You're right. He is Smerdyakov embodied. Smerdyakov might well be a Prime Minister." However, Can did not seem to hear what she said, or if he did, he did not understand what she meant. "Come, let's not abandon our Prime Minister to evil spirits," he said, rushing toward the room where drinks were served.

No sooner had he entered the room than he halted petrified.

Doğan, thanks to his security guards, made a way for himself through the crowd, approached Temel, greeted him warmly, and spoke, his hand resting on his shoulder. Can felt dizzy and had to hold on to Gül to steady himself. "No! This is impossible! I can't believe my eyes!" he said. "I'm sure they have met before, and more than once, just look at them!" Gül did not understand. He saw Doğan embrace Temel before heading to the door with a smile frozen on his face. He was surrounded by his security guards, who looked as if they could be extensions of himself. It occurred to him to rush towards the Prime Minister and accompany him to the roof and wave goodbye until the spaceshuttle left. But he felt exhausted and didn't move. "Do you think I've done the wrong thing by not accompanying him?" he whispered to Gül. "I hope he does not make me pay for it!"

At this moment, judge Halis, with his tricolored gown and cap in hand, accompanied by his corpulent spouse came forward. He introduced his wife first and expressed his thanks for Can's help. Can himself was searching for Temel and saw him talking with judges, telling them that, since their caps and gowns were designed to fit the requirements of the job, they would facilitate to a great extent the lifestyle not only of themselves but of the community as well. As soon as Temel ended, Can approached him and, placing his hand on Temel's shoulder, said, "Let me introduce you to Judge Halis. Judge, I'm sure you know our famous architect who is trying to recreate Istanbul," he added.

While Temel was trying to recollect the man's full name, the judge, in unalloyed delight said, "Who doesn't!" and stretched out his hand. With a sardonic smile he asked, "Temel. I have been told that every morning on your way to your office it's your custom to look at Şirin's house, to see whether it's still there or not?"

Temel remembered the man's name. "Not every morning, but I often pass by. It's a place I like," he responded.

"I suggest that you continue to look for a few days more," said the judge, "since, as Can may have already told you, in a short time, say in a couple of weeks, it may not be there anymore."

For the moment Temel was radiant, but his pleasure soon began to dim.

"How?" he asked. "Can said how difficult this would be."

The judge smiled. "Initially, we planned to settle this affair with a trial," he said. "But, as our leader well knows, there are problems that cannot be settled in court."

"How so, as a judge, are you not settling affairs with judicial proceedings?" asked Temel.

"I can't say that justice isn't involved."

Can cut in, "Judge, you have a mysterious way of expressing your thoughts. We can speak openly since there is no one likely to hear us."

Yet the judge kept talking to Temel and paid no attention to the remark.

"Well, you must have persuaded him to yield to our request then?"

The judge smiled. "I have tied, believe me. But to no avail. He is as obstinate as a mule."

"Well then?"

The judge, gathering up the skirts of his tricolored gown, moved to a somewhat secluded part of the room, followed by Temel, Can, and Gül.

"I had before me the case of the son of the mayor of Istanbul. It was a hard case. The decision at the end of the trial might not be what the defendants anticipated," he began. "I told the mayor that if he could arrange for the expropriation and demolition of Şirin's house and sell it to Temel to enable him to erect a skyscraper, he might have a chance. Well, my proposal was eventually accepted." He smiled enigmatically.

"The mayor has, of course, the professional experience of long years behind him," stammered Can, frowning with disgust. "Once you've done something corrupt, you breathe a different kind of air. Incredible!" he said.

Temel felt elated. "I had thought of it myself. I've told Can about it over and over again, but he seemed reluctant to do as I suggested," he said.

Can took Temel's arm. "We didn't have the privilege of a case against the mayor's son."

Nonetheless, at a time when his importance should outweigh all other concerns, he felt that he had been humiliated. No one responded to his comment.

"Could the mayor convince Şirin?"

"You speak as if you did not know him!" said the judge. "He refused point-blank."

"Then?"

"Whereupon the municipality decided to expropriate the house and demolish it. If the old man continues to resist, the security forces will do what's necessary. A writ has already been served on him, and the deadline is approaching."

"I congratulate you," said Can. "It is a great achievement indeed! Clever judge. Two different cases finalized under a single umbrella."

But Temel was staring at the judge with a perplexed smile. "What will Şirin get out of this? Do you think it will be a fair deal? I mean his cats, birds, furniture, and the hazelnut tree?"

The judge looked baffled.

"Have all these things been taken into consideration? Will Şirin be accommodated comfortably?" insisted Temel.

The judge tried to smile. "That is not my concern, Sir, but you can be sure that everything will be done in due conformity with the law," he said.

Can shook hands forcefully with the judge. "We are grateful to you, your honor. You've done a good job. Now we've cleared away everything we begin. Hail the conquering hero!"

The judge, exhilarated, said that he had done his duty and promised that he would keep serving in the coming term as well as he could."

Can shook hands again, expressed his gratitude, and said brusquely, "Thank you, good evening to you. I hope to see you again."

The judge was appalled. His face turned white. "Thank you! Good evening," he stammered and, having shaken hands with Gül and Temel, he headed to the door.

Gül looked after him till he reached the doorway and then turned to her husband. "Why did you do that?" she said, "You nearly showed him to the door! Why?"

"Indeed!" said Temel, "You looked as if you were upset at his solution to the problem."

Can shrugged. "Why should I be upset? No. I did not dismiss him on purpose, to settle this business. Yet I can't say I was indifferent to the way he behaved, very sure of himself."

"Why on earth didn't you say anything to me about the case?" asked Temel.

Can shrugged again. "Because I wasn't sure that he could win the battle. Because I did not want to disappoint you. Because ..." He had flushed and seemed unable to find the exact words. Then he changed the subject. "What have you been talking with Doğan about?"

It was Temel's turn to be upset, although he pulled himself together quickly. "Skyscrapers, of course. I told him that business did not progress as fast as he desired. I said that if Istanbul is going to assume the look of a modern city soon, we have to work quickly."

"How do you suggest making things go faster?" asked Gül.

"You know well, and so does Can. There is a great demand for apartments. People have understood that they can no longer live in anywhere else other than in a skyscraper. They sell whatever they have in order to get an apartment in one of the skyscrapers. We have no problem with that. The biggest obstacle now is that the old skyscrapers are ugly."

"Well?"

"Can must have told you about it. These ugly skyscrapers were built toward the end of the last century, of various heights and shapes, some narrow, some not, some angular, some round, some downright crooked, without the least similarity to each other, unshapely, ill-proportioned. Gruesome. They stare at each other as if in utter disgust. Conceited, contemptible contractors won't have them pulled down. When we suggest that it would be to the benefit of us all to do so, they turn a dead ear. But Doğan promised that he will be defeating them soon and will, in case there is no other way to convince them, pass a law that will make them change their minds. Then, yes, then ..."

Gül listened, bewildered, but Can was tired. The subject had already become irksome. "

I'm sure that you haven't discussed all these things with him today. You must have talked about this earlier?"

Temel did not deny it. "Yes," he said

"How often?"

"Oh, I don't know. Perhaps four or five times."

"And where?"

"Not at his home. At the ministry, of course. Middlemen arranged the appointments."

Can was worried, but he did his best not to let on. "In short, you have already come to an understanding?" he asked.

"Yes, but it was he who asked me to visit him. He told me that I should keep it a secret and not tell you."

"And you did as you were told?"

"Yes, I did keep the secret. Since I am resolved to re-build this city, I had no other choice. I had to comply with his wishes."

"What exactly were those wishes?"

"Not many. Roughly one apartment per skyscraper."

"Profitable business! An apartment at every corner!"

"However, he is considering exchanging them in the future for a single skyscraper at Maçka."

Gül, flabbergasted, looked from Temel to her husband.

"What a passion! A nice way to make ends meet!"

Temel shrugged. "After all, that man has been Prime Minister for the last three years. He may be richer than I am, but this does not concern me. My job is to erect and sell skyscrapers, and to get this done, I am prepared to do anything. Don't think that we have joined forces against you," he added. "You are my friend Can, my friend first and then my lawyer."

"Thanks for the compliment," said Can and became silent.

Temel also grew silent. He looked over the remaining ten or fifteen guests. He drew closer to Can and said, "I have asked another favor from him which you may not like."

"What is that?

Temel seemed pleased and drew closer still. "The use of numbers instead of street names."

"I see," said Can.

"He stipulated, however, that his street have the number 10!" said Temel, laughing before he realized that Can had turned pale. "Damn it! Have I made you angry? Did you want number 10 yourself?" he said laughing, but could not make Can smile. "Anyway I must be going." At the door, he suddenly turned around. "The first thing I'll do tomorrow morning will be to see Şirin and make sure his new place will be comfortable."

Gül was astonished. "I see you are tender hearted," she said. "While on the one hand you spare no effort to get the old man's house, you patronize him on the other."

Temel smiled as he turned the knob. "Şirin is a very good man, and we happen to be from the same part of the country." So saying, he looked at Gül. "What do you think, would I have abandoned him to deal with things alone?" He said nothing else and left.

Gül turned to her husband. "What do you say to this?" she asked.

"Oh, I don't know. If I had the passion he does, I would like to bury this city in the depths of its own filth together with its skyscrapers of all sizes, all the houses, including the house Temel wants so much, and have everything razed to the ground with a bulldozer. I'd see to it that no trace was left from the old city. But I have no such passion."

"So much the better!" said Gül. "In a way, he destroys the old city in another way."

"Correct. There's no denying that, but he does not walk away. He is resolutely rebuilding it. He is ready to sacrifice everything for his cause."

"What do you think will happen to that old man? What was his name again?"

"Hikmet Şirin."

"Do you think Temel would give him an apartment in the sky-scraper?"

"He might," said her husband without hesitating. "Not just a flat, perhaps a whole skyscraper."

Temel was indeed ready to give Şirin a skyscraper. He called him that evening to ask if he needed anything. Şirin thanked him for his kind interest and said that he needed nothing. Temel told him about the court decision and reminded him that within a few days he should find a place to move to. Şirin's response was categorical; as long his mind functioned, his eyes could see, and his hands worked, he would not give up his house. Nothing in the world would deter him from his decision. "Don't worry, Temel," he said. "I'll take care of everything," and thanking him once again, he hung up. There was not the slightest trace of worry or anger in his voice. Temel was fidgety, he was not sure whether Şirin would be able to take care of himself, yet Temel's mind was full of multi-colored skyscrapers. In his imagination, he also saw Nokta's blown-up beautiful face on the statue he would erect. Without coming to a defini-tive solution about Şirin, he said to himself, "Perhaps he has something on his mind we do not know about."

Actually Şirin *did* have something in his mind. At 10:03 a.m. on Sep-tember 3rd, 2073, without the least resistance, he opened wide the garden gate for seven officials, some in uniform and some in civilian clothes. They entered without even saying, "Good morning," but when they began to look around, he warned them that this could have serious consequences. He made it clear to them that he had no intention of abandoning the house in which his two sons were born and his wife had drawn her last breath. He was determined to maintain the current situation. He waited and looked at the men who were stripping covers off from the chairs and the table and beginning to carry them into the garden. These could always be replaced. They told him to collect his valuables. But then a swarthy man with thick eyebrows dared to take down the picture of his son from the wall and throw it on the ground. Hurrying over to the picture of his wife, Şirin shouted, "Don't you dare touch it!" When the man failed to listen, Şirin reached under his sweater and took out an old revolver and, without waiting, fired it at the offender. As the man collapsed, the others ran. He shouted after them, "I'll shoot all of you all if you dare bother me anymore. Come, take your fucking friend and get out!" The men stopped, then returned to help their friend, whose hand was now a red blob.

Şirin, revolver in hand, walked resolutely toward the picture of his wife, lifted it from its nail, and after wiping off the dust, hung it back on the wall. Gingerly, he also took down the picture of his son, and having dusted it, too, hung it back. Then he went downstairs and locked the gate and returned to his room on the top floor. He took a kitchen stool and placed it in front of the window overlooking the gate. "They will return, armed this time," he muttered. Revolver in hand, he lay in wait. His prediction proved to be correct. Two hours later, the men were back, this time brandishing machine guns. Şirin did not loose his composure, but he let them force the garden gate open. But when they broke into the house without knocking, he shot one of them in the right leg, and another in his left. The number of men with machine guns increased. Şirin stood, revolver in hand, facing the gate but never had the opportunity to shoot again.

He was now the target, and a minute later, his identity could have been determined only through chemical analyses. Neither the police, nor the law, nor the municipality, nor Temel had time enough for anything like that. Identification rested on the testimony of three old janitors. The rest of the job was undertaken by junior officials and the gigantic machines of Diker Co. The house and the garden were bulldozed, and the site smelled of fresh earth.

XI.

TEMEL THOUGHT LONG ABOUT THIS MATTER, always arriving at the same conclusion. Had he known that he could acquire the site almost for nothing but the cost of Şirin life, he would probably never have done what he had. In fact, he suggested as much in the days that followed the disastrous incident. Seeing that nobody claimed Şirin's remains, he gave orders to his men to buy a beautiful grave site overlooking the Bosphorus and to arrange for a sumptuous funeral service. With an expression of deep mourning, he took part in all the rituals up until the moment of the burial. He had planned on a solemn ceremony for the laying of the cornerstone for the new skyscraper, but now he abandoned that and deferred work on the building for a week. In short, Şirin's death caused him to rethink everything.

As if the entire city, in order to assume its new identity and shape, had been waiting for Şirin's death and the levelling of his property, no district, no street, no road, no construction now challenged the advance of Temel's bulldozers, which raised a cloud of dust that covered everything. Sumptuous old buildings collapsed with a deafening sound in a massive cloud of dust, followed by machines that swallowed up the rubble. This yielded to a third battalion of machines that dug into the entrails of the earth, leaving behind a land cleared of all human traces. Cars and pedestrians continued on their way after a momentary glance at the work going on. People in power and prominent CEOs, who considered travelling between their homes and their offices in private spaceshuttles to be an indispensable indication of their class, were compelled to give up this privilege temporarily for fear of losing their way in the clouds of dust and had begun to use surface transportation like everyone else. Temel was glad to see that his plans had gathered momentum, and to those who complained about the dust and noise, he said to consider such inconveniences the harbingers of an age of serenity and peace. They need only be patient a few more years.

In point of fact, there was no need for such statements, since once they were engulfed in the demolition and construction of buildings, residents had begun to share his great ideal and did as he desired. Although there had not been the slightest research or study of the subject by the media and the press, nearly everybody saw a direct connection between the rapid development of the skyscrapers and the privatization of justice. Despite the fact that justice had not yet been transferred to the private sector, people, believing that the weak can never prevail over the powerful, believed that Temel, as the greatest shareholder in the TBLPC, must always right and so always sided with him.

Contractors, regardless of their business acumen, were the first to side with him. After seeing the demolition of the sixty- or seventy-story skyscrapers constructed at the beginning of the century — a reason for pride among their owners and architects at the time — they understood that there was no sense in trying to impede the course of events, especially considering Temel's unwavering determination and his privileges. They asked him for permission to imitate his designs. He was only too willing to do so. What is more, although the applicants did not ask for it, he offered them the use of his machinery and his specialists. He even offered to lend them money, provided, he said, that their buildings were made available for his inspection, so that there may be no difference between skyscrapers. To those who could not conceal their admiration and wonder, he said, "My only concern is to re-create this city. Once I have realized my objective, I may walk away, hands in my pockets, and not look back, not even seeking something in return." At all events, within three months, Istanbul became a vast demolition site and the possibility of constructing anything incongruous was eliminated. The example set by his contractors was followed first by the prominent entrepreneurs in the city and then by those in the country in general.

Except for buildings that were public property, people increasingly began to see their own buildings as inferior, decrepit, and unseemly compared with the gigantic structures that were close to their own places and so razed to the ground everything that didn't look like the new structures. People who, until a year before, considered their homes spacious and comfortable and who would not yield to proposals for change and ignored the slightest criticism of their furnishings began to refer to their homes as "huts" or "shanties" and preferred to sell them at very low prices to contractors in hopes of acquiring apartments in Temel's skyscrapers. Desirous of realizing his great ideal, Temel was very generous in this matter. He ordered his staff and the contractors who used his designs to assist these people as best as they could. Thus some were granted reductions in price, others exchanged their homes for apartments in any of the skyscrapers, and some were offered mortgages. In the meantime, members of Istanbul's middle class invested the entirety of their assets in skyscraper apartments, thinking that this was "a golden opportunity." For the notables of Bursa, İzmir, Ankara, Adana, Kayseri, Eskişehir and Manisa, to purchase a spacious apartment in an Istanbul skyscraper and fly there every Friday evening in their private spaceshuttles for the week-end, became a sign of the "ideal lifestyle," an indication of opulence and superiority.

Every middle-class family that could afford a skyscraper apartment purchased one and rated themselves according to their distance above other apartment dwellers and the pedestrians, who from this point looked like ants. Later when they were close to the ground they began to see themselves, their spouses, and their children as ants and wanted only to hurry back as soon as possible to their accustomed height. Home again, they would give a sigh of relief, not having to be caught in a traffic jam. But they also felt lonely up there but knew how impossible it would be to escape from their height and anxiety. On the other hand, the same height, the same dimensions of their apartments, the same construction, and the same roads and sidewalks everywhere gave the impression that no matter how far or fast they went in their cars or how high they flew in their spaceshuttles, they could not escape. To climb or descend a hill was only a dream. Since Temel hated uneven surfaces and geographic irregularities, he had done his best to level the ground, so that the skyscrapers could see only each other. A few historical monuments, for which permission to demolish could not be obtained, lost their meaning and beauty amidst this uniformity and seemed to be aberrations.

Veysel Çakır, in his column in the *Illustrated Agenda*, often spoke of this situation in a sarcastic tone, saying that Temel's skyscrapers had brought equality to the city at least, if not to the entire country, and having done away with all the vestiges of the old order, including the notion of neighborhoods and social relations among neighbors, thus leaving no room for the poor. He added that Istanbul with its skyscrapers had become the city closest to God. But in his article under the title of "Great Triumph," which appeared on September 17th, 2073, he stated, "Given the fact that this levelling could not be attained until the last quarter of the twenty-first century, we must own that humanity is progressing, but at a very slow pace." For this, he was banned from writing, and his column was henceforth filled with editorials advertising the skyscrapers.

However, this was due to interventions by Temel's employees rather than Temel himself, since Temel spent most of his time supervising the work on the Statue of Liberty and the skyscraper to be erected on the site of Şirin's house. He forced the workers to work overtime in order to finish his opus magnum as soon as possible. He especially encouraged the men working at the site of Şirin's house, saying, "Come on, get moving! Get moving! I want to move in here as soon as possible!" He was still under the spell of Şirin's murder, however, and could not keep from thinking about him. Every so often, he would feel a grudge against Can for having chosen a devious and dubious route to privatizing justice, which had included Şirin's murder. "I could have settled it by turning to the Mafia," he said. "It would have been much easier, and it wouldn't cost Şirin his life." He told Can this, fifteen minutes before the beginning of the TBLPC's Board of Directors' Meeting on September 21st. "We messed up the whole thing. Not only did it take a long time to get the site, but we lost Şirin as well. And now we are wasting our time in this lousy board meeting."

Can turned red, saying, "We still have some distance to cover. We have not come to the end of everything. Quite the opposite. Everything is just beginning. Let's tackle the items on the agenda first."

Temel seemed to hold himself aloof at first. He kept saying to himself, "Everything is just beginning, huh?" He thought more than once to leave and never return, resigning his membership. When he saw Tolga Caymaz, the supermarket CEO, take the floor, he listened. The subject was "How to Benefit from the Existing Buildings of the Courts of Justice in Istanbul." he addressed the audience as "a learned friend who had studied law and as a long-time Istanbul citizen." He pointed to each of the buildings in question on the large city map on the wall, highlighting their historical and artistic characteristics, and put forward suggestions for each of them, proposing that none of those left to the TBLPC should be left derelict. Temel repeated to himself the word "derelict" before banging on the table. "I would like to take the floor," he said, "about the procedures to be followed, and immediately!"

He was given the floor and explained in five minutes what was on his mind. A new order was being established in the country in the wake of the privatization of justice. It would be a mistake to preserve the antiquated short buildings of the past. That would hamper the uniformity and harmony of the new city being developed. Under the circumstances, it would be incumbent on the members not to fall prey to Caymaz's suggestion and to see to it that the functions performed in the said buildings should be continued in one of the skyscrapers of Istanbul currently being renovated. He emphasized that in case the Board considered the project too onerous, he, Temel, was prepared to donate to the TBLPC one of the skyscrapers nearing completion. His words were received with applause. Sabri, who took the floor after him, said that he warmly supported the proposal and that he did not doubt that the Chair also shared this view, stressing however that at present the TBLPC needed no donation; in other words, it could afford to pay the cost of the skyscraper into which they would move and suggested in deference to justice that the regional courts have their headquarters in skyscrapers.

Temel, as was his custom, leaned his chin on his left fist and was lost in thought for a minute or two before standing up with a smile. "I would like to repeat my offer, I do not want any money from the TBLPC. Just leave the old derelict buildings to me," he said and, after a moment's consideration, went on, "Not in order to use them but rather demolish them, erecting skyscrapers at their sites."

After two hours, elsewhere in the TBLPC's offices, while toasting the decision with Can and Sabri, he said that he was at a loss how to apologize for his behavior during the meeting. In the end, he embraced Can. "You are a rare intelligent person," he said, "You said that everything was just beginning. I resented that at first, but before a couple of hours passed, you proved to be right. You knew beforehand that it would turn out this way, didn't you?"

Can looked puzzled. "What do you mean by 'this way'?" he asked.

"I mean the state of buildings related to courts of justice, of course."

Can smiled wryly. "Not exactly," he said, "but the only reason to be involved in this business was certainly not that house you wanted so much. I thought, however, it would help us to attain our objective."

Temel was staring at the floor. He raised his head and looked from Can to Sabri and back again. He had a mysterious smile. "Come on," he said. "I've got a surprise for you."

"At this hour?" Can asked. "Gül is waiting for me for dinner. She doesn't eat until I get home."

"Give her a call and tell her you'll be a couple of hours late."

Can looked at Sabri, who was smiling. "I see he's resolute. No use contradicting him." He turned to Temel and asked him where he wanted to take them.

Temel laughed enigmatically. "To the place everybody will want to go. To the Statue of Liberty!"

"I can't refuse that, can I?" Can replied excitedly. "As a matter of fact, I have been expecting that. They say that the monument is not Temel's work but the invention of Americans or devils."

"Good," said Temel, turning to Sabri, "You come along as well."

"I'm afraid, I can't," Sabri replied. "I would certainly like to, but we're going to have a meeting this evening with our members back from their Anatolian tour. I am expected to submit the relevant report to the Chair by tomorrow morning."

"Can't you put that off for a day?" asked Temel

"The fact is that the Minister of Justice keeps pressing us."

"Then we'll have to go without you. You will see it another time. Come on, Can. We'll go!"

They took the elevator to the roof where they boarded a spaceshuttle made in America and four minutes later approached a gigantic cylinder of light, nicknamed 'Vertical Rainbow' by the citizens of Istanbul. At first Can relaxed, but inside the cylinder, he felt his heart to be heavy in his breast and instinctively covered it with his hand, closed his eyes, and for a long time felt himself being whirled downward in the circle of light. At last when he opened his eyes, he asked Temel, "Where are we? Where in heaven's name are we?"

"On the pedestal," Temel replied

After disembarking from the spaceshuttle, they boarded a roofless vehicle car driven by a small man who looked human but who Can felt was an illusion. The car stopped in front of an elevator. The small man swiftly got out and, like a soldier, saluted Temel, who stretched his hand to Can.

"Come," he said, "let's go."

Can did as he was asked with a pounding heart, stepping into a huge elevator car and fixing his eyes on the panel of buttons. He didn't hear what Temel said. Judging from the number on the panel, they were on the seventh floor. "Yes," Temel confirmed, "we are in fact on the seventh floor, level with the ground." The elevator took off and soared higher and higher. Its walls were glass through which, however, nothing could be seen, not a person, not a vehicle, nothing. All that could be seen was dazzling light. "What is this exactly? No workers? Has their work day ended? Or is all automated?" Can asked.

Temel laughed. "All right," he said, "since you want to see men on the job, you will." He pressed a button, and the elevator stopped on the 27th floor. They exited. Temel took him by the arm and led him through a glass door into a large room illuminated by a white glow. There were six people sitting before their computers, watching images and now and then typing things on their keyboards.

Can watched them for five minutes or so without understanding what they were doing. "Well, anyway, there are a few people at work!"

Temel smiled. "Isn't this enough? You don't think that I would have filled three floors of a skyscraper floors with a lot of workers, did you?"

"Is this the whole work force?" asked Can astounded.

Temel, taking him by the arm, led him to the door. "What did you expect?" he asked. Once out of the room, he added, "These are but the things that make it all work. Two floors up is the master mind."

"And who besides that? "asked Can.

"Isn't this enough? Construction has already begun," he said, leading Can to the elevator.

It seemed to Can as if were being swept forward by something other than his own will power. It seemed as if something were flowing beneath the floor, in the ceiling, and in the walls around them. He was nervous. The lack of people made it seem as if it were the end of the world, and he remembered Rıza's statements about the lack of jobs. "Incredible!" he observed in the elevator. "He's lived as a castaway and knows better than I."

The door of the elevator opened, and they were ushered into a spacious covered area lit with a soft light. Can took Temel's arm and said that the pedestal of a statue might itself be compared to a skyscraper. Suddenly, Temel opened a glass door on which were the words in capital letters "NO ENTRY." "Let's go in," he said. "The master mind is here, Perihan Söylemezoğlu, the towering intellect!" There emerged a dwarfish, hunchbacked, middle-aged dark woman, with an enormous head. "Welcome, Sir," she said as he shook her hand, "it's a great honor!" When Temel told her that he had invited his highly regarded friend to

184

enlighten him on the construction of the monument, she resumed her seat and pressed a few keys to create a wide screen on which one could watch the prototype of the statue in New York, contrasting it with the monument in the process of construction. The new statue was three times the size of its prototype. Aside from the size, the sole difference was the face, now covered, where Nokta's face would be. As she began going into detail, Can interrupted her to ask, "Where is the artist? I mean the sculptor?"

The woman replied with a smile, "Actually there is none, Sir." After some hesitation, she pointed to the computer before her. "Or it's this," she said, "if one may call it so." Continuing to point to the computer, she said, "This small machine is the artist. All we had to do was to enter the image of Nokta. The rest was done by the computer itself."

Astonished, Can turned his gaze from the computer to the woman. "I don't understand how the work progresses so swiftly. There is no hardware in sight. The slabs of stone to create the pedestal are gigantic. Where are they, where are the workers anyhow?"

The woman laughed. "Our colleagues below arrange everything through their computers, shaping and designing the slabs of stone, the girders, and the glass."

Can's astonishment continued. "You're not joking, are you?"

It was the woman's turn to be astonished. "Haven't you seem the process that building a skyscraper involves? Diker Housing is the leading firm in the world in this field."

Can, confused, turned to Temel. "Goodness gracious!" he declared, "I'd never ... But you have told me nothing about these things."

Temel stroked the head of the hunchbacked little woman: "The leading element is this lady. Here she applies a technique even more advanced than the one used in the construction of skyscrapers."

Can said nothing. The little woman and Temel, in the presence of Can's wonder, preferred to add nothing else and abstained from going into details. They imparted him the fact that if they wanted they could complete the work within two weeks and the reason for their seeming reluctance was the fear that the advanced technology might be copied together with their concern about the simultaneous completion of the privileged skyscraper they were about to erect at Cihangir. At last, Temel proposed to take their leave, and not keep Gül waiting. As they were about to quit the place, he turned and reminded the little lady of something that Can could not make out, other than the pronouncement of the word "trick." He had been shown so many things in the course of the last three quarters of hour that the word "trick" meant nothing. "Perihan Söylemezoğlu," he pronounced in a low tone, "her name is even taller than herself."

In the spaceshuttle, he closed his eyes and leaned his head against the headrest. A few minutes after the takeoff, he heard Temel say, "Look to your right," drawing his attention to something in the air. Whereupon he saw in the air at a distance of some ten metres, Nokta more beautiful than ever accompanying them. "Nokta! Nokta!" he called out in a low tone. Yet, as if she had been waiting to hear her name called, no sooner had he pronounced it than she vanished.

Her image did not abandon him, either on the way, or back at home. Not only did she not vanish from his sight but also transformed a human being into another human being. Whenever he resumed the depiction of her image, Gül remarked:, "There is something funny about you this evening," to which he replied, "Had you seen that image you wouldn't make this remark".

When the next morning as Sabri entered his office with a thick file under his arm, he still seemed to be in a dream. He wanted to tell him about his dream and said, "I wish you were there with us yesterday evening."

But Sabri did not seem to be interested in the details related to the Statue of Liberty and the image of Nokta. He said, "I hope you've solved all the problems and the new system of justice will begin to operate smoothly all over Turkey within six weeks." Whereupon he placed the file on his desk and, with a sigh, said, "Nothing has been solved, Sir," said.

Can, as if he woke from a deep slumber, was staring at the general secretary in astonishment. "Is it a joke?" he asked.

"No, Sir, it is not," he replied. "It's not the time for jokes!" He sank into the chair indicated by Can. After a moment's silence during which he formulated in his mind what he was to say, he began, "We have screened all the applicants. Well, in monetary terms, none is poorer than the other. Some among them can stretch their network to comprise more than one region, but everyone of them is a Mafioso. Each one of them is involved in more than one criminal case; each one of them happens to be a contractor representing one or two international firms."

"Representations of ?"

"America, Germany, France, Italy, and so forth and so on." Here he named many organizations.[1]

"If they were only contractors of foreign firms, I'd understand. But, they are behind all sorts of organized crime in their respective regions. What's more, they operate there openly. Frankly, I didn't know that the country had sunk so low."

"How about summarizing the situation facing us?"

"In short, these men can only pass judgment on innocent people. I warned you, Sir, we should not have entered this business."

"But now that we are have, what can we do?"

"The only thing to do is to turn down all applications and set up our own organizations to maintain tight security."

"That's incredibly difficult!"

"I know, but I see no way out!"

As Can tried to come up with a solution, İnci entered to say that Prime Minister was calling. "Shall I put him through, Sir?"

Can turned pale.

"I'll take it," he replied, and as soon as his phone rang, he picked up the receiver. His answers to the Prime Minister were curt. "Yes, Sir." "All

---

[1] Since these establishments are still operative, we abstain from naming them, given the fact that we have no members of the Mafia to protect us

right, Sir!" "Right, Sir!" "I see, Sir." "As you say, Sir, it's a bit difficult, but we'll do whatever we can. Yes Sir. Good day, Sir." He hung up and turned towards Sabri who had been trying to interpret what he had heard. "News update," he said, "a new alternative. Veli Dökmeci is sending the Prime Minister's list."

"What list?"

"The list of the individuals and organizations he recommends."

It was now Sabri who turned pale. "Good news, indeed!"

İnci entered and gave Can a paper. Sabri took it began to compare it with the list of applicants. "Strange!" he said. "Very strange, indeed! Exactly the same names and establishments who have applied with one exception."

"The ones you called Mafia?"

"Exactly."

"You know, the fax is coming from the Ministry of Justice?"

"Yes, I know," said Sabri. "What are we going to do now? Shall we entrust the jurisdiction of the regions to these people?"

Can stared at him for quite a while, then said, "I'll examine your file first before taking the matter to the board of directors. I might even convene a general meeting, if need be." He brooded over the issue for some time before adding, "This is the right thing to do, I hope?"

Sabri was sullen. "I don't think so, Sir," he said. "My opinion is that you should use your authority as chairman. Even though this may be against the rules, you've got to act. The board and especially the general meeting may give the green light to these men. On the other hand, please take into consideration that this list has not been sent only to you. Quite probably the rest of the members have a copy of it by now."

Can looked at his general secretary with growing astonishment. "How did you come to this conclusion?"

"From the way that the men acted while talking with us, Sir. They seem to have been convinced that their applications would not be turned down."

"Am I to understand that you and I are the only honest people in this country?" he asked.

"Nor have we made up our minds about the whole thing, Sir," he said with a smile.

Can made no reply. He took the file that his assistant had brought and began to skim through it. He noticed that the names of the people, firms, and cities were similar, but he was so confused that he could not draw Sabri's attention to this. His silence lasted about five minutes. Then he noticed that İnci had entered. "What's up?" he asked.

"The Minister of Justice is on the line, Sir," she said. He was asking whether the list of applicants had been approved.

On the phone, Can began to answer the Minister with forced laughter and said that he had been examining the applications for the past three quarters of an hour, or at most the past hour, making it clear that before making any comment it was necessary that the general secretary and his advisors visit to the regions concerned and investigate. Such an operation, he indicated, would take at least a week, and that only then could he give a positive or negative answer. He heard the Prime Minister cough before replying with a laugh, "My dear Can, what do you mean by a positive or negative answer? The Prime Minister is expecting a positive answer. In other words, you have no alternative. Under the circumstances it is pointless for you to go over the files. It would be a waste of time. Am I clearly understood?"

Hearing this, Can was swept back to that bright May morning when he had grabbed the pistol of the policeman and pointed it at him. "Under the circumstances, dear Minister, let me not keep you waiting; my answer is no!" When the Minister wanted to know whether he was joking, he replied, "No, I'm not joking. I am perfectly aware of the fact that I am addressing Veli Dökmeci, Minister of Justice of the Turkish Republic". Without waiting for a reply, he hung up.

Sabri looked at his boss with an expression half-glad and half-frightened. "I believe we have settled the matter once and for all, or, at least we are about to do so."

Can made a gesture that meant 'Don't worry about it!" "Yes, we are about to do so. However, since we have not come to the end, let's tackle first the file for the city of Adana. Read the lines underlined in red."

"Right, Sir," said Sabri.

But just he picked up the file, İnci half opened the door to say, "The Prime Minister is on the line, Sir."

Can, his hand trembling, picked up the receiver. The Prime Minister, contrary to expectations, sounded quite different from the previous call. He inquired first about Gül's health, how business was going, and so forth before coming to the subject at hand. He did not change its tone. "You have been sharp with Veli, I see, and you may have been right to do so. He is a tactless, but you must overlook his shortcomings." He went on to say that he understood perfectly well Can's reaction after the great exhaustion he must feel after his hard work and caused by hard efforts and expenses. "My name is Mevlut Doğan," he said, "I show respect to the feelings of people like you, although not openly. Therefore, I have made a considerable reduction in my stipulations. I, as your Prime Minister, who has been instrumental in clearing the path that has led you to your present position, I ask you to spare for me three regions only, namely, İzmir, Konya and Diyarbakır. Right?"

As Can realized later, Sabri might have sanctioned this offer, and so would he for that matter, had it been any other day, but this morning it seemed to him as if were he to close his eyes he would see Che Guevara standing in front of him.

"Sir! There is something you should consider. Turkish justice depends henceforth on a private and autonomous establishment and cannot share its authority with anybody else," he replied.

Doğan's answer was followed by laughter. "Can, my dear man, which country do you think you live in?" he said. "Turkey is replete with private and autonomous establishments, our universities in particular. So long I maintain my position, all of them comply with my wishes and consider anything I say as a decree. Just think, I am not asking you for something beyond your powers. Out of sixteen regions, I only ask three. Right?"

"Not quite, Sir," Can replied. "I can't spare even a single region. It is incumbent upon us to make the selection. The law is clear. We may, if we deem it so, give up regional courts all together and institute courts of justice of our own there and appoint our judges."

Doğan was silent for a while. Then he coughed and said, "You remember that we signed a confidential agreement?"

"Indeed, Prime Minister, but there was no such provision in the agreement," he replied.

Doğan coughed again. "There should be, Can," he said. "My name is Mevlut Doğan. I never err in these matters. If I say, 'there is,' it means 'there must be.' If you don't trust me, consult the document yourself. Good day to you," he said and hung up.

Can, receiver in hand, was petrified.

"What's the matter?" asked Sabri, "Your face is white. Can I get a glass of water for you? Did he threaten you?"

"No, thanks." He was short of breath. "The scoundrel claims that there is a provision related to the sharing of authority, but I know for certain there is no such provision. I am positive!" He took a bunch of keys from his drawer, and opened the cabinet behind him and the safe in it. He took out a file with a leather cover. "Here it is. Let's examine it." So saying, he turned over the pages, only to remain baffled and as if turned to stone.

Sabri immediately ran to him. He looked at the so-called agreement, which was but a blank sheet on which there was nothing, neither a text, nor a signature, nor a seal, nor a date, nothing. Can was holding a blank sheet of paper, which he laid on the table.

"He had a copy of it," he remarked. "All the stipulations, dates, and signatures were exactly the same."

Sabri cursed and swore softly. "His must be intact, but altered, no doubt. Anything should be expected from the crook that has done this," he commented. His eyes fixed on the blank agreement, he brooded before saying, "That one's intact." Then he went to the window and looked at the clouds as if searching for inspiration. He returned to Can. "For the first time in my life I'm witnessing such a trick," he said. "It appears that science itself is being transformed." He sank into an armchair, his head between his hands, and meditated for a while. "I think we are at the end of our adventure, Sir," he said. "And it has not taken much time. Henceforth we have to beware of every step we take, every word we utter, and comply with at least part of what these men say. We are in a mess!"

Can was frightened but imagined that he still had the pistol he had snatched from the policeman." Don't be so quick. Just wait. Let's not give in so quickly. The law is on our side, and it's dispensed by us!" he said.

Sabri laid the blank sheet on the table. "Don't rely on our position, Sir. Everything may change. Anything can happen. I remember you saying once, 'The situation of a free individual in Turkey is like the situation of a healthy individual in an epidemic. He may find himself in a hospital at the least expected moment.' We must take precautions. We must grant concessions, if you want my opinion."

Can was not impressed. "Let's not be so submissive. We must not underestimate our own power. The law is on our side, and the rich are our associates." He noted that Sabri had recently been keeping track of incidents more intently and assessing the situation better than he himself. "Let us not overindulge them at least," he added.

"Yes, Sir," said Sabri. "Let's not give these men an occasion for more than they have."

Can was roused by this remark. "What did you mean by that?" he asked.

"What I meant is clear enough, Sir," he said. "I know that you are deeply attached to your friends and loyal to them and that you will spare no efforts to be at their side. This is all very well. But I fear that if you continue to deal with Varol Korkmaz as you have, to insist on freeing Rıza from his cell and remain adamant about the Prime Minister's request that he have exclusive control of İzmir, Konya, and Diyarbakır, you might bring about your own end," he said, pointing to the blank sheet of paper. "This man is capable of doing anything. He may find a place for you or me in the cell vacated by your friend Rıza's release," he added.

"What makes you think that Rıza is in jail? "asked Can startled.

Sabri did not seem surprised at Can's response. "I thought you knew, Sir," he replied. "His new book *The Overbidding* is selling well all over the country. There's no reason to be surprised at him being arrested," Sabri said calmly.

"Do you know this for certain? Do you think he's got arrested and imprisoned again? If so, where?"

"I don't know exactly, but it would be the natural consequence of writing such a book," said Sabri. "Have you not read the book yet?"

"No. It's the first time that I've heard of it."

Sabri was doubtful about this. "I understand you've been travelling recently only by spaceshuttle," he said. "Well, if one does not travel by car, even if in an armored car, through the streets …"

"They advised me to do so for security purposes," said Can.

Sabri tried to tell him about Rıza's recent exploits of his comrade-in-arms. *The Overbidding* was a booklet like Rıza's other works, 64 pages long. Despite its secretive distribution, it looked as if it were going to become a bestseller. Every day from morning till night in every corner of the city, children sold piles of it. Whenever they caught sight of a policeman or were informed of the arrival in the neighbourhood of someone in uniform, they collected their money and booklets and ran away. The frequent confiscations, the detention and interrogation of those who were caught, together with torture by the police and occasional raids to certain hideouts did not discourage them. It followed that there was more than one secret base of operations. The booklet was published by at least four different printing houses and distributed by at least ten distributors. The number of boys, jobless adolescents, young girls, and elderly men and women who sold *The Overbidding* in different parts of the city steadily increased. What is more, his other books were also displayed for sale. Apparently the same thing took place in İzmir, Bursa, Ankara, Konya, Antalya, Kayseri, Diyarbakır, and Trabzon. Especially after the publication of *The Castaways*, the name Rıza Koç became a 'brand,' the voice of the silent masses, and people began to say, "Let us see what has Rıza Koç has to say about it." In short, Rıza Koç had become a celebrated person and a famous author. Had his works been distributed under normal conditions, he would have been the richest writer in the country. Without mentioning him by name, certain newspapers had begun to speak about his achievements. Some linked this to the failure of security forces, some to "certain minor shortcomings in the government," and some to the decline of taste in readers. Nevertheless, according to Sabri, those who printed and distributed his book in defiance of all the bans were potential castaways, who tried to perpetuate a last hope of a "humane tomorrow." Even if they hid themselves among the "intellectual" castaways, their eventual arrest was certain.

Can listened without saying a word. "Did *you* see it yourself? *The Overbidding*, what is it about?" he asked.

Sabri, after hesitation for a few moments, said, "It's about the privatization of justice, Sir."

"Is that so?"

"It is, Sir."

Can fixed his eyes on the floor and remained in that position for a while. Then with a deep sigh, he thought, "Whatever he said has come true, so must it be so in this case, too." He continued to brood. "Let's stand our ground as best as we can," he thought without having in his mind either Varol Korkmaz or Rıza Koç, but he considered that the first thing he should do, once the justice was acquired would be to take Varol Korkmaz and Rıza Koç under its protection.

"Happen what may, the first thing we should do is to remedy injustice. Giving priority to our friends does not mean that we would neglect other miscarriages of justice," he said.

Sabri could not help smiling. "He still has his head in the clouds," he thought. "You are right, Sir. but it seems that neither Temel nor Cüneyt would be willing to support us anymore."

"How do you reach that conclusion?" asked Can despondently but without waiting for a response added, "Let's not discuss this further."

He went to his spaceshuttle and boarded it, taking stock of the situation, and flew home.

No sooner had he arrived than Gül astounded him. Without welcoming him and asking what he had been doing during the day, she returned to her seat and continued to read the booklet that lay open on the coffee table. Can approached her and tried to see what she was reading, then coughed to attract her attention.

Gül did not seem to come back to the real world from the one in which she was immersed.

"What are you reading, dear? It's a long time since I last saw you so engrossed in a book. Is it Dostoyevsky or Kafka?" As no reaction came from her, he took the booklet from away from her and read the cover: *The Overbidding* by Rıza Koç, banned publications, No 42. Then he glanced at the color photograph of the guards of the TBLPC in their new uniforms with pistols and batons. In a fury, he threw the booklet toward the nearest window. "Oh, no! No!" he cried. "To challenge me! The idiot!"

Gül picked up the book.

"Where did you get this filth?" he asked her.

Gül held it tightly.

"Don't jump to conclusions before reading it!" she said. "Although he occasionally attacks you, he shows you to be a man who acts impulsively without considering the consequences, a learned, highly intelligent man, a man lacking tenacity, and exposed to all sorts of influences. He claims that you have fallen in Cüneyt's and Doğan's trap. In other words, you've been deceived by them."

"Can there be a worse thing to say?" he replied angrily. "To censure one who's been a friend his entire life?"

Gül laughed. "What he says about you is nothing compared to what he says about Doğan. "You should read how he describes his moustache, his appearance, his words, and the contents of his brain. You'd be reduced to fits of laughter. Read it. It's not like his other books. It's a monument of comedy! To produce his masterpiece he'd been waiting for his closest friend's great achievement!"

"And what would that be?"

"A revolution in law, the privatization of justice."

"Bravo! Excellent!" he said, and pointed with his chin to the book. "Where did you get this filth?" he asked. "You said you'd stay home today."

"I haven't gone out. This morning a woman that looked like a housemaid brought it, with a dedication to us both."

"How kind of her!" Can said before sinking into a chair and holding his head between his hands.

"The woman looked exhausted, I invited her to come and rest a while and have a cold drink, but she refused. She snuck off as if she were afraid of something. When she left, I began to read it. I didn't stop for lunch. I finished reading around 4 p.m. and then began to read it again."

"Fascinating?"

"Fascinating indeed! He predicts that once you've become the president for the administration of justice, you'll abandon it in less three week or less."

"Oh?"

"That's what he says. Anyhow, even if that turns out to be the result of your efforts, it won't have been for nothing. You'll have been a pioneer in the creation of a masterpiece."

Can grimaced. "How lovely!" he remarked but then remembered his conversation with Sabri. "There is no end to this man's predictions, and this time he may be right," he muttered. "I wish I had never gotten involved with these things."

"As a matter of fact, what you have done has been to have others do the work. You've been the one who initiated things," she said, but thinking that she had gone too far, she backed off before taking up the book again. When at last she closed it and turned to him, she saw a man looking blank, despondent, dejected, and in despair. She was sorry, thinking that she had neglected him recently. She got up and hugged him. "I think you underestimate the book. It's not so bad. Just read it! It's easily read." she said.

Can furrowed his brow "No! I won't!" he said. "Never never in my life shall I read that idiot's book!"

"Let *me* read it then for you, not the whole of it, of course, just certain passages I've found interesting," said Gül and, not waiting for an answer, began reading. Can, his face buried in his hands, and his eyes fixed on the floor listened. He felt exhausted, taciturn. When the doorbell began to ring insistently, she was still reading, and he was listening. The bell startled them both. They looked at each other, wondering who it could be. Can pressed the intercom and asked who it was, then opened the door. He turned to Gül, saying, "It's Rıza. He must have a problem. But how come he is outside at this hour?" Gül looked confused and said nothing.

Rıza entered and greeted them both.

"Are you insane?" asked Can. "At this hour? Do you want to get caught and arrested again? You must know that they're looking for you!"

"Dear Can, you have become the most prominent and reputable person in the country, but your ignorance of your country and city is appalling!"

Can frowned. "What do you mean?"

"Truth, nothing but the truth, as they say in America," he answered. "As matter of fact I waited until now before setting out."

"Do you know what time it is?"

"It was a little after midnight when I rang your bell."

"And?"

"That means the critical hours have passed."

"Are you kidding?"

"No, my dear Can, are you really unaware of the conditions in this city? It's been years that the streets are deserted at this hour, and there are no policemen around."

"But, why? Occasionally I look down at the streets, and although it's true that I don't hear voices, I can still see a lot of people passing by or talking."

"Yes, but this district is especially crowded. There are lots of pedestrians at night, women, girls, young boys, suspicious looking men, but there are no police in sight."

"Why not?"

"The police protect only the wealthy middle class. These people are hardly ever seen on the streets at this time of night, and when there are none of them around, you can't find any police either."

"No police either?"

"Almost none, for people with money wander among the clouds in their spaceshuttles, and when they land, they land on top of skyscrapers and patronize roof bars."

Gül watched the two men. "Not all of them live in skyscrapers, do they? Nor do they all have spaceshuttles"

"Sure," said Rıza, "but they all have bullet-proof armored cars. When they have to go out during the early hours of the morning, they travel very fast and do not pay attention to pedestrians whom they hit and continue their journey."

"But I have seen many drive slowly and stop for pedestrians," said Gül.

Rıza burst into laughter. "I've always acknowledged your view of things. You're not to be compared with your husband's, Gül," he replied and went on, "You're correct. Some even get out of their cars and start bargaining with men and women. They're customers, Gül," and they have practically nothing to fear."

"How?"

Rıza smiled. "Gül dear, I hate to talk about such things, but take your binoculars and you'll see up close what is going on. These are jobless people, jobless, in the sense of unemployed, who prefer to remain in the city until late and engage in all sorts of illicit things. They are thieves and murderers, but their main occupation is pandering to women and boys. Drivers slow down and bargain with a boy or girl whom they find attractive. Eventually an agreement is reached, and a woman gets into the car. When I say woman, I mean a girl of twelve, even eleven. It's tragic certainly. It doesn't take long for her to become wasted and worn and, eventually, join the castaways."

As he listened to Rıza, Can remained silent and tried to be patient, but finally he could not contain himself. "All right, but how come you mix with these outcasts?" he asked.

"They can spot me if I'm on a rooftop," said Rıza, "They recognize me, and they love me. Some make a good profit selling my books. In general prosecutors leave them alone. If someone were to knock on your door now, it would certainly be the police, but now that it's past one, that's not very likely."

Can made a gesture of indifference. "The only house where they wouldn't look would be this one," he said, "especially after your lousy book. You have ridiculed me and my objectives."

Rıza Koç laughed. "You're angry at me, I see," he said. "Well, aren't you going to show me to the door?"

"Wouldn't you be angry if you were in my place? Using my money to defeat me!"

"What about you? Had you remained loyal to the ideals of our youth, wouldn't you have acted the way that I have? Once you were among the most ardent Marxist militants. Then, what happened? You preferred to take sides with the people in power and work for the privatization of justice!"

"Tell me how often have you been taken before a judge and jailed? You must have seen how the law operates in the hands of the state, haven't you? Did it never occur to you to think about what has happened to Varol?"

"Varol was sent to prison by the judges."

"Have you seen, in this our year 2073, any judge who did not serve someone? Who do you think the judges who kept Varol in jail work for?

"The bosses, but my duty is to criticize, and as long as there is criticism, there is hope."

Can screwed up his face. "Nonsense!" he said.

"Now, are you going to show me the door? Are you, or not?"

Can smiled. "Personally, I would have done that, but I hate upsetting Gül. She says she liked the book immensely!"

Rıza replied, "All right then! Give me permission to lie down. I'm dead tired."

XII.

CAN ALREADY HAD MUCH TO WORRY ABOUT, and now there were new problems to deal with. He couldn't take on additional burdens, nor could he put up with new acquaintances. He arrived at his office without even greeting Sabri, but İnci approached him saying that Cahit Güven had been trying to speak to him for the past day. "At the end, he flew into a temper," she said, "and reproached me for failing to reach you."

Can thought for a while. He didn't remember the name, nor could he connect it with a face. "Who is he, anyway?" he asked.

"The chief judge where Varol Korkmaz is on trial."

"Oh, yes, I remember. But what does he want with me?"

"He said he was going to present his apologies. He says unless he did so, he'd never be able to rest. He said he'd call us again today. Should I put him through in case he does?"

"Don't. Tell him I don't want to speak to him," Can said and hurried into his room.

He stood by his desk and remembered Cahit Güven in his gown talking down to the accused and the witnesses. He remembered Güven's warning that he would dismiss Can from the court. What else could someone in Can's position do but refuse the judge's appeal? "A person subjected to such treatment feels himself to be as humiliated as the accused," he said to himself.

A half hour later, he told Sabri how he felt.

"You are perfectly in the right, Sir," Sabri said. "I had the same feeling, believe me, when he begged me to arrange a meeting with you yesterday. He almost made me dislike myself."

"I don't understand this wish to make amends after such a long a time."

Sabri laughed. "Apparently, there is a year and a half before he can retire." He rose and left but returned a few minutes later with a mysterious smile, announcing that there was a middle-aged gentleman outside with the features of someone from northern Turkey who spoke Turkish flawlessly with an American accent and who introduced himself as John Smith, professor of law. "He would not leave unless he saw you. I suggest that you speak to him. One does wonder what such a person may want with you."

Can, who didn't know whether to invite the man in or ask him to leave, finally opted for the first alternative. "All right," he said, "show him in." When a minute later, the man briskly came toward him and extended his hand, Can immediately felt frightened.

"My name is John Smith, son of Şirin, younger brother of Tufan Şirin."

Can was stunned. The brother of a companion from his younger years, with whom he had lost contact years ago, stood before him, and he realized that this man was none other than the son of the same person who had been riddled with bullets while defending his home. For an instant, he thought he was in a dream. John Smith came closer and warmly shook his hand.

"You do remember Tufan Şirin, don't you?" he asked.

Can took a deep breath, and his face flushed. "How could I ever forget him!" he replied. "We were the closest friends. I knew many of his poems by heart."

"He used to tell me about you frequently, and he admired and imitated you in every respect," said John Smith "whether in a fight or in love, in everything. His poems were full of references to you."

"I know, I know," Can stammered as felt tears rush to his eyes. He took a deep breath.

"He is no more, and I happen to be here," he went on. "Urged by my father, I escaped and went abroad. I could not even attend my brother's funeral. The fact that he had been shot dead was something that I didn't learn until much later. You once rescued him from policemen by grabbing the gun …"

"Yes," said Can fixing his eyes at a distant point, "the foolish years of our adolescence. But I failed to rescue him from the hands of fascists." He was reliving his past experience. With a smile, he observed, "You resemble him. When I set eyes on you I thought for an instant I saw him."

"Those who knew us used to say we were like identical twins. When he was killed I was at the eighth grade," said John Smith. "But didn't my father's name have any associations for you?" he asked.

After a moment's thought, Can said, "We hardly ever talked about our parents those years. All that we knew was that there was a revolution going on, and of course, we spoke of our loves. Further, I don't recall Tufan talking about you. This is the first time that I realized he had a brother."

John Smith suddenly came closer. "Nevertheless, you could not possibly have forgotten the name Şirin. You and your cohorts filed a court action against him."

Can was baffled. "I tried to find a way to delay things, put things off as long as I could. and find a way to settle the matter amicably. Believe me, even when you said you were Tufan Şirin's brother. I had difficulty seeing a connection between you and him and realizing that you were Şirin's son."

John Smith did not seem to believe that. He leaned against the table with both hands and said, "Your men have murdered my father. It was a cold blooded murder."

Can frowned. "No," he replied, "my men had nothing to do with the incident. For that matter, I have no such men, never had any in fact. The official who did it did not do so because of the court said. The court had nothing to do with it, and the men you refer to were not my men. No one asked my opinion. None would have wished such to happen. I learned about it much later."

John Smith smiled sardonically.

"A misunderstanding," said Can.

"I see, yet for such a misunderstanding so many policemen, guns, and bullets."

Can stared at the ceiling and considered what his visitor had said. "You're right," he concluded. "But I knew nothing about the affair. I heard about it much later when he chose to defend his house against the security forces."

John Smith did not seem impressed. "I don't really care about that," he said. "Assuming that the account you give is true, I would like to know your opinion about the following. Were I to go to court now, would you side with them or with Tufan Şirin and his father?"

"You're asking such a question is humiliating, mortifying," he said angrily. "Let alone the fact that I am no longer a lawyer. I am …"

"I have heard you will be soon taking over the administration of justice," replied John Smith. Then?"

"You may consider the probability of winning your case to be very high."

"I am not thinking of any monetary compensation," said John Smith. "I demand that my father's murderers be punished."

"I haven't implied monetary compensation. You are perfectly justified in your claim. We can do everything within the confines of the law."

"What would your attitude to the case be?"

Can considered the case for a while before answering. "I'd assess the case on the contents of the file brought before me," he said and added, "provided, of course, it is submitted to me."

"Is there a possibility that it might not be brought before you?"

"Everything is possible. This is Turkey, you know."

Smith, after staring for quite a while at his brother's friend, stood up and stretched out his hand.

"Even though under such circumstances, I am glad to have known you. I am sorry to have been suspicious of your friendship and loyalty. Good day!"

Before he allowed Can to respond, he left.

Can could not take his eyes off the door through which Smith left. An hour later, when he had recovered, he called Sabri and told him about the incident. "What do you say? Can we do something for him?"

Sabri considered the situation. "We have already enough problems on our hands, Sir. I think that we should stay away. Let's not cut off the limb we're sitting on. After a moment, he added, "Had we not gone in for this business of privatization, you could have defended the case in such a manner that it would become legendary."

"You think so?"

"That's how I see it, Sir."

Can looked as if he had a foretaste of the case that would never be brought to court and never tried. "But despite your opposition, I was the first to bring court action against Şirin," said Can as tears came to his eyes.

"Don't be unfair to yourself," said Sabri before he left.

That evening as his spaceshuttle landed on the skyscraper, Can began thinking how he would tell Gül the story about his encounter with the American professor of law, John Smith. The moment he realized that Smith was Tufan Şirin's younger brother, he felt a shudder run down his spine. He felt a heaviness that weighed him down. He asked the pilot to circle the building a few times before landing. As the spaceshuttle did so, he recalled Smith's words, "I see, yet for such a misunderstanding so many policemen, guns, and bullets." His memory of Smith's brother would not go away and kept haunting him. Only after he was home and Gül, seeing his distress, asked, "What has happened to you, darling? Did you have an accident or something?" did he recover. Without believing in what he said, he answered "I'm all right!" Then he saw Rıza in the living room with a glass, smiling at him. He felt somewhat relieved. "Please, Gül darling, get me something to drink, too," he asked.

A quarter of an hour elapsed as he sat, glass in hand, without speaking. When Gül said that she was going to send for a doctor, he recovered himself. "No need for a doctor! I'm all right!" he said before sinking back again in apathy.

Only after his third drink did he fully recover. He told her disjointedly about Smith, who had visited him. "But, who is John Smith?" she asked, puzzled. Unable to explain what he was thinking, he began sobbing like a child. Gül felt tears rush to her own eyes as she said, "I understand nothing, nothing at all"

"Something has happened to this man," she cried before kneeling before him and taking his hands in hers. "Come. Tell me. Who is John Smith?"

"He is Tufan's brother and Şirin's younger son," he explained. He turned to Rıza. "I didn't know that Şirin was Tufan's father. I never set eyes on him. But I liked it when he challenged Temel. I did my best to prevent his property from being demolished. I tried to postpone the whole thing, and I called the judge, but I didn't tell him to do what he did. Şirin's death was a serious blow to me." He was about to dissolve in tears.

Both Gül and Rıza Koç held their breath while they listened. Then Rıza approached him. "Come, come," he said, "you mustn't let this overwhelm you. You knew that Şirin had been shot. You were also aware that it was a disaster, but you were not so upset then. Now that you know that he was Tufan's father, your world are miserable, but the incident is the same incident. Don't you think that's something of a paradox?"

Can was plunged in sorrow. "I'm more upset by my situation that by Şirin's," he said. "Everything seems to go opposite to what I expected. I had thought that I could do everything as I wanted and just the opposite happened. I was thinking that once I became the head of the justice system, I would be able to do the right thing, but now that I am about to become the head, I realize that the reverse is happening. There is something absolutely wrong in all this."

"No!" cut in Rıza Koç. "These are but the result of the age we live in. You are not to blame for this. Actually none of us can be said to be responsible for our actions, and our actions prevent us from fulfilling our objectives. Both of us are prisoners of our thoughts. You are in pursuit of so-called ideas. You are trying to establish justice in a world where money is power. I write those books at the risk of my liberty in the hope of transforming the established order. Yet nothing happens, and nothing will happen. Our sole consolation is that we are not among those who submit. Both nature and society are dying. A French author has written in a book entitled *The Future Will Last Very Long*. Now, the future has no future anymore."

The doorbell rang. Gül glanced at her watch.

"A quarter to two," she said. "Who could it be at this hour of the night?" she said.

Rıza smiled.

"Well, Şirin may have come back to thank Can for his empathy," he said.

"Şirin would not be so insistent. Now whoever is it pounding on the door?"

Can walked to the entrance way. Just as he was about to open the door, Gül cried, "Stop! Wait, don't open it!"

Can drew back." Who is it?" he asked.

"The police! Open the door!" was the unexpected answer.

Can switched on the closed circuit camera and saw at least half a dozen policemen outside.

"I'm afraid you're at the wrong address. I have nothing to do with the police. Moreover, I enjoy immunity," he said.

"We have not come to raid your house or arrest you, Sir," said one of the policeman. "We are after a wanted man, who — as we have been informed — is staying in your house, a man by the name of Rıza Koç."

Can deepened his. "I said that this place enjoys immunity!" he shouted. "Further, I don't believe you are from the police. I'll call security."

Then he heard the voice of the security officer, who said that the police had in their hands a warrant for the search and had the right to force the door open.

"Yes," said the person who had spoken before. "We have a search warrant issued by the chief prosecutor of the Republic. We have complete respect for you personally. Our duty is to obey our superiors. If you do not open the door, we'll have to break it down. We are ordered to get the man."

At that moment, something unexpected happened. Rıza himself opened the door. Raising his hands, he walked out. Can trembled as if he were in the midst of a horrible nightmare. He tried to see his friend among the police. He saw Rıza being handcuffed by two of the police while a third held him down by the neck and then dragged him to the elevator. Can called after him, "Don't worry Rıza, you'll be free very soon." Rıza turned and said, "Don't interfere! Mind your own business!" He saw the police thrust him into the elevator. After a while Can and Gül went back into their apartment and bolted the door.

They said nothing. Later, however, in bed, before falling asleep, Gül held her husband's hand and said, " It seems to me that this is the end of the story, dear. Accept defeat and get some sleep. It's three o'clock."

When Can said that he wanted to get up at eight thirty at the latest, she replied that she could not and would not wake him then. Nevertheless, exactly when he said he wanted to be wakened, she took the newspapers from the doorway, glanced at the photographs on the front page, and read the headlines. She ran to the bedroom and began shaking her husband. "Up! Come on! Wake up! Look at this scandal!" Can straitened up and cast a quick glance at the headlines and the photographs. One of them showed Rıza, handcuffed with the police leaving the skyscraper, and another showed Can arguing. Aside from minor details, nearly all of the articles had similar contents and almost the same words. The headlines were different though: "Justice Protects the Accused," "Justice and the Accused in Collusion with Each Other," "Judge and Culprit Bound Together." It was all too clear that one author was behind all of the articles. The fact was that Veli Dökmeci, the Minister of Justice, had told reporters at 2:00 a.m., before the arrest had in fact taken place that "We have not touched Can Tezcan in any way, but we had to restrain his guest in order to handcuff him," proved as much

"Everything is plain. They are resolved to do away with you," said Gül, straitening up and dropping the papers into her lap. She drew close to her husband and stroked his hair, then took his chin in her hand and raised his head to make him look at herself. "Don't worry!" she said. "This adventure was destined to be short-lived anyway. It is better that it come to an end. The sooner the better."

Can pushed aside the newspapers in her lap and looked straight into her eyes, thinking that she was still beautiful and attractive.

"Maybe so, but as long as nothing stops me, I'll carry on my work and get Rıza out of their hands as soon as possible," he said resolutely and began dressing.

A half hour later, he was in his office. İnci put aside the newspaper she was reading and rose quickly. She seemed afraid of something. He smiled at her, and she smiled in return. "Good morning, Sir," she said.

Can acted as if he had not noticed the newspaper she had been reading. "Good morning, İnci. Will you please ask Sabri to stop by, if he's available."

After a couple of minutes, Sabri arrived.

"What do you think of what's happened?" Can asked.

Although at first Sabri was going to use the word 'imprudent,' he said instead, "Things are going from worse to worse, Sir, and it seems that there will be no end to it. The die is cast. There is no turning back, Sir," he added in a trembling voice. "The men had the audacity to search your house!"

Can sighed. "The worst of it is that Rıza was caught because of me."

"Not because of you, Sir," interrupted Sabri. "You're in quite a mess because of him."

"Do you think we can do something for him?" Can asked.

"I'm afraid not, Sir," Sabri replied. "You know better than I, they have the right to prosecute. Justice has not been officially transferred to us yet. Actually there *is* a solution. But, I very much doubt that you would be willing to …"

Can understood what was being implied but insisted on hearing it. "Tell me this solution."

"To do unreservedly what Doğan wishes."

"In other words, cut off the limb we're sitting on."

"In a way, yes."

İnci entered suddenly without knocking.

"The Prime Minister is calling from Ankara."

The Prime Minister asked him how he was and said, "The tone of your voice sounds distressing. I am grieved at this. Really I am. You remember, I'd told you at our first meeting that I had taken an interest in you. my name is Mevlut Doğan. If I say something, I stick to my word. Therefore, I have one last offer. By the way, are you alone?"

"My general secretary, only. I have no secrets from him. He shares all my secrets," said Can.

A laugh followed. "You're close to Rıza Koç, I understand. All right then, if you do not see any inconvenience in talking now, I have no objection. Here it is, my last offer. If you turn it down, we shall henceforth be free to do as we like, OK?"

"Yes, Sir; hasn't that always been the case?" Can answered.

"Listen then," said the Prime Minister. "Here is my request. You shall not dismiss the ten judges I am going to name."

Can seemed to hesitate at first but became resolute. "The law is clear, Sir. Our establishment is an independent organization and is free to nominate the judges it deems best."

The Prime Minister's grew somewhat more coarse. "Actually, I do know. But we are not discussing law now. We are speaking of an agreement. Moreover, I can change the law at any time."

"I'm a man of law, I abide by the law, Sir."

There was no answer until the silence was broken again by a laugh.

"Don't you think that you are exaggerating," the Prime Minister said. "In the meantime, we've got a present for you. Koç will be set free, all right?"

"Much obliged to you, Sir," replied Can. "I'd do anything for my friend, but this is out of the question."

"But why?"

"I'm restrained by the great responsibility I have assumed."

For a while, the Prime Minister did not speak. The he said, "Strange! Strange indeed!" and in a louder voice," Try to remember the things that you accepted in our first interview!"

Can sighed. "I don't have to remember it, Sir, since it is fresh in my mind."

"Well then?"

"At the time I had not yet assumed responsibility."

"Is this your final opinion?"

"It is, Sir. You have your prosecutors, and we have our judges."

He heard Doğan laugh again. "Well, nothing doing. We have failed to reach an agreement, but our friendship will continue. Good day!"

Can searched for an answer but failed to find one and heard the click as the Prime Minister hung up the phone.

"He hung up," Can said to Sabri. He stared at the floor for some time without speaking before banging on his desk. "Yes!, Yes! Yes!" he shouted.

Sabri looked puzzled. Anxiously he stared at his boss.

"Yes! I am positive now! At first it seemed to me that his voice and personality resembled Smerdyakov's voice and figure, but I was wrong. The men is Smerdyakov himself. Mind and heart included!" Breathless, he stood immobile for some time before turning Sabri with a smile. "Ivan Karamazov portrayed him beautifully," he said. "'You seem an excellent idiot or a perfect scoundrel.' Something like that."

Sabri smiled. "I think this is not a rare kind of character, Sir," he said. "It's enough just to raise our heads and take a look around. We'll find ourselves besieged by these figures; political parties, associations, chambers, universities, magazines, newspapers are full of idiots and scoundrels. People who play guitars and dislike poetry."

XIII.

SABRİ PUT THE DOCUMENTS that he had been carefully holding, on the table and sat down. He watched Can, who skimmed over them. As Sabri knew, Can's reaction to them would be different from his own.

"What do you make of them?" Can asked.

Sabri looked upset as if he had not understood the question.

Can smiled. "Yes, Sabri, what do you make of them?" he repeated.

Sabri was discouraged. He looked exhausted and could find no proper answer. "It appears they have found the easiest ways out," he commented.

"The easiest, huh?" replied Can. "They're just beating around the bush!"

"Why do you say that?"

"To collect so many signatures and talk to all these people trying to persuade them. Do you think that's an easy way to handling the thing, especially since these men had elected me chair unanimously. Am I wrong?"

"You are not, Sir."

"How about counting the signatures. Let's see how many have signed?"

Sabri did as he was asked. "Sixty-seven exactly," he replied.

After some thought, Can drew a deep breath. "Sixty-seven, huh?" he said. "Approximately ninety per cent of the shareholders. I never would have thought so many would give in."

Sabri clenched his fists. "I don't think that this was a matter of giving in or not, Sir," he said. "They didn't doubt that this would be so easy. Our shareholders knew well from experience that they could not challenge either Doğan's or any other Prime Minister's will. I believe that our shareholders signed without hesitation. Didn't I warn you that these men were pliable?"

"You did in fact, but I never thought that they would yield so easily. A good many of them have been my clients. They should have known me better," said Can.

Sabri tried to smile. "They may have thought that you'd be useful as a lawyer, Sir."

"You have a good sense of humor," said Can. "The best thing is perhaps to carry on with my profession as lawyer, and let them pay for it. Life is full of conflicts."

Sabri was visibly upset.

"Don't worry, Sabri. You should be amused by all this. You're perfectly justified in doing so. We have been defeated. We tried to be honest in the middle of a crowd of crooks and have ended in defeat simply because we won't abandon our principles. We have lost and caused of poor Rıza's arrest. Now, let's go over things again."

According to the documents, the fact that Can had hidden a wanted man for days had not only given him a bad name but the TBLPC as well. Under the circumstances, those who had signed the documents suggested that a general meeting be convened as soon as possible in order that all legal efforts be made, including a new election for Chair, in order to re-establish the organization's prestige and trustworthiness.

"May I remind you that among the accusations brought against Rıza," said Sabri, "the principle charges include the charge that he humiliated you and and the new order of justice you pioneered?"

"That may well be. Justice has been dispensed so far. Actually those who accuse Rıza might well be the prisoners themselves."

"We have worked in vain. After all, this should have been expected," Sabri said.

"Why?"

"In order to create a new judicial system, didn't you work twith powerful representatives of an unreliable and hostile class of people who were absolutely opposed — not to you necessarily — but to your view of life?"

"Viewed from our current position, your interpretation is correct. You are right and you have been so from the beginning, Sabri. Our mistake has once more proved that our values are correct."

"At any rate, to have been unable to accomplish what we wanted is awful, Sir."

Can, focused on the ceiling, seemed lost in thought. After a while he turned to his assistant. "You are absolutely right!" he said, "Leaving something as important as this undone is awful! But you can never know when and where something will reach its end. What is important is to be able to carry on, to go as far as one can, and that's what we are going to do now!"

Sabri was stunned. "Can we go further considering the number of signatures?"

"To hell with signatures. I'll go on until somebody stops me." Can's tone was resolute and loud. He caught sight of Sabri's wonder and smiled. "Yes, that's it. I'll go as far as I can," he confirmed.

"There are thirteen days before justice is turned over to us. We should convene the general meeting within the next three weeks at the latest," said Sabri. "That means we can't announce our appointments before October 3rd. October 3rd will be the date of the general meeting "

"So much the better, Come on. Let's hurry and set up our courts."

Smiling, Can tapped at his desk. "You seem quiet today. Do you think that this way of handling affairs is really dumb?" he asked.

"I've been thinking about the bleak future in store for the judges we'll appoint," said Sabri with a sigh. "They'll surely be dismissed by their future superiors simply because we appointed them."

Can meditated for a while. "We'll act as if nothing has happened," he said determinedly with an enigmatic smile. "If you say that the judges we will appoint will end up joining the mass of starving people, let's appoint those judges that are close to them and let those who will replace us — namely, the Prime Minister's men — dismiss them at the beginning."

215

"Sir, you know that five out of the ten board members have signed this document calling for a general meeting and elections. If we exclude you and me, there are only four people left. If one of the four takes their side that will be the end of us," he said, "let alone the probability that all four of them will join the opposition. Is it worth taking that chance?"

Can smiled bitterly. "So long we are in charge, we'll do what we are supposed to do. It's a matter of ethics!"

"Right! As you say, Sir, "Sabri replied.

"Let our staff work hard and form at least the courts with jurisdiction over the Istanbul, Ankara, and İzmir regions."

"All right."

"Let's carry out a final project and bring our work to an end."

"If you say so, Sir," Sabri replied.

Barely twenty minutes had passed before the project was under way.

By 4:00 in the morning, the judges for the regions of not only Istanbul, Ankara, and İzmir but also Adana, Trabzon, and Diyarbakır had been named. Can, reviewed the files of the chosen and declared, "Excellent! You've done a very good job. You have a highly skilled group of assistants." But he saw that Sabri was troubled and said, "Sabri, you seem to have something that troubles you on your mind. Do you disapprove of your own selections?" he asked.

Sabri bowed his head like a guilty boy. "I have some reservations, Sir," he said. "Leaving aside the special courts and judges, the institution that operates best in this country is the judicial system. If the laws permitted, it would operate even better. Now and then we hear people speak in favor of Turkish justice. My concern is that this impression may soon vanish."

"How do you reach that conclusion?"

"Our list comprises all the experienced and learned judges. If they were to be dismissed because they are the ones we chose, one could no longer speak properly of justice."

Can, with his chin propped up on his fists, meditated quietly, then turned back to Sabri. "You're wrong," he said. "One must trust in human nature. More often than not, injustice prevails everywhere. People say, 'If this has been so in the past, it will be so until eternity. One can't help it.' At the most unexpected moments, at times of crisis, justice appears, and no public outcry stops it. 'Things can't go on as they have!' they protest."

Sabri did not seem convinced. "An apt observation, no doubt!" he said. "However, if you ask my opinion, justice is the prerogative of the strong. The weak hardly know what justice is. Assuming that they do know, they will never believe that it may be theirs someday. Therefore, they are not hopeful. They remain content with the laws of nature. When I think of the conditions of the castaways …"

Can halted and coughed before he said, "Let's go ahead and submit our proposal to those in power. The fact that those who want new elections are in the majority does not mean that they will reject our proposal. They're two different issues."

"All right, we'll submit it," Sabri acquiesced, "but I am not optimistic."

"Let us do what we are supposed to do and leave the rest to others," replied Can.

"Maybe you are right, Sir, but I haven't the slightest doubt they will vote against it. They won't even discuss the issue."

The result was as expected. Except for Sabri himself and one young member, all of the members voted against the proposed list. Given the fact that in a few days a new board would be elected, the majority unanimously agreed to have the future board carry out the appointments. One member noted that the Chair himself had failed to attend the meeting and ended his speech by saying, "If our honorable Chair considers this issue important, why did he not take part in and present his views?"

Can listened to the account of the meeting with a smile while Sabri gave gave an exact report. "All right," Can said. "I understand. No need to go into detail. I can see the meeting as if I attended it myself. If you've hurt someone, they'll retaliate sooner or later. Tell me though, did Temel speak?" The answer being no, Can simply smiled, although he wanted to know who the person besides Sabri who had voted for the appointments was, but eventually he gave up, saying that it was just as well not to know who the opponents were. He all but forgot about the TBLPC, for the formation of which he had worked so strenuously. If Gül or a new acquaintance mentioned the subject, he dodged the issue. Yet he did not look crestfallen. When, on October 11th, 2073 he took his briefcase and started to leave the apartment, Gül asked where he was going. "Fifty-Fifth Street, building C-54. Did you forget? I have a meeting at 4 p.m.!"

Gül hugged him. "I forgot. Sorry, darling," she said. "Please forgive me!"

He kissed her. "Don't worry. I'm all right," he said and turned to the door.

At 4:05, he opened the regular meeting meeting of the TBLPC. First he delivered a short speech, which was followed by the election of the Chair to preside over the meeting, and his assistants. Then he invited the elected Chair to preside over the meeting and warmly congratulated him and showed him to his seat. "It's yours," he said. He then walked quietly to the door, accompanied by applause and a voice that shouted, "Don't go!"

But before he reached the door, Temel jumped to his feet and ran after him, grabbing him by the arm as Can was leaving "Where in heaven's name are you going? The meeting is just beginning. Aren't you going to defend yourself? Aren't you going to be a candidate yourself?" he asked. When he saw Can looking at him serenely, he added, "I was obliged to sign. I know I am greatly indebted to you, but I had to do what I did and vote for him. I knew that you would be the winner in the end. I have not lost hope. I've talked with many of the people here. Just come back and say, 'I'll be a candidate!' and that will do it."

Can, with the same smile, listened but said nothing.

"I understand. You don't have to justify yourself and apologize for anything" Can said as he tried to free his arm from Temel's grasp.

Temel took the other arm. "Don't think that I am cross with you," he said. "I promise I'll stand by you whenever you run into difficulty. You know well that I'm a regular part of your office. You know, of course …" He suddenly stopped talking.

Can did not listen. "The law office is there, and nothing has been decided as yet. You're surely not to abandon the thing you yourself created."

Can tried again to free himself from Temel's grasp. "No, Temel, even were this desired by all of the members, you may count me out. I can no longer work here. I've lost all my confidence."

"If at least you were to attend the meeting. Can I go and announce it?"

"Gracious, no!"

"Are you positive?"

"I certainly am!"

"Aren't you curious about the deliberations and the result?"

"Not in the least? Good day!" he said, heading for the door.

Temel caught him by the arm once again. "Can I do anything for you?" he added.

Can thought for a while and said with an enigmatic smile, "No," then added, "Wait, perhaps you can."

Temel beamed. "Just tell me!"

"Instead of giving numbers to streets, how about giving them names."

"What for?"

"For instance, one of the streets at Cihangir might be named for Nokta, another after Hikmet Şirin."

Temel stood immobile. "That's good of you to say so," he replied, shrugging his shoulders, "but principles are more critical for me."

"It's up to you to decide!"

Can shook hands with Temel before once again heading out. Just as he was about to exit, however, he turned around to cast one final glance at what he was leaving. He saw Temel, looking back at him. He walked briskly towards him. "You've turned down my first request. Let's see whether you'll do the same for my second," he said.

"I'll do it for sure. If it's in my power, of course," he replied.

"All right. Here it is. I would like you to buy my shares in this organization."

Temel, without even considering the offer, said, "I don't want you to abandon us. However, if you are determined, I am ready to buy them, not because I want them, but for your sake."

"All right! You can have them at half their face value," said Can.

Temel smiled. "I am not an opportunist. I'll buy them at their face value," he said. "You've really given up, huh? Aren't you at least curious about the results of the election?"

"Not in the least," said Can. "Further, Sabri is here. He'll tell me all about it."

Sabri did so before noon the next day, October 12th, 2073. He said that many members had taken the floor and that the meeting had lasted quite late. At least half of the original members of the organization had praised Can's know-how and skill in his efforts to privatize justice and establish the TBLPC. They expressed their disappointment in his objection to the new nominees to the board. There were those who expressed their suspicions regarding the possibility that a trap had been set up to catch the notorious criminal in the house of the Chair. The fact that there were some twenty votes in Can's favor, although he was not a candidate, suggested that the speakers were sincere.

"Who was elected?" Can asked.

Sabri took a paper from his briefcase and handed it to the ex-Chair, who glanced at it before putting it aside. "Excellent! Splendid!" he said, "and you're here."

Sabri protested vehemently, "I'm not, Sir!"

"Your name is there!"

"Yes, but I told them to count me out! After the elections, I told them that and confirmed it with a written statement. I'm not going to serve!"

"Why not?"

"I told them, I had set out with you on this journey with you, and I would end with you."

"You shouldn't have done that, "said Can. "You know well that the function of the secretary general is of utmost importance. That place cannot be filled by any other person as qualified as you."

"It did not occur to me to think about it, Sir. Moreover, there was another important reason."

"How so?"

"The board of directors appointed a non-member as the Chair."

"Anyone we know?"

"Indeed! Cahit Güven!"

"Cahit Güven! Cahit Güven! Can kept repeating. Looking at the ceiling, he stood stock still before suddenly turning back to Sabri. "What are your plans now?" he asked.

Sabri smiled. "I haven't decided on anything yet, Sir," he said. "I have had no time to think about it. I think I can find some kind of job elsewhere."

Can was furious. "We'll resume our work and have a fresh start. We'll begin with even greater enthusiasm."

Sabri was delighted.

"Excellent idea, Sir!" he said "I'd thought you'd begun to dislike your profession. Well, we'll carry on!"

"You bet we will!"

"Yes Sir! Splendid! We'll be even more active than before!" he said.

Can laughed. "You bet we will! But one of our main associates will no more be with us. Temel is leaving."

"Why?"

"How can he carry on his business properly in his capacity of the major shareholder of the TBLPC? He no longer needs us!"

"That's not important. We can carry on our business without him," said Sabri. He was lost in thought for a while: "Just think, the new judges will provide us with so many new opportunities. We'll be very busy!"

However, when Sabri entered Can's office around 10:00 a.m. on October 15th, 2073, with a file under his arm and a few newspapers, he was somewhat nervous. He didn't know whether he should be glad or upset.

Can had been reading the sports page of the *New Agenda*.

"You haven't read the news, have you, Sir?" he asked. "The news about our list."

"Of course, I have, Sabri," said Can. "They haven't thrown it away! As a matter of fact, they've appointed many of our own nominees."

"To be precise, all of them, Sir. I have checked them all. They're exactly the ones on our list. See for yourself, Sir," he said setting the list before him.

"You've checked it all, I'm sure. There's no need for me to go over it," he said. "They must have thought they couldn't prepare a better list."

"Can there be a secret reason behind this?" he asked.

"Possibly," said Can. "One has to be prepared for every contingency in this age of paradoxes."

"Is it that simple, Sir?"

"One can formulate as many hypotheses as one likes. You may suppose that the reason they have approved of our choices may have been so that they can dismiss them one by one, for instance. You can multiply this example. You may make your own scenario."

"Yours is good enough, Sir," he replied.

İnci knocked on the door and entered. "Sorry, Sir, there is lady on the phone. It's the third time she's called. She says she is one of the newly appointed judges for the Istanbul region. Apparently she has an important message for you."

"Her name?"

"Zeynep Bulak, Sir."

Sabri looked at the list before him. "In the fifth column," he said. "I know her. She is a very good judge."

Can's interest was aroused although he didn't show it. "I'll take the call," he said.

The voice on the other end of the line said, "Sir, we are twenty-three judges from the Istanbul region." As soon as he heard this, he pressed the button on the phone that would allow his assistant to hear. Sabri and Can learned that twenty-three of approximately seventy judges appointed to the Istanbul region had decided to resign their positions and they expected quite a number of others to follow suit. When Can suggested that they should think it over again, taking into consideration that justice should be maintained at all cost, Bulak confirmed that they were determined and would not change and that in the days to come there was every likelihood that there would be more doing the same. Her statement was corroborated a short time later by a call from İzmir. Can and Sabri could not decide whether they should be pleased or not. Can began pacing up and down before stopping in front of Sabri and saying, "We are witnessing the fact that once more, despite the Herculean efforts of capitalists and the continual corruption of human values, justice itself cannot be obliterated, no matter how much pressure is exerted on it. It finds its way and surges once more to the surface. Our judges have demonstrated this once again. For the sake of truth, they opt for starvation. They have forgone the comforts that a high salary would have secured for them."

Sabri recalled an earlier conversation he and Can had had. "The proportion is fifty-fifty, Sir."

Can did not seem perturbed. "This may be a sign of vitality. It shows that truthfulness has not vanished. It is proof of the fact that every individual ... ," he continued. His enthusiasm grew, but was interrupted when İnci entered again without knocking.

"The Prime Minister is calling, Sir," she said.

Can hesitated whether to pick up the receiver or not, but finally did so. "Yes, Prime Minister?" he said.

There was much laughter, followed by Doğan's shrill voice. "You have lost an excellent organization that we were about to transfer to you almost for nothing. I want nothing from you. However, when I tell someone, 'I like you.' I mean it. You know, I like you. That's why I just want to say how sorry I am on your account."

XIV.

IN TEMEL'S ELABORATELY DECORATED AND COLORFUL LİVİNG ROOM, Gül, Can, and Sabri were silent, and so were Temel and John Smith. If anyone expressed a personal opinion or tried to tell a story, he was interrupted and asked to be silent. They prefer either to listen or pretend to. And if they felt it was important to speak, they would keep their comments brief. Temel, who had arrived late that evening and found everyone quiet, was surprised. "The best lawyers in our country and one of the best lawyers of America seem to have forgotten how to talk," he said, laughing. Seeing that none of his friends responded, he added, "Are you talkative only when there are judges around?" But seeing that there was still no response, he himself became quiet.

Despite the fact that they had dinner later, they continued silent, hardly touching the delicious dishes prepared by Temel's Italian chef. Even Sabri, whose metabolism kept him thin, was no exception. The one thing they did not refuse was wine.

"Look!" cried Temel. "It's three already! Time to go to a bar!"

Gül rose to her feet. "No more liquor. We've got to get some sleep. Tomorrow is a big day," she said.

Tomorrow was the inauguration of the Statue of Liberty. As usual, Sabri was able to distinguish between the important from what was unimportant. "It's not only a big day, it's an historic one. Just think, a Statue of Liberty is to be unveiled for the first time in the Turkey, vastly bigger than its prototype and with a face even more beautiful. We must congratulate Temel for this. He looked around, but Temel had already gone to bed. "He's going to be a historical figure along with his mother," Sabri added.

Whether the following day, November 17th, would make Temel an historical figure or not was uncertain. History that would decide it. What was certain, however, was it would be the happiest day of his life. He dashed around, exchanged a few words with those he chanced to meet and, seeing that everything went according to plan, felt elated. Everybody seemed in the right mood and was conscious of how extraordinary the occasion was. Nearly all of the citizens of Istanbul and even the wealthier people from the provinces, were there to see the historical inauguration of the monument, which itself had long generated great expectations. On both the Asian and the European sides of the city, especially in the windows of the skyscrapers, crowds with flags in one hand and binoculars in the other, were vigilant, anxiously waiting for the moment when they would be able to see the magnum opus lit variously by spotlights that turned from green to red and from red to a dazzling white and from white to yellow and to blue. In order to avoid accidents, spaceshuttles were grounded despite protests by the wealthy. However, special spaceshuttles from four different places carried people to Seraglio Point, where functionaries in showy uniforms like those worn by Italian officers escorted them to their seats.

Only Doğan was an exception, arriving in a spaceshuttle four times as big as the others. In view of the number of his guards surrounding him, no one except they could see him. However, the red carpet on which he marched brought him to the point where Temel waited. He embraced Temel.

"When are we going to unveil it?" he asked.

"Very shortly, Sir. As soon as it is completed," said Temel.

Doğan didn't know how to respond. "Completed did you say? What do you mean? Not completed yet?"

"Not quite."

"Am I to sit here and wait while your men finish their work?"

"Not my men, Sir. The monument is automated," said Temel, pointing to a big number lit in green. "A few minutes to go."

Doğan looked and saw that the green number seven was changing into a six.

"In other words, in six minutes it will be ready?"

Temel, with a radiant expression, took a blue device from his pocket and showed it to the Prime Minister. "In five minutes, during which you can please deliver your speech, the monument will be ready. At the end of your talk, please take out this device from your pocket and announce, 'I am opening the Statue of Liberty. I hope it will bring good luck both to Turkey and to the world,' and press this green button. Then an illuminated mass will begin to rise and the monument will be revealed to onlookers from its base up." He handed the device to the Prime Minister, whose hands were trembling. "Everything will be all right as you'll see, Sir." When the one becomes zero just press this button and say what I told you."

Doğan's hands trembled even more. "Do it here? It there no podium?"

Temel smiled. "Just press that yellow button, Sir, and you'll find yourself standing on a podium."

The Prime Minister pressed the yellow button. No sooner had he done so than the image of a huge podium, magnified at least fifty times its actual size appeared in the air. Cheers were heard not only from the crowds in the vicinity but from all over the city. Doğan felt so nervous he almost collapsed, but put the device back in his pocket and drew out the text of his speech, thinking, "I did well to listen to Temel and have my speech in writing. Otherwise, I don't think I'd be able to speak a single word. I have the feeling that this gigantic replica would have the same effect."

He started to read his speech. Whether because his situation was so novel or because he felt comparatively insignificant in the presence of the gigantic apparition, he stammered every now and then as he spoke, and his speech could not be heard clearly. However, the crowd cheered as he said, "The year 1789, which marked the creation of the United States, was the greatest beginning in human history, and the date October 18th, 1886, which marked the inauguration of the Statue of Liberty in New York, was the second greatest." Even louder were the cheers when he said that the Statue of Liberty's summit was a hundred yards above sea level and that it was the apex of art and technology of its age.

Can, who watched the event on the television, said to Sabri, "That man knows well how to excite his audience with numbers."

The Prime Minister went on, "Temel Diker, known to every Istanbul citizen, is a man of great wealth whose inspiration is American. One of his country's most successful and loyal citizens, he has made given a second Statue of Liberty to Istanbul, a city of skyscrapers. He has spared no expense and has given great effort beyond imagining. The Turkish Statue of Liberty is 300 yards high, three times the size the one in New York. In other words, it has far surpassed the original."

These words were taken by storm. People began to shout "Temel! Temel!" and the cheering did not stop until Doğan took Temel's hand and raised it high in the air, a gesture magnified many times over in the mass of light that enveloped them. The audience was elated, and the Prime Minister then added something that was not in the original text. He quoted a couplet by the great poet Fuzuli:

Rise higher and higher, this is not your station
To have come to the world is not itself a meritorious[2]

"Our brother Temel has realized the words of our poet, dear friends!" the Prime Minister concluded. His words received a thunderous applause.

Doğan, meanwhile, had become dizzy. He was anxious in the presence of his own image fifty times bigger than himself. He put the paper back in his pocket and continued, "Our brother Temel has enabled us to feel pride in realizing what our great poet wrote. To be exact, this statue which will secure a closer connection between us and the Statue of Liberty in America, thanks to which peace could be established not only

---

[2] This couplet is not by the poet mentioned, an instance of the frequent errors made by the Prime Minister

within this country but the world at large." He added that everybody would soon possess an apartment of his or her own in a skyscraper, plus a spaceshuttle.

At the moment when the figure one was about to change to zero, he took out the blue device and pressed the button. Until this point, the statue was hidden by a mass of colored lights that now assumed the colors of the rainbow and then soared into the air. The onlookers, utterly silent, saw the pedestal, three times bigger than the original, followed by the feet, skirts, and body, and on its shoulders the face of Nokta, creating wild excitement throughout city, followed by a deep silence. Nokta's face was so beautiful, pure, unprecedented, natural, and vivid that it seemed as if she might any moment leave the earth. All held their breath. Not a word was spoken by the Prime Minister, the American ambassador, and the governor of Istanbul. When the ceremony came to an end, they were still silent and did not want to leave. The fact that Nokta's apparition was still there was interpreted as a miracle and so long as this miracle lasted they wanted to admire her.

Diker-38, the fastest of Temel's spaceshuttles with its pilot and two copilots, took off with Can, Gül, and Sabri on board.

The voice of the pilot was heard saying, "Your captain Demir speaking," followed by information regarding their flight to Florence.

But Can pressed a button and interrupted him. "Captain!" he said, "don't bother with all the data. Just tell us if you can circle the city three times before leaving for Italy."

Demin answered immediately, "Yes, Sir."

"There is no risk, is there?" asked Can.

"None whatsoever," said the captain. "Diker-33 is one of the four or five aircraft with permission to hover above Istanbul. Just to make sure that there's no question about your escape, we have started the formalities of selling this aircraft to an Italian. In three days, I will be heading back to Istanbul with a new aircraft."

"Temel had not mentioned this to me."

"Perhaps to save you from unnecessary speculations, Sir."

"Let's start circling the city now."

"Right! I'll try to fly at the lowest altitude allowed."

"Let's have a look at the monument before we leave for good."

They did so. They saw the monument for the last time.

Tears rushed to Can's eyes. "An exact replica of her face! Just like the photograph, as if she were brought back to life."

"Indeed, but all alone in this city!" said Gül.

"A monument of loneliness," said Sabri.

Can sighed.

"You always try to cover your feelings, Sir, but you are sentimental."

"All right, Captain. Thanks. Let's go!" said Can

Can looked at the flood of people was flowing toward the city, "No! How can this be?" he stammered and asked the captain to fly a bit lower.

Sabri shouted, "Look, Sir!"

Can looked in the direction indicated. Another mass of people was coming from the south and converging towards the centre of the city with a deafening sound.

"The castaways!" cried Sabri. "There are the castaways, Sir!"

Can remembered what Rıza had said long ago, "It's as if the world is returning to its essence."

After reflecting a while, he said resolutely, "Captain, we are not going to Florence. We are going back to Istanbul!"

Pronunciation:

Written Turkish includes letters not otherwise found in the Roman al-
phabet: ı (undotted i), pronounced as in "fit"; ş, pronounced "sh" as in
"short"; ç, pronounced "ch" as in "choose"; ğ (soft g), which extends the
length of the vowel that immediately precedes it. "C" is pronounced like
"j" in "June."